Mike Nicol

THIS DAY AND AGE

Born in Cape Town, South Africa
in 1951, Mike Nicol is the author
of three novels, *The Powers That Be*,
This Day and Age, and *Horseman*,
and a book of nonfiction,
A Good-Looking Corpse.

THIS DAY AND AGE

THIS

DAY

AND

AGE

Mike Nicol

VINTAGE INTERNATIONAL

Vintage Books

A Division of Random House, Inc.

New York

ACKNOWLEDGMENTS
For some stories, images and ideas, I am indebted to the
work of a number of historians, particularly Charles van
Onselen, J. B. Peires and Robert Edgar.

All rights reserved under International and Pan-American
Copyright Conventions. Published in the United States by
Vintage Books, a division of Random House, Inc.,
New York. Originally published in Great Britain in
hardcover by Bloomsbury Publishing Ltd., London,
in 1992. First published in the United States in hardcover
by Alfred A. Knopf, Inc., New York, in 1992.

The Library of Congress has cataloged the Knopf edition
as follows:
    Nicol, Mike, [date]
    This day and age/Mike Nicol.
    p. cm.
    ISBN 978-0-679-74200-5
    I. Title.
    PR9369.3.N54T47 1992
    823—dc20 92-53054
    CIP
    Vintage ISBN: 0-679-74200-X

For Des and June, my parents

CONTENTS

Prologue

One

Two

Three

Four

Five

Six

Where yesterday, that is in the happy days of Enlightenment, only the despotic power of the monarch had seemed to stand between man and his freedom to act, a much more powerful force had suddenly arisen which compelled men at will, and from which there was no release, neither rebellion nor escape, the force of history and historical necessity.

Hannah Arendt,
On Revolution

When people rally around the word of God, people must die.

Enoch Mgijima,
Leader of the Israelites

We hold this nationhood as our due, for it was given us by the architect of the universe. His aim was the formation of a new nation. The last hundred years have witnessed a miracle behind which must lie a divine plan. Afrikanerdom is not the work of men but the creation of God.

Dr. D. F. Malan,
Prime Minister of South Africa,
1948-54

PROLOGUE

Afterwards

Between the time that was before and the time that came afterwards there hung a brutal moment: a moment that was simple, brief, that changed what had been and altered everything that was to come. It may have lasted no longer than twenty minutes but it sits in the lives of us all, afterwards. Afterwards when the secrets were told, when the confidential files lay exposed upon the table, then, afterwards, there was no way out.

Of course afterwards there were causes, effects, explanations and excuses, blame, relief, the truth according to one, the way it was according to another, rumours, gossip, stories about what happened or what may have happened or what people say happened. On the one hand heroes and martyrs, on the other hand terrorists and perverts. Here the innocents; there the guilty.

According to this the president had no alternative, according to that he was the worst of sorts. Some said Enoch Mistas was a prophet, some said he was the devil.

How can you argue freedom when it was clearly subversion?

Ah, but if you consider their circumstances, didn't they have every right?

An ear for this. An ear for that. Who to believe? Who to trust? On the one hand. On the other hand. My story. History. The struggle for truth continues ever afterwards.

Because afterwards is where we live, where we can resolve what happened, according to one, according to another. Afterwards is real. Afterwards is where stories begin.

His Story

It was the day after his birthday and the heliographed message. It was only hours after the doctor had changed the dressings on his bum-boils. It was merely minutes after he had taken the salute, bald-headed, hat over heart, lips smirking, eyes unblinking. It was during a military parade that the president's heart, still wearing the Homburg, struck once, twice, and he collapsed on the platform among service medals, gold braid, jugs of water, pulling the green baize tablecloth over himself like a shroud. Curtains.

Pandemonium. Generals, brigadiers, captains, all the top brass bending down, Oh my God. Call a doctor.

Yet through it sits the first lady, his wife, chiffoned, pleated, larger than life, waving a puffy hand at the state photographer, headless under a black cloth.

What's happening?

It's just the heat.

Undo his collar.

Stand back.

Give him air.

But air, undone collar, a ring of worried faces, are no longer enough.

The president had seen it coming, spent the first night of his short new year looking out across the trees at the distant lights of city and harbour imagining his funeral: the black procession – his coffin on a gun carriage draped with flags – leaving the presidential palace, going into the streets lined with people, through the city closed in his honour where businessmen, bankers, brokers, hands clasped before them, heads bowed at his passing on to the

5

boulevards and wide avenues lined with palm trees, the sun for the last time warming his body, perhaps hearing faintly through his death twenty-one guns and some quiet words of praise before the first clods close out this world for ever and ever amen.

At least, that was what he had tried to imagine, grimacing at the pain of his boils, pacing from window to bookcase, bookcase to window, trying to conjure up the last grip of power, the strength to move a nation. But always a dark figure intervened, always among the people on the street there was one in a black frock-coat who looked on and smiled. He was there between the bankers and businessmen professing mildly: I am just an honest broker, sir, paying my last respects.

He's not, shouted the president, he's an impostor, an agitator, a snake in the grass. He's Enoch Mistas. Arrest that man, guards, arrest that man.

But they couldn't hear their dear departed president.

This man waited, too, at the cemetery: always respectful, a tower of strength, moving back for members of the family, giving up his place for cabinet ministers, offering a steady arm to the grieving.

Keep him away, do you hear, he's the man you want. Handcuff him. Try him. Hang him. For heaven's sake listen to me this is your only chance, yelled the president from his coffin.

But they couldn't hear him. Couldn't see the sweat on his brow, the tears of frustration, the clenched fists where before had been praying hands.

And despite security men, friends and prelates, the tall man couldn't be kept away. He was the first to sprinkle earth, to show who's myth, who's mortal.

Hence the president's anger before his death and after it.

Before, when he raged down the hall of portraits, called the generals fools, morons, witless, not worth the price of their commissions because why wasn't there more news than this useless heliographed message – which he waved in his secretary's face, complaining: Johan, get me the chief of staff, I want a report. I want to know what's going on. Birthday or no birthday, we do not lose touch with a division, they must be somewhere, they must be out there. I want them found. I want an explanation.

And afterwards: Dammit, Trotter. Dammit. Dammit. Dammit. Where's the officer commanding? What about Mistas? Is he alive? Did he escape?

And Captain Trotter, a mere shadow of his former self, haggard, wild-eyed, unshaven, in tatters, lost with a division of Cape Royal Fusiliers, having given up the ghost, even so snapped to attention: On Field Marshal Hedley Goodman's conclusions, presumed dead, sir. The field marshal himself is badly wounded.

Conclusions, Trotter. I don't want conclusions. I want facts. Is he alive or is he dead?

We couldn't find the body, sir, replied the captain, disheartened, demoralised, dispirited. But . . .

But me no buts, captain. Is he or isn't he?

There were strange stories, sir.

Strange stories! What do you mean, strange stories? Explain yourself, man.

Miracles, sir.

For God's sake, Trotter, talk sense.

There are men who say he levitated, sir, Mr President.

Levitated. People don't levitate, Trotter.

No, sir. Of course not, sir. My opinion, sir, for what it's worth, is that he escaped on horseback heading for the swamps. We found the tracks.

Trotter, sighed the president, Trotter. Do you know what you and that wretched field marshal have done? You have failed, Trotter. You have failed me, your colleagues, your family, your nation. And not only have you failed, you have done worse, you have created a monster. Whether Mistas is dead or alive, you've let him escape. When you and I are gone and forgotten, Trotter, he will always be somewhere waiting to stir up trouble. That is why I sent you to arrest him, and all you do is bring back tales of miracles and levitation. That's rubbish, Trotter, that's the sort of rubbish people die for. We could have avoided that. So easily we could have avoided that, Trotter, sighed the president, sad, sadder than ever during his life, preparing himself for another reluctant question. Did you find the government agent?

After all this, after everything, wondered Captain Trotter,

searching for words, picking his euphemisms, why should he show such concern for one man?

Because, Trotter, small things make great presidents. We all know that is how history remembers.

Perhaps, allowed the captain, but I was just a soldier, sir.

And he was just an agent. He, too, could have helped, but perhaps that was expecting too much. My decision to send him out there was against the odds. Yet whoever wins otherwise?

We didn't find him, sir. He is presumed dead.

Of course he's dead, I don't need you to tell me that. But he's unburied, man, he needs a Christian funeral, some honoured spot to rest his bones. Poor man. He had a wife and daughters, you know. Young girls, a young family with everything to expect. Such a shame. Such a great, great pity: a real tale of woe. But I warned him there would be no glory, that the most he could expect was for someone to say he did his duty. That when he was called he acted selflessly and did his duty. We will look after his family, of course, it is the least we can do, to honour and remember him.

Which in the end is what it's all about: who gets to be told, who gets to be in the story. Who is hero, who is villain. Who lives, who dies.

Some say the president died on the platform at the military parade, that any other announcements were a cover-up. According to one, it was assassination; according to another, he answered God's calling.

Officially he fainted but recovered enough to pin on medals. Officially he had a mild stroke and was admitted to hospital for observation. Officially he'd had a heart attack. Officially he was in intensive care. Only afterwards, on the next day, was he officially dead.

The nation mourned. The nation was jubilant.

Afterwards so much seemed possible.

Afterwards it was easy to cover up rumours, gossip, stories. Where was the evidence? Where the signs of outrage? The heliographed message lay shredded in the bin and no one could find the president's copy. So it was enough to say there'd been no message, or, yes, we did get something but it was garbled, there was too much cloud, but we have no reason to expect an irregularity.

Until afterwards.

Until, after the lying in state, after the funeral, after his portrait had been hung in the hall, after a decent interval, but before the new incumbent moved in, a maid dusted the presidential desk and found the president's copy with other papers slipped beneath his blotter.

ONE

This Story

If there is any single beginning to this story then it's to be found long, long ago deep in the time before, in the extravagant years of a president who built mansions and palaces out of the budget for public works, who financed yachts and racehorses with funds from social pensions, who entertained kings and statesmen from the coffers of national education while his citizens laboured under the imposition of higher and higher taxes. What an age of patriarchy and enslavement! What days of desperation and unhappiness! . . . When on the quayside men changed owners like cattle, and women were traded for jars of Eastern spices; when parents bound their daughters against the rent, and travelling salesmen hawked a boy for a kettle's price. While this president ate *pâté de foie gras*, the people ate slops. In the cities debt, which was too high a wage for freemen, let alone those born to bondage, enslaved them all. From the hostels and the poor houses people fled, most empty-handed, some carrying bundles of food and clothing. In broad daylight they took flight, disappearing into the veld at the end of vineyards, bolting high fences, praying they would not feel the lash of the overseers' whips. At night they slipped out, breaking the curfew, dodging soldiers, hoping not to be counted among the morning's dead. For those who made their fearful way through the streets, keeping to the shadows, skirting pools of light, their babies smothered against them to muffle chance cries, and eventually found themselves crossing the fields into the bush, there may have been quick thankfulness to have got this far but most were too worried about where to go next. Because no one could travel the roads by day for fear of capture, and at night the veld seethed with passing bands of violent men.

So little wonder Enoch Hemelswerd, bootmaker, husband, honest man turned criminal by an impossible debt of three months' rent, victim of recession, inflation and a president's lavish spending, breathed a sigh of relief to have evaded the city's clutches but, in the early light, looked about at shadows beneath the trees and the dark mouths of caves among the rocks and felt the prickle of a new fear. What terrors lurked in the backlands? he wondered as his wife lay exhausted on the ground and the others he'd gathered along the way huddled near him. Yet in the months to come, as they were chased by government patrols and hounded by bandits, as they gasped with thirst in baking valleys and shivered with cold on the bare mountains, never once did Enoch Hemelswerd betray the alarm that so often swirled within him. If danger threatened he got them to safety: each day, steadfast, he faced north, heading ever deeper into the mountains where only prospectors and hermits had been before them. When people despaired that they were lost among the crags, Enoch Hemelswerd led them to a green and shady field; when the weak or the ill fainted from fatigue, Enoch Hemelswerd carried them until they could once more go on alone: he led them, he encouraged them, his strength was indomitable. Enoch the Ox they called him, in praise and wonder at his tenacity.

Then came the day when Enoch Hemelswerd brought them to the edge of those bald and granite mountains, and below swept a valley fringed with trees along the lower slopes that ran to veld and hazed hills in the distance. Here, he said, this is the place we've been seeking. And they looked at a stream that ran out of the high buttresses, collected in pools among the trees before casting itself thin and silver across the land. Buck moved in the further scrub and the refuge was without a sign that men had ever been there. Down an eland trail that took them out of the mountains and through the foothills Enoch Hemelswerd led the refugees, until they came to a place that was shaded by huge cedars and watered by the stream. There he founded a mission station: built a church to which came a young Pastor Melksop in answer to God's calling; and across from it a house (where for so many nights the founder tried again and again for sons). Soon the dusty patch between his house and the church became market square, festive square, a place of meeting, and the mission thrived with vegetable gardens laid out along the river, cattle among the reeds, sheep and goats on the scrubhills. Here those who had followed him and others who sought his sanctuary put up shelters, huts, cottages, whatever they could afford. Here he taught men and boys to make boots which no merchant buyer could refuse, no matter how they might complain about his being off the beaten track, about the dangerous pass, about his high prices. When the tally was drawn they always paid up because no one else made better boots.

In all this Enoch Hemelswerd took great pride, and who would have said, to see him working, haggling, laughing among the goatherds, that within him a stone hardened? Yet during his later years, those shortly before the birth of his daughter, there was a bitterness in Enoch Hemelswerd, and he no longer rode out over the mission's lands or tooled leather in the shed with the other men. Instead he wandered on the lower slopes, became a creature of the trees or haunted the dragonfly pools, chasing off the children who went there to play. In that time his eyes sank, his mouth turned down, grew thin and shut. If he spoke, it was to admonish or warn against neglect and sloth. People avoided him, hurried off at his approach, withdrew into their houses at the grate of his step on a path. Only Pastor Melksop did not run from his benefactor, if anything became even more obsequious: said special prayers for the Hemelswerds on Sundays, sent Enoch illustrated copies of the psalms. Such kindnesses were wasted. The prayers annoyed him and the presents he hurled aside. Nor could his wife offer comfort, except to bear the burden of his wrath. On her Enoch Hemelswerd spent his pain, needing neither the violence of his strength nor the leather of his belt to pitch them both into misery. Each evening he forced himself upon her, undeterred by menstruation or, eventually, pregnancy. Think of the child, his wife begged in the last weeks, but he ignored her. Only when the girl was born did Enoch Hemelswerd turn away from the woman who had loved him. Why? she pleaded then. If we can have one we can have the other . . . But her husband refused to listen. It's all over, he said. I won't be shamed by the chance of another girl.

For five years those words soured within him. He would talk to no one, never acknowledged a greeting, said nothing to cheer the ill, had no comfort for those who mourned. And so his last words turned putrid. They chewed at his intestines, grew ulcers on his stomach, coloured his water with blood, but he would not relent to ease the pain. His mouth was sour with gall. Only on the day of his death did he speak again, and then, had it not been for some children peeping through the window at the dying man, no one would have heard what he said. Even so his words were almost lost. People thought the children had made them up: that it was nonsense, this business of ever needing to leave the valley, because didn't they have it all – a good business, a humble life, peace and quiet? And weren't they God-fearing people who caused harm to none and loved their fellow man? Didn't they thrive in His bliss? Wasn't that why there was always water in the furrows that fed off the stream? Wasn't that why fruit grew in abundance and the crops never failed? How could he say there would come an end to this when neither greed nor avarice nor evil thoughts entered their minds. No, it was just children's fantasy. But even so, the things they came out with . . . like this idea there'd be great hardships unless a boy with Hemelswerd blood was born to save them. Where did they get such strange ideas from? But then, children were children, they lived in a different world.

No one would admit it, but the passing of Enoch Hemelswerd was a relief to all at the mission station, especially his wife and daughter. If everyone felt they could laugh again without his scowling face appearing to spoil the joke, then it was particularly the laughter of his family that rang loudest. If again they danced on the square, then it was Ma Hemelswerd who danced longest. Even Pastor Melksop was more at ease: no longer so servile, in fact, now a man with a mission. And although it was many months before those in that valley behind the mountains knew it, in the city people were smiling once more because the spendthrift president, his gut rotten with rich food and heavy wine, had passed on too. A relief to all and the national economy. Things can only get better, everyone said, casting their ballots for the one and only presidential candidate who was to succeed him. We've been through the worst. So they voted into high office a young man wearing a Homburg, clean-shaven and with true ideals. No hedonist this. He thought of wise government, justice, the dignity of human rights. He wanted development, productivity, foreign capital, a trade surplus. These are my desires, he told Johan van Rooyen, as they gazed out over the city that was being prepared for his inauguration. And I'll take whatever steps are needed to ensure no saboteur gets in my way.

Affairs of State

On the eve of the new president's inauguration, when the city stood decked in flags and coloured lights and the guard of honour polished their toe-caps until they shone like brown mirrors, when the archbishop prayed for justice in high office after years of fiscal embezzlement and the trumpeter practised his scales in ceremonial anticipation, the president-to-be called for his secretary and ordered a staff car to pick him up at the side entrance.

Just a plain car, Johan, he said, and I want you to drive. I'm not having any old sergeant with a loose tongue on this business.

To his wife he said: Get a good night's sleep, my little lamb. There's affairs of state I must see to.

And thirty minutes later a nondescript black car drove out of the grounds, unaccompanied, unacknowledged, the dark figure at the back crouched into his collars, hidden beneath his hat but unnoticed by the sentry who waved them through.

Down to the docks, said the incoming president. I'll be more specific when we get there. And stay off well-lit roads.

They kept to lanes that ran between trees, passed grand houses locked and barred in the darkness of shrubs and ivy; then, shooting the intersection separating rich from poor, dived into those mean streets where nags tore at the grass on vacant lots, disturbing neither drunks nor dead babies. On among stores, warehouses, factories, past the Seaman's Mission and the Custom's House, through the back roads of stained hotels on to the quiet wharfs where Taiwanese fishing-boats slopped and stank.

Keep on, said the presidential incumbent, we're almost there – and they bumped over railway lines, hooked around packing crates, seemingly lost in a maze of quays and cranes until before them loomed the gates of the whaling station.

Hoot, Johan van Rooyen was ordered.

There was no response.

Hoot again.

And out of the dark came a young woman, tidy, bare-foot, not yet fat, her hair hidden in a doek. She squinted against the car lights.

Hoot, said the voice from the back.

The woman opened the gate and the car drove in.

Are you Maria? asked the presidential candidate.

Yes, sir.

I want to know the future, he said.

Consulting the Oracle

In the shack the young woman placed a candle on the table. She looked up at the man before her: the small head, the tight eyes, the fat lips still waiting for the years to curl them in a sneer, the large hands that would hold so many empty gestures, and felt fear at what she could foretell.

Does sir want bones or cards? she asked.

Neither, he replied. I have come here for the truth, not interpretations.

Sorry, sir. Please, sir, I must know at least what sir dreams.

He laughed. Do you know who I am, woman?

She hung her head. Sir is my president.

He laughed again. Only tomorrow. Only tomorrow will I be your president. But now I want you to help me, Maria. I want you to tell me what will happen so that I can issue wise laws. So that the people can live in order and happiness. Isn't that what we all want? The people have had enough trouble, now they want peace. I can bring peace, Maria, if you will do what I ask. I am not here to learn about my life or my health or how many children I shall have. No, Maria, I am here because of the people, my people. This is important business so you must not ask me silly questions. It doesn't matter what I dream of. If last night I dreamt of dragonflies and peacocks, that means nothing, absolutely nothing. It is trivial. You must tell me about the state of affairs.

She was silent.

Then: Sir knows, I'm just a poor woman, sir, not even this is mine – and she waved a hand into the darkness of the shack, at mattress and basin, bundles and metal scrap.

Consulting the Oracle

The practically-president glanced about him, sniffed. God looks after everyone, Maria, especially poor people. You are rich in other ways. But when I am president I will build homes for poor people. I will build a home for you. He took two banknotes from his pocket and put them on the table. Here, take this. It is not much. But if you are truthful there will be other rewards.

The woman looked away, did not reach out for the money. He stared at her, puzzled, moved the notes towards her.

Go on, take it. He doubled the payment.

Still she said nothing but left the money lying on the table, too afraid to touch it.

Go on.

Sir knows, she said at last. Sir knows. I am a helpless woman. I only speak what is given to me, they are not my words. I mean no wrong. I am not to blame.

Yes, I understand that. You must just tell me what's going to happen. All I want is the truth.

It is always the truth, sir, because once it is spoken it cannot be untold.

Of course. Whatever. But go on. Go on.

Whispering, fearing every word, she said: Sir, I can tell sir this, never pick up a peacock's feather in the afternoon. Never put them like flowers in a vase.

It was so quiet in the shack, so quiet that neither the rising wind nor the slap of loose ropes could break in. The man, the nearly-president, looked at his hands spread out – thick-fleshed, hairy – on the table. The woman, Maria, whimpered, making him think of a pit bull-terrier he'd once seen dying in the ring.

Maria. Maria, he sighed. I am a reasonable man, but if you say such things you will make me angry. I want to hear about matters of substance, not old wives' tales. Are you with me?

Sir, please, sir. She was almost crying, trembling with fear. But it's true, sir. Sir is going to pick up a peacock feather and give it to sir's wife. Then . . .

Then what?

Then it's all going to happen, sir.

What, Maria? Tell me what?

Bad things, sir. Very bad things.

Like what? he yelled suddenly, reaching across, clutching her dress, pulling her towards him. Like what? Tell me, dammit! Tell me!

She felt his spit, smelt lotion, saw the tongue behind his teeth, and cried out: Sir, please, sir, let me go.

Slowly he sat back, opened his hand and set free the torn material. Maria stepped away into the shadows.

Eventually he said, I am sorry, Maria. You must not be afraid. Don't worry. I won't hurt you. You must just tell me what you know. Come. Come closer.

Drawn out of the dark, summoned by the power of his calling fingers, she approached, sat opposite him on an upturned bucket, her face turned away, her hands locked like marble in her lap.

She told him this, in a voice softer than the passing of a dragonfly. She told him about a time of great dissatisfaction, when cattle coughed a yellow froth from their muzzles and died bellowing, nostrils wide, tongues thick with flies, little more than covered skeletons rotten, putrefied. For this was the time of a strong sun that hardened the earth against maize, corn and all tubers; turned brother against brother, father against son, burned witches in their huts, made men mad who found nothing but dust in the rivers. A time that set fire to the pastures and the hills, and led to the slaughter of cattle. A time when people looked to their prophet and heard his command to cleanse themselves, to purge the plague from their cattle and the sorcerers from their midst.

Prepare yourselves, he says, because the new people are coming to cultivate the fields, bringing with them healthy cattle, and they will return the land to those from whom it was stolen and put to death all tyrants. Power will be ours.

Maria told of this time: of how in the valleys fires flared, fed by plague carcasses, dead dogs, the new flesh of bulls and cows, fires that would not die, that burned at night like stars, that hid the day beneath a brown blanket. She told of how the stomachs of children swelled with hunger and mothers' teats dried; of men who chewed mimosa bark and women who ate acacia thorns; of the smell of the starving as they passed from house to house begging potato peels or onion skins, receiving nothing but beatings and abuse.

Consulting the Oracle

Of how thousands left their homesteads for the towns, crawled into churches, town halls, on to verandahs in bougainvillaea streets where they died among the purple flowers. And of those who never got that far, fallen by the wayside, picked over by starlings and crows.

A prophet speaks to the people: Prepare yourselves, for these are our days. The Lord has looked on us with mercy, He has shown the justice of His way. He has said that the dead will arise. In the sun, in the rain, they will be there, our fathers, our ancestors, with new weapons and the strength of young bulls to march us to victory. Believe in me, the shades have awoken, the power will be ours. And he takes his followers on to a flat mountain that is like a fortress.

And each night come more bands to his camp. Groups, exhausted and rank, eager for the succour of his words, his provisions, leave their broken huts, struggle across vulture desolation and scorched earth to this refuge. His name is heard wherever people have given up hope, wherever they lie down to die. Softly it moves from lip to lip like a kiss: Enoch Mistas, Enoch Mistas, Enoch Mistas. Let me show you the way, he tells them, and all suffering will cease, we will be freemen in this land, untaxed, neither spat upon nor cursed, the power will be ours. And they respond, the power will be ours, in a cry that goes through the hearts of farmers with the precision of ice.

Because the farmers are afraid. For weeks they have watched men, women, children, little more than ghosts drifting across the veld. They have chased them from the lands, offered neither sour milk nor dry bread to the pleas for mercy. Jackals! Vermin! they shout, bearing down with Mausers and sjamboks, slashing, whipping, trampling, shooting stragglers like buck. Death to all trespassers, no quarter for vagrants, they vow, riding out in commando to patrol dams, stock, crops. Confident men, they are enjoying new adventures with a laugh and tales of killing until the day whole flocks go missing, a son is raped, a daughter wounded. Enough, they say then. Grim, worried now, they saddle up to petition for help.

Enough, they demand of magistrates, arriving at outlying towns in delegations of sweat-stained, small-eyed men with bad skins.

We can't go on like this, being plundered, chasing thieves, guarding chickens and lambs, our children assaulted, our women afraid, our lives in danger. It can't go on. We've done your work for months, but now we demand you send troops, police, call up able men, there's trouble out there we're telling you. This is no small matter. It's an uprising. Rebellion. Sedition. A plot to overthrow the president. They must be put down. Once and for all.

All right, say the magistrates, fanning themselves to move the smell of sheep-loving men, opening windows to entice in whatever breeze will brave their courts. All right. Just don't get excited, don't crowd the bench, let's see if we've got this straight. A priest, some religious nut, and his starved followers are holed up in the hills, stealing eggs and the odd lamb, trespassing, and thereby breaking the sacred laws of property, preaching insurrection, enticing your slaves to revolt, wounding your daughters and raping your sons . . . Er, you do mean sons? Or should that be wounding your sons and raping your daughters? Which we could understand, because daughters do entice with short skirts, low necklines, provocative smiles, too much thigh, the suggestion of round buttocks in their walk, the lure of firm breasts, tight nipples . . . We could go on, but you get our drift and know yourselves how these things affect us men! How God tempts to strengthen our resolve, giving beautiful daughters to fathers with haggard wives, laying them before us like ripe plums, stirring such bitter-sweet thoughts in our trousers . . . We could go on, these temptations are well known. Some of us may even have succumbed! Lord have mercy on us mere mortals for we know not what we do. After all, we are all innocent sinners striving for God's grace, aren't we? But you do mean sons, do you? Yes, yes, that's what we thought. And you do mean rape? You do mean . . . actual . . . How shall we put it? Actual sodomy . . . Sticking it up . . . We see. Yes, yes, that's what we thought. Up the back passage, you say. That's worse than rape, that is violating everything men stand for. All dignity, all rights, all self-respect. This can't go on. We'll deal with these perverts, these bum bandits. We'll send soldiers.

Which, as Maria foretold, they did: a small commando of local regulars more used to rounding up drunks or quelling belligerent slaves than dealing with religious rebels. But all the same they go quite willingly, for the hell of it, glad of a break from guard duty, thinking this nothing more serious than chasing bushmen.

Get one for me, shout fathers and uncles.

Remember to bring skulls, call out little boys.

And their beads for us, laugh mothers and aunts, as the frontier's finest clip-clop out of town, their hearts crossed with bandoleers, rifles shouldered, waving their hats to applause.

What's the good of this? sigh the farmers, ever scornful, derisive, gathered to one side. You can't pit youngsters against those fundamental types. And where are the big guns? Why hasn't anybody listened to us?

And at the end of the second day's march when the adventure has worn off with saddle sores and insect bites (much to the amusement of the sheep-shearing men), they are spied by Dead Das and Allermann, who sit high up a kloof enjoying lamb chops with a jug of strong wine, keeping watch.

Didn't I tell you they'd come this way? sniggers Dead Das, picking sinews from his teeth.

Ja, says Allermann, sucking marrow, tossing away bones. It's good, ja – and he could have been referring to the meat or the display of state force picking its way over the debris of smashed meteorites and extinct volcanoes.

Now these men, Dead Das and Allermann, are the redeemer's lieutenants, the prophet's right-hand men, the perpetrators of unrest on the farms and unease in the farmhouses following egg raids, chicken stealing, flock disappearances, cattle rustling, the wounding of a daughter that occurs when she snags her arm on a newly cut fence and the rape of a son that happens in a ditch when no one is watching because he is enticed in with offers and sweet words and spends the whole afternoon there crying violation only when, late getting back, he is faced with the wrath of his elders. Nor has it ever been told that this young, no longer virgin boy has forsaken all: grandfather, mother, father, sisters, brother, a slice of the farm, the comfort of stiff porridge to make his way, at night for fear of patrolling neighbours, across the miles into the arms of his never-ditched lover. But that's another story.

What Maria revealed to the as-good-as-president on the eve of his inauguration was how Dead Das and Allermann waited until the troop passed into the narrow kloof before they dislodged a boulder that dislodged others that sent down a shower of stones, rocks, chunks on to the veldhat heads below them. Faced with no alternative, the state's finest had to run this gauntlet, which knocked out horses, concussed men, smashed rifles and rations, which didn't stop until they had all been bloodied. Only the farmers, rolling with laughter, wiping tears from their eyes, escaped the pounding by taking the long route round the hills.

Damn, says Dead Das, those boers have lived among baboons for too long.

Their meal finished, the entertainment over, Dead Das and Allermann lead their horses – which just the week before belonged to one of those now taking the long route – down a narrow track that passes within hearing of the commandos (who can hear nothing but their own distress) and disappear along a river-bed before the farmers come galloping up. Not that their departure goes undetected: but by the time a sharp-eyed sheepman scanning the veld notices a smudge on the horizon that isn't a dustdevil and sees in his telescope the unhurried pair it is too late.

Damn, he says, and we thought it was baboons caused the landslide. Now they know we're coming.

Which is not a happy thought for these farmers looking down at young men crying. If all it takes is a stony shower to produce such scenes of mayhem and rout, what will they do in the zing and spit of bullets?

And Maria told how it took the commando another two days to cross those plains. Two days in the sun and flies knowing that just out of rifle-shot they were being watched every inch of the way. Two nights fending off mosquitoes, midges, moths, tossing on ground harder than duty before they rode through the last range of hills on to the flats that led to the rising fortress mountain and wondered goddammit how the hell they were supposed to lay siege to that for Chrissakes! Exclamations that brought a smirk to the farmers' faces.

Didn't we tell you to bring cannon? they taunt. Didn't we tell you a Long Tom would make short shrift of this? But no, you're the experts. You know best. And they unsaddle, stoke up a fire for coffee, pare sticks of meat from their biltong.

Consulting the Oracle

Damn you, curses the sergeant commanding, still smarting because the magistrates turned down his request for cannons.

Out loud he shows his mettle. There's only one way, men: we'll scare the shit out of them with drills, target practice, parades, marches, combat displays, the stuff of army life. A couple of days of that and they'll be gone like spooks at first light. Any questions?

None from his men, but one from the farmers: Sergeant, please tell us, are you going to use live targets during shooting practice?

Silence, except the stomp and snort of horses. Sergeant Bloodstock spits, draws the back of his hand across his mouth, says: No.

. . . Because if you don't, they'll have your arse . . .

. . . We'll see about that . . .

. . . It's just friendly advice . . .

. . . Well keep it to yourselves. Troop dismount. Pitch camp.

Relax, tease the farmers, you're not impressing anyone, least of all the stinking hordes.

We'll see, replies Sergeant Bloodstock. We'll see who laughs loudest.

Through binoculars Dead Das and Allermann watch the white tents mushroom on the plain below, see a kraal of thorn surround the official horses, see sentries posted. While beyond the military ropes, their horses grazing free, the farmers lounge, smoking, chewing the fat, laughing at such army antics.

Fetch Mximba, orders Dead Das. I've got a plan.

Which much later that moonless night works perfectly as these three, treading lighter than dragonflies, come down off the mountain, cross the darkling plain and lead away the farmers' horses. Not once does an iron shoe strike clink against a haphazard rock, not once is there a sudden whinny to disturb dreams of wives or lovers, sheep or little boys and girls. Not once. The farmers sleep on. The sentry nods off. The men breathe easy in the depths of sleep. And each moment the horses are further away, following their rustlers quietly up the mountain.

Until in the vague hour before light, some farmers fumbling at their flies look about for their horses. Jiggling with the need to pee, alarmed at this audacious theft, giving way too soon to that craved release which wets fingers, trousers, boots, until in regulation order their seven fountains arch on to the veld, and they, relieved of so much, can go storming to Bloodstock demanding: Where are our horses? What's the good of your sentries? How are you going to get them back?

And he, suppressing a smile, says: Gentlemen, gentlemen, you're in good hands. Everything will be all right.

But this is a stain on their standing as farmers, as men who know the veld, that is not going to evaporate. They have been done, defamed, diddled. They want action.

What they get is an impressive display of square-bashing.

Left right left right left right ooh, left right left right left right aah, sings out Sergeant Bloodstock as his khaki platoon in white puttees marches to the base of the mountain. Squad. Squ-ard. A-bout . . . turn. Up, two, three, four. Left right left right left right ooh, left right left right left right aah, until in the middle of nowhere they are about turned . . . up, two three foured and ordered: Squad. Squ-ard halt. Squad. Squ-ard, pre-sent arms. One, two three, one. Fix bayonets. Squad. Squ-ard, chaaarge. And they go howling a hundred yards to slash and stab the hot, shimmering noonday heat.

Through his binoculars Dead Das sees the farmers shake their heads and shakes his head too. All afternoon he watches target practice, drill and mock charges, the cut and thrust of readying for war.

They mean business, he says to Allermann. Let's call their shots.

And Maria told how that night – when the exhausted platoon were at ease among their blankets, muscles sore, dozing off, and within the ropes the farmers lay muttering of useless mock parades that frightened no one as much as would have done a single cannon-shot – how that night all the people of the prophet, those who had lost herds, homes, husbands, children, who had lived on thorn and bark, who had dreamt of the coming of the new people and revered the redeemer's promise, took firebrands and like lava poured down the mountain on to the plain.

In the still night the only sound is the whisper of bare feet over rocks: sibilant, hardy as they encircle the soldiers. Nor can the sentries, terrified, ramming bullets into breeches, believe their coming. Only Sergeant Bloodstock, called from his tent to view the spectacle, dismisses fears of bloody battle.

It's nothing, he says, they're just showing off.

What'd'you mean showing off? howl the farmers. Shoot now or we'll be crow's meat tomorrow.

No, shouts the sergeant at all nervous men. No one shoots unless I order, is that clear? And to the farmers quietly says: Leave me. This is a military matter now.

But despite his nonchalance, Bloodstock takes no chances. Ride, scout, he commands, fetch the magistrates, this needs more than guns – and he smacks the horse's rump and watches intently until the man is through the pincers of light closing about them. Right, he sighs, that's that, but what's this about?

It is about a little knot of men on a vast karoo plain with only a rope between them and the firebrands that often seem to float, disembodied, that occasionally cast a faint glow on forms that could have been the bodies of the dead so thin they are, their skin so tightly stretched across their skeletons. It is about a sound, a moan, that could be from pain or from sadness, that could have welled in years of human bondage, deep, raw, an agony rolling from where the lights are dimmest, gathering strength, breaking in throat after throat, howling from mouth to mouth until it has passed in a circle about the commando and only the echo comes back again and again to protest the despair of all men bound. And as the cry dies, the firebrands go out. Beyond the ropes is empty veld.

But not so to each green troop or farmer. They see a horde of devilmen, hear the ululations of women, the cries for blood and murder, and open fire. Round on round on round. Muzzles spitting flames. Hot lead striking rocks. Cutting air. Falling softly at the end of point three-oh-three range.

Stop, yells Bloodstock, running from soldier to soldier, knocking down rifles. You're wasting ammunition.

But no one will listen.

Blam. Blam, go the retorts.

Hold your fire.

Blam blam blam.

There's nothing out there you goddamned fools. Listen to me.

And when they do it is to forsake all dignity. It is chaos, a rout. Where before there had been an enemy there is suddenly nothing. Where before their bullets had cut down the hordes there are suddenly no dead. Holy Mary Mother of God. Ghosts. Spooks. Devils. Jesus Christ there is no fighting this. They run. Through tents, cooking fires, thorn-scrub kraals they run, abandoning rifles, dumping ammunition, screaming blue murder. They run, green troops and farmers, across the plain, trip over anthills, fall in dry river-beds, pick themselves up and run until they can run no more, until a day of heat and displays of arms get the better of them and they collapse, sobbing for mercy.

What a fuck-up, remarks Sergeant Bloodstock alone in the wrecked camp. What a goddamned bloody awful fuck-up.

Well who would have thought it would come to this, says Dead Das to Allermann when a new day throws some light on the scene. Just look at that, they're pulling back.

Ja, but they will return. Next time it will be blood, says Allermann grinning, running an oiled cloth over the Lady Schwarzlose . . .

Visions of Acclaim and Burning

And now? asked the all-but-state president after a long silence. Go on. Tell me what happens next.

Sir, please, I can't, replied Maria, agitated, drawing into herself. Please, sir, it's gone white, it does sometimes. I can't see any more.

Try. I'm sure you can. Try again.

No, you mustn't ask, sir, please, sir, don't ask – and she reached forward to clutch his arm.

He felt the woman's fingers grab him like a bird's foot and flinched.

All right, calm yourself. If you calm yourself it may come back.

She shook her head.

Sir mustn't be cross. Please, sir.

No no, Maria. You tell me. Tell me whatever is there.

It's white, sir, like a mist. Sometimes there are figures, men in black coats, ssh, ssh, they are talking, they are talking about sir, about sir's heart which they say is weak, they are talking to someone who has drawn the picture of a dragonfly. It is a strange dragonfly with wings on the top and bottom. They are talking about one who turns everything he touches red. It is the only colour, sir, this red. White and black and red. Sir mustn't be cross. Please, sir.

What are they saying, Maria? Can you hear what they're saying?

Ssh, ssh, they're saying that sir is a good man, that sir looks after his people, that sir feeds them when they are hungry, that sir has even given his coat to a beggar in the streets, that sir will not allow evil men to shape his way.

Yes, it will be like that.

You see, sir, everything will be all right. People will love sir. They will cheer when sir drives through the streets. They will send sir presents and pray for sir when they worship the Lord. Everything sir does will be for the good of sir's people. Sir is an honest man. Sir will be like a father to all sir's children. Long may sir be president.

How long, Maria?

Many years, sir. Many, many years.

And you can tell me nothing more about this trouble?

Maria hesitated. No, sir.

I see.

He stared hard at her.

Look at me, Maria, he said. But she wouldn't meet his eyes, kept her head bowed as she had done when they first sat down. Then he relented. All right, let me hear what it is you wish to tell me.

Sir! She glanced quickly up at him. Sir, it's this. It's important, sir. It shows how sir is honoured. Sir is in a bright room with many people, beautiful women in long dresses and men in uniforms. Sir is also in a uniform, a smart uniform with medals and bars.

And she told of an occasion in the state room at the presidential palace when all the generals with their bare-shouldered wives came to eat and dance and drink and listen to Field Marshal Hedley Goodman praise thirty-five years of peace and prosperity, of the building of harbours and highways, the manufacture of weapons and the mining of gold. Of how cities had spread, rivers been dammed, fields ploughed, of international ties and diplomatic relations, the strength of the currency and the gilt holdings of banks. But mostly about the peace that had followed years of war on the borders and unrest in the country, of how under the wisdom and guidance of the president there had been no slogans demanding democracy or the freedom of prisoners, no treasonous graffiti sprayed on street walls. For his presidency had been a time of conciliation and negotiation, of compromise and human rights, a period of nation building: during which and without exception we have enjoyed the fruits of good government, the privilege of easy living and so, fellow officers and good ladies, it gives us, mere servants in the defence of our nation, great pleasure to honour the president with the rank, general of the armed services.

Into the applause and the congratulations, the hands to be shaken and the beaming faces, steps the honorary general, the president, stilling the accolades with outstretched arms: Friends, he says, friends – and waits until there's not a shuffle. None of what the field marshal has talked about would have been possible without your devotion to duty and country. When anarchy prevailed among the shack people, when thugs and gangsters went rioting through the streets murdering people in their beds, setting fire to poor homes, and the innocent were axed to death, then, at great personal risk, you restored order, not brutally, but with fairness and justice brought about the calm that has graced our years. And if we have heard rumours of discontent, of uprisings, if we have heard talk of voices raised in anger, then confidently I can say it has only been rumours and talk, slander spread by those who could not abide our happiness, who felt they had grievances when we had given so much: tractors, medicine, aid, cattle, the compassion of our humility and humanity. The state has not discriminated. The state has looked after all without favour or prejudice, fed the needy, nursed the ill. These are achievements history will acknowledge. It will be said that we governed wisely and well. And for your service, those lives lost, those loved ones who never returned, there will always be our monuments of remembrance.

Again the officers and their wives applaud. And the waiters go among them with thin glasses of champagne until everyone stands delicately poised for Field Marshal Hedley Goodman's toast: To our president.

To our president.

The virtually-president coughed. Yes. Well. Yes, Maria, that is all most interesting. Very flattering. I'm sure it will happen as you've told. But as I said, I'm not here to learn of personal matters so I must ask you again: can you tell me nothing more about that other business?

Maria tightened her hands in the fabric of her dress. Please, sir, she begged, shrinking away from her prophecy of good fortune.

For some moments they sat in the silence of the whaling shack while the words grew faint and small noises came creeping back like cockroaches into their ears. The soon-to-be-president shifted uncomfortably on his chair and exhaled a long breath across the table: the candle flame guttered, steadied, recast its shadows against the walls. He picked at the outer edges of wax; in those still moments Maria knew the terror of prisoners. She waited for more questions. Outside, so close and sharp they both felt it in their fingers, Johan van Rooyen cleared his throat and further off a drunk sailor called: Isabel, Isabel, come here you bloody maid – but even that died away as if suddenly a fog had settled, a damp whiteness in which men moved back and forth, sometimes visible, sometimes grey, but always lost. It was in this moment, this brief minute which became a world within the night, that the imminent president, held spellbound by Maria, foresaw an event which was not an affair of state, which was not even an event because it existed only in his mind, was never reported, never for him turned real.

He saw a church, white, with a flickering yellowness at the windows as if lamps or candles burnt inside. The doors were closed against a rasping wind. Across the ground leaves scratched like lizards. It was not a church he knew, not a place he had ever been. He went closer, coming out of the dark edges into the middle of the square, hugging his body for warmth, an elderly man awkward in a suit and tie as if he should have been at dinner or expecting a deputation, been anywhere conducting affairs of state, anywhere other than in this raw world. Faintly he could hear the congregation singing, gently the words reached him: Oh Lord our help in ages past, our hope for years to come – and softly they faded behind him among trees, buildings, shacks, it was too dark to see because only the church gleamed in that bright celestial light. Yet he felt there were houses in the shadows: houses where those who were not at church sat in their dim rooms, waiting. He could sense them, knew that in some a man sat alone, or a woman, or two friends, or a wife and her husband. He knew, too, that they could hear the hymn but were listening for another song. Was he, too, with their invisible witness, waiting for that song? For words that were strange yet always known, for a stirring that was neither wind nor shifting leaves, but an excitement that raced in his heart? It would come, he knew, from the darkness opposite the church, and as he listened it was there, within him, without, demanding, taking hold. All about the night moved, coming down through the trees. At first it was too dark to see them, but they were there, more and more, brushing against him, touching his trousers, letting the discord gather force. He saw young children in frocks and shorts, without shoes, and older boys and girls, eyes alight, smiling, laughing, calling him to join their dance. He took their hands, stamped his feet as they moved into a slow phalanx, a many-headed beast that rippled, rolled, swayed to the stridence in its belly. Ay e ay a ee, ay e ay o oo. With them he raised his arms, sang again: ay e ay a ee, ay e ay o oo, moved to their rhythm, gathered up, no longer the bystander, now part of the crowd. Ay e ay a ee, ay e ay o oo. He took up the chant that had always been within him, had lain torpid in presidential meetings and official functions, waiting to tear loose here, now, wild, grown suddenly rampant. Arms linked, surging this way and that between the houses where people sat in dread, he gave himself to the children. Sweat-damp, hard-pulsed, bent into their chant, they circled the church one two three four times – ay e ay a ee, ay e ay o oo – beat on the walls with fists, sticks, stones that smashed glass panes to release the smell of victim, of sacrifice, pungent into the night. That was the moment. That was what they wanted: the falling glass and the hunted's fear. Snorting, violent, into the church broke the monster, crawled over pews, crunched ripped tore, searched, nostrils wide for the odour of dread. Have mercy, beseeched the praying few. Take pity on helpless ones. This is the sanctuary of God, defile not his holy place, ordered the priest. But he, they, were shoved aside as the hell-hag wrenched from the knot of cowering people one woman who neither shrank back nor fought for freedom. She was lifted up, her head held briefly above the crowd, her face, Maria's face, contorted, mouth open in a scream that could not be heard, before she drowned down down down among those arms. Out, back out into the night, they pushed, he pushed, trampling those smaller beneath his feet, crack of rib, splinter of bone, crushing, tugging, fighting until he, too, snatched at clothes that tore, hair that his fist uprooted, grabbed hold of flesh colder than ice as the woman was dragged back between the silent houses where the witnesses closed their eyes to ease their guilt, back through the trees to the field where sheep cropped at winter grass. There, flicking sweat from his eyes, he swung an axe until his arms ached and the wood was cut. And all the time they danced and laughed, sang round and round the field – ay e ay a ee, ay e ay o oo – happy as children at games. Then leaves, grass, twigs that had been dry all winter became kindling, released the rage within them, crackled into furnace. Flames licked around logs, flowered in the heart of wood, sparked into a single spear of fire upon which they impaled the woman. Picked her up from the grass that was damp with dew, swung her like a carcass into the blaze. Here they let her burn. In the noise that was now only fire they watched her disappear. Clothing, hair, eyes, skin, bone. And at the edges of the field a man, a woman, two friends, a wife and her husband, others, members of the congregation, the priest, those who tended sheep and those who made boots, those who dug potatoes or crocheted tablecloths, came to stand. They stood, one there, a group here; some close enough to feel the heat, all of them frozen like statues: an arm half raised, a head bent, a hand reaching forward. He, too, had become stone; watched only the woman before him, burning. Then the flames went down. One by one the frenzied drew back, became children once more, fled across the field into the streets of open doors and silent houses, fled past the church where the lamps burnt low, fled to their homes and beds where nothing had happened, where if there were dreams and nightmares they were a terror that waking would wipe out. But only when the fire had become embers that glowed now red, now white, did the others, the parents, the elders, break their attitudes and go home. Alone, in groups helping one another, or as couples holding hands, they left the paddock to the sheep cropping in the shadows, the coals that tomorrow would be ashes and the two still standing beside that white and cooling ring: a man in a suit and a youth in a black frock-coat, a Bible dangling by a chain from his wrist. The man let fall the axe he'd clutched all through the burning. Side by side in the light raining from the stars they stood, maleficent, spectral.

No, shouted the president-to-be, standing up, kicking over his chair. It can't be. It won't be.

It is, sir, wailed the woman. It's what we cannot escape: neither you nor I nor him, Enoch Mistas.

He turned on her. It is your doing, these lies. You want to malign me, to sow confusion in my heart to show that I am like this fiend. Is that why you put such horrors in my head? I will not be a part of it, do you hear? I am your president. I am the first citizen. Men honour me, women seek my favours, children kiss my hands, these same hands, clean, unsullied, guiltless. I am not a beast like those savages. Do you hear me, woman? I am not a murderer.

Sir. Please, sir. I don't know what sir's talking about.

He stared at her, shook his head to dislodge that last image of the woman's face framed in flames. It couldn't be. Such things didn't happen any more. People lived by civilised values, Christian ethics, the rule of law, they had respect for human rights, for property, for freedom of association, for the sanctity of the Church. They did not burn women they thought were witches. No, that was impossible. Intolerable. He would right such wrongs, give protection to the vulnerable, the sinned against. He did not burn people.

Calmer now, reinforced by the logic of his high office, he realised what had to be done.

Maria, he said, Maria, I need your help. Earlier you spoke of a prophet, a man they call the redeemer. You must tell me where he is.

She broke into sobs.

Come, Maria, it's important. We must stop him. We cannot have this chaos, this anarchy, this disregard for human life. I'll have you protected, no one will know what you've told me. But I can't have him running at will. He's barbaric, savage, he's beyond reason . . .

He stared at the woman, her head on the table, deep shudders passing through her body. Come, he said, almost reaching out to touch her, then quickly drawing back his hand. Come. There is room in my kitchen for you. There you will be safe.

But Maria shook her head.

Yes, he said. This is the way I want it.

No, sobbed Maria, it will only be the way I've told sir, and the way sir has seen it.

Never. I am warned. I know what's going to happen.

But that's all. She looked up at the grey face of the man hours from adoration. Now sir knows, but there is nothing sir can do. Nothing. And again she buried her head.

There is, he said. There must be. Events aren't fixed. We have the power to choose, to change. You've told me the future that would have happened if I'd never known. But now the power has been transferred. Now I know the story I can change the ending, I can make it anything I like. So these things won't happen. None of them. It will all be very different. But you must tell me one thing. You must tell me where this man is, this Enoch Mistas.

Maria dropped her arms, spoke as softly as she had done in the beginning. He is nowhere, she said. He is not yet born.

Enoch Mistas

But even as they stand in the flickering candlelight, Maria can see Enoch Mistas. She can see him years hence with his sister Simple Martha on the veld outside the mission, herding goats. He is a boy of about ten, gangling, dressed in tattered clothes, his hair stiff with dirt, his bare feet hardened to thorns and stones. All day, a hot, unrelenting day, they've been wandering with the goats over these black rocks and scrub, squatting wherever there is shade, squeezing warm milk from the goats to ease their thirst. Soon their day will be ended by Nick the Herd's shrill whistle, penetrating even here where neither voice nor another human sound has reached them, where the only noise is goats and wind and the occasional clatter of locusts beating from bush to bush. Then they will crawl off the rock, run after the few animals that have strayed down a gully, and start back for the mission, not hurrying, dawdling into the shadow sliding towards them. From a distance two children herding goats: from close up Simple Martha's loose eye rolling with fatigue, a slackness about her mouth where only once will words be formed; from close up Enoch Mistas with scratched legs, snot smeared across a cheek, a dry scab on his belly visible when the breeze tugs open his shirt. Then he hadn't heard the voices. Then she hadn't seen the licks of flame. Then they were two children bringing in the goats, two children who afterwards ran free for an hour's quick:

> Hide, hide, he's got the flu
> Tishoo, tishoo,
> So have you

THIS DAY AND AGE

Don't let him in
Don't touch his skin
Death death death
Waits for you

with the other children, round the back of the church, among the latrines where a sullen sheep's head glares from the bottom of the pit.

But of this she says nothing, nor warns the president of the fatal stroke that strikes old men. He pushes more money across the table, turns to go, and she is left in the faint, fainter, faintest throb of the car engine disappearing down the wharves and quays.

The President Commands

On the day of the president's inauguration, when the streets were lined with crowds waving flags and the guard of honour sat perfectly on their horses, when the archbishop waited at the altar and the trumpeter held the brass to his lips in anticipation of that first triumphant note, the president, about to climb into the carriage alongside his wife, motioned for his secretary and said in an undertone: Go alone and fetch the fortune-teller. Find a place for her in the kitchen.

Right now? queried Johan van Rooyen.

Yes, now, hissed the nearly-president. Get it done before the swearing-in.

But the day had passed before the dictates of ceremony, the new demands of state, allowed the president and his secretary a few private words.

All done, Johan?

Not exactly, sir, the secretary replied.

What do you mean, not exactly? What does not exactly mean, Johan?

The private secretary swallowed. She was gone, sir. She wasn't there.

Gone. Gone! She couldn't have gone far. Have you had men looking for her?

Johan van Rooyen nodded.

And?

Nothing yet, sir.

They'd better find her, Johan. I don't care how long or how many men it takes. Just find her.

TWO

Consummation

Before the epidemic, at the birth of each of her six children, Ma-Fatsoen's curses echoed through Pastor Melksop's mission church like a premonition of disaster.

Everlasting heaven, he would pray, looking up at a picture of the Blessed Martyr, Benedictus qui venit in nomine Domini. But it never helped.

Six times in six years, always at the end of winter after the last frost, those curses jerked his eyes to that source of divine inspiration as he clapped his hands over his ears. Only at the birth of the last three did he think of tolling the bells as if in celebration. But that didn't help either. He could still hear, clearly, unremittingly above the clangour, the blasphemous rollcall that brought tears to his eyes and made him want to run out for miles and miles into the flylands.

Surely heaven must be ringing with that irreverence: the saints more angry than wasps; the martyrs, the burnt, quartered, crucified, adored martyrs, shouting for revenge. Why else this drought that had begun with the birth of the first child and worsened each year with the death of sheep or a plague of locusts, as Ma-Fatsoen's curses got louder and more coherent?

But those yearly curses, heralding summer yet containing a hidden prophecy which Pastor Melksop sensed but could not understand, were not all that disturbed this man of God. There was also the laughter. A high, hysterical laughter which began as a low moan on each New Year's Eve, like wind among scrub, then dropped off until it was just audible, more a feeling than a sound, only to come back in sucks and moans and chuckles, eventually

45

to break in a laugh at first wicked then purely joyous that had everyone who heard it laughing too. Except Pastor Melksop.

When it first happened, seven months after Ma-Fatsoen's marriage to Fat Eddie, he lit a lantern and ran bare-foot across the square in front of the church to Ma-Fatsoen's house. He paused once in his mad dash, nightshirt billowing, dust swirling, to make sure he hadn't dreamed it, but there it was again: moan, moan, snigger, laughter. Without another thought he began pounding on the door: Is everything all right? Is everything all right?

For a long time nobody answered, no matter how hard he pounded, but the laughter got wilder and wilder until the old lady, Ma-Fatsoen's mother, opened the door.

Before Pastor Melksop could speak she put a finger to her lips and said: Ssh. Ssh. It's happened at last – and closed the door.

But is everything all right? he shouted. The door opened again, the sunken face appeared, grinned, cackled, disappeared.

Bewildered, Pastor Melksop recrossed the square and went back to bed.

What, he wondered when the laughter suddenly stopped, had happened at last?

The question kept him awake all night and it was only the next day that, with a deep flush, he realised.

But on the morning after Ma-Fatsoen's outbreak he was none the wiser, although the villagers clustered together and broke up giggling when he approached. Neither was Ma-Fatsoen, who usually strode around the village kicking hens and chickens from her path as she saw to the women in the vegetable gardens and the men making shoes, up and about at her usual early hour. Nor was Fat Eddie to be found slumped in his chair on the stoep eating dough cakes with coffee.

They're probably resting, he overheard Mrs Naald telling Maria, his kitchen woman, in a whisper when they thought he was out of hearing. It just goes to show, storytelling's not all he's good for.

And, strangely, the old lady, Ma-Fatsoen's mother, who hadn't left the house in months, took out a stool and sat in the sun to shell her peas. When Pastor Melksop came up she worked her mouth into an empty smile. It was such a beautiful wedding, she said.

The Last Virgin of the Sourveld

Such a beautiful wedding and what a bride: the last virgin in the sourveld, the lust of boys, husbands and old men, the dream of slobs and gallants who had come riding from distant plains, vleis and mountains only to know the disappointment of guttered candles and her mother's harsh send-off when Ma-Fatsoen, still Hemelswerd, in a dazzle of lace and calico took her henna-haired, pool-eyed, peach-lipped, melon-breasted desire scornfully off to bed.

And in the end, the shame, the waste, the dreadful shamewaste of rampant nights, to think she chose Fat Eddie: a nothing, a nobody with soft hands and clean fingernails who couldn't catch sheep or kill jackals, who could only tell stories, and those milk stories without any blood.

But he told them better than the Bible and so charmed the lovely daughter Hemelswerd she said: Ma, I want this man.

Never, came the quick retort. He's nothing, a nobody. He's so fat you'll never have children.

The gorgeous daughter Hemelswerd shrugged: Tell her about whales and boats, Fat Eddie, she said. Tell her about deep jungles and bright birds. Tell her. Tell her.

And Fat Eddie did, until there were no more candles in the cupboard, but the old lady wouldn't go to bed and he had to go on telling stories in the dark. When the sun came up, the old woman bared her gums: All right, daughter, she said. Maybe he can't ride a horse for a week across his land, maybe he can't even ride a horse, but he's got a tongue for a dull night. And I should know, God rest your Father the Ox, that's probably worth more.

Over the weeks word got around to distant plains, vleis and mountains where fathers looked at their long-legged sons and said: Ag shame, man, to think she thought you worse than Fat Eddie. Ag shame. Ag shame.

The wide-eared sons hung their heads and walked out into the veld disgraced. Some saddled horses and went off to plead one last time, only to be told by the old lady, Ox Hemelswerd's widow: My daughter's betrothed, humble your spirits.

One by one they crawled away, leading their horses through the scrublands. Soon news came of one found hanging from the only tree on the plain, another drowned in his tears at a vlei, a third fallen from a mountain. Even some fathers, rumour had it, took to their wicker chairs and stared over plains, vleis and mountains in the direction of the mission trying to overcome their humiliation.

But none of it worried the luscious daughter Hemelswerd, blushing bride-to-be, radiant radiance, full of smiles, swishing among leather, tacks, eyes, tomatoes, cauliflower, carrots in her best dresses kept waiting in boxes for all these years. But even that wasn't good enough.

From now on, my girl, it's nothing but the best, nothing but the finest, said her mother, calling in dressmakers, knitters, cobblers to You-each see she looks even better than when those hairy-nosed suitors were keeping us up night after night.

Which they did, with dresses for morning, afternoon, evening; skirts for market-days and festivals; white, cream, red, purple, green blouses; suits for church; cardigans; jumpers; coats; boots; shoes; sandals; a fashion all her own.

Holy Father, muttered Pastor Melksop, are there so many ways to cut cloth? when once again the future Ma-Fatsoen flounced into the square like a peacock in full fan.

Now she's showing her blood, said her mother, now she's showing we're not from the common herd. Just look at the blue in her, Fat Eddie, despite the Ox, God rest his soul, her father and all his tribe before him. And Fat Eddie dipped another dough cake in his coffee and smiled with a mouth of jam.

But dresses for morning, afternoon and evening weren't all the old lady was after.

The Last Virgin of the Sourveld

That's mere feathers, she said. I want a creation.

So the dressmakers designed and cut, patterned and pinned enough wedding dresses for more than a hundred brides, yet nothing satisfied the old lady.

There'll be no wedding until you get it right, and you'd better get it right soon because Fat Eddie's said no more stories until he's a husband. And my daughter's getting more impossible by each dull night. So hurry, even if it takes your fingers to the bone.

Long hours, dawn to dawn, design cut pattern pin until . . .

Now that's a creation, marvelled the old lady. That's *haute couture*, what I call out of the top drawer. But you keep it a secret, hear, this one's going to have them all gasping. This one's going to make even Pastor Melksop lose his words.

Day on day, cloth was cut, lace made, gloves embroidered. Once, twice, three, four times the bride-to-be, more radiant than ever, went down to Mrs Naald's room behind the trading store where, among skeins of wool piled high and racks of cotton, tweed, linen, worsted, woollens, calico, gingham and silk, she was measured and fitted as the creation took shape: full, beautiful, lovely.

The women clucked their satisfaction; the old lady, her mother, proud as a peacock, said: If only your father, long may the Ox rest in peace, could see you now. We've got to set a date.

So a date was set, a date in May when warm winds drifting down the dry lands blew between the hills on to the mission turning green leaves brown, shrivelling the wings of dragonflies, burning nostrils, scouring eyes, hot, listless, filled with crying babies.

Oh Pastor Melksop, oh Pastor Melksop, lamented Maria, things always go wrong in the hot winds. They must not marry. It's not a good day for a wedding.

Nonsense, Maria, said Pastor Melksop adjusting dog-collar, fitting mantle, pressing his hair down with licked fingers. That's old wives' tales, superstition, what better day could a bride want? Look at it: blue sky, birds calling – it's a good day, Maria, the day before rain.

But even the old lady, the betrothed's mother, wasn't so sure. Maybe tomorrow would be better, she said, pressing studs, fastening stays. It's an ill wind that blows this hot. Listen to me, daughter, I know about these things. And what's one more night in an everlasting marriage? Nothing I tell you. It's neither here nor there. Let's call the whole thing off, just for today.

Nonsense, Ma, said the bride, lifting her veil, putting on lipstick. It couldn't be better. Not everyone gets a warm day in autumn to marry. And look at me, look at this creation, it's time to show it off.

In the church, the congregation shifted anticipating feet, craned necks, strained to see out of the ice-box church into the hot blaze where the daughter Hemelswerd, radiant radiance, a mirage in white, wafted in chiffon and froth across the square, small explosions of dust clouding her shoes. Pastor Melksop, fumbling for the marriage service in his hymnal, looked up, opened his mouth in wonder, for a moment convinced of a divine visitation, and did not shut it again until five minutes later he stammered into the solemnisation of Uh, um, Dearly beloved we are gathered here together in the sight of . . . Because there, sweeping past the long table laid out for the celebrations, past the kitchen women bringing loaves, cutting mutton, the vintners fetching sweet wine brandy port sherry from beneath the church, her peacock train held up by twelve dainty hands, her pool-eyes cast demurely down behind the veil, her slim white glove resting beneath the arm of the old lady, her giving-away mother, her whole entourage shaded by a lace umbrella, came Fat Eddie's future wife, the only child of Enoch the Ox and the now toothless Mrs Hemelswerd. Women paused in mid-cut, men stopped bringing wine, howling babies suddenly smiled as her beauty the bride shimmered out of the hot wind into the cool, dark church. At the communion rail Fat Eddie licked his fingers still sticky from the last dough cake, said softly to all the short-haired boys on distant plains, vleis and mountains: Eat your hearts out, boers – and gave a wait-until-tonight smile to his rapidly advancing spouse. Behind him the congregation heaved a collective sigh of admiration.

Pastor Melksop closed his mouth, opened it again, saw the gummy smile of the old lady Mrs Hemelswerd and was at a loss for words.

Fat Eddie thought of a story. His bride shifting her eyes beneath the veil said: Tell me. Tell me. The congregation sniggered; Pastor

Melksop cleared his throat, asserted his authority, began before Fat Eddie could begin.

Uh um to join this Man and this Woman uh um wilt thou have uh um wilt thou have . . .

I will. I will. I will I will I will.

Those uh um whom God hath joined uh um let no man put asunder uh um. Let us pray.

But no man woman or child was in a mood for prayer. It was confetti time, snow in the cool church, snow on the baking square, it was hip hip hurrah hurrah hurrah, it was a triumphal arch of spades, hoes, walking sticks, rakes, it was accordions, mouth organs, tambourines, whistles, bugle, it was good luck, handshakes, kisses, neighing horses in the fields, bleating goats on the hills, cocks at their doodle-dos in the middle of the afternoon.

May the Lord bless you all, intoned Pastor Melksop, drawing an imaginary cross in the air as his flock disappeared through the white rectangle at the back of the church.

What an afternoon evening morning. Wine, food, music, dancing, sweet nothings whispered, ears nibbled, love, lust, quarrels, fists, knives, blood, tears, accusations, I warned you no one should marry in a hot wind, stories the best Fat Eddie had ever told, laughter laughter and more crying. Which all began when Fat Eddie and his unveiled bride came out of the spade hoe stick rake tunnel of honour, out of the snow into the sun and sat down at the head of the long table that went right across the square.

I love you, said Fat Eddie through a mouthful of dough cake.

Let's dance, said Ma-Fatsoen putting down a drumstick.

Slowly they waltzed between the tables and the food, her ear to his tales of sherbet and diamonds, bokoms and bread, fishing villages and tyrants, while everyone ooh'd and aah'd what a lovely daughter you've got Mrs Hemelswerd and a clever son-in-law too. What a handsome couple. Aren't they the perfect pair? If only my Dora, John, Cynthia, Robert could be like them.

Sighing mothers, lecherous fathers, boyfriends, girlfriends took to the square dancing, whispering, hugging, kissing those they should've and those they shouldn't until one husband saw a strange hand cupping his wife's buttock. At least that's how some say it started. Others say it had nothing to do with love at all but how a cardsharp cut the pack where they were playing Dead Men under the bluegum tree with aces high and wild jokers and one of them saw the cards up his sleeve.

At first it was push, shove, raised voices, then a punch and some men, whether on the square or under the bluegums, decided there was honour at stake and went in too. Others didn't stop dancing, nor did Fat Eddie so much as pause in the midst of his story. Some women raised their eyebrows, shook their heads, then went back to discussing the bride's dress, while a couple who were married but not to each other took advantage of the distraction and one another under the table.

Only Pastor Melksop, surprisingly strong for such a slight build, tried to stop it by laying out five, six, eight men with his mace. But by then the damage had been done: Nick the Herd lay bleeding in the dust from a stab wound in his shoulder.

Pastor Melksop raged, Satans. Dark hounds. Sons of serpents. Whose knife? Whose knife is this? And he picked up a small blade, the sort used for cutting dried meat or whittling twigs.

No one owned up although they all knew it belonged to Augustus Niemand, who was neither playing cards nor dancing when the fracas started, who was even now stretched out on the ground, felled by Pastor Melksop's mace. But no one whispered that fateful name because people thought Augustus Niemand had once murdered a man called Mackenzie and fed his body to hyenas. And everyone knew the taste of blood kept a long appetite.

Oh I told you, Pastor Melksop, didn't I warn you no one should marry in a hot wind? howled Maria washing out the wound with tears. Poor Nick, poor Nick among these jackals.

Some looked on, others drifted off to dance or back to the table where the old lady, Mrs Hemelswerd, beat out a rhythm on the plates with her spoon.

Pastor Melksop, suddenly alone among the bodies, threw the blade on the sand and turned his eyes to the darkening hills to pray.

From out of those hills, leading a horse that had thrown a shoe, came the young P.T. George, gentleman traveller passing through on his way to hunt rhino, sable, giraffe.

The Last Virgin of the Sourveld

Excuse me, Pastor, he said, may I rest here a few days?

Everyone is welcome at God's mission, replied Pastor Melksop, pouring wine, cutting bread, offering refreshments to a dusty face. Do you come from far?

From the coast. From distant countries, said P.T. George through a mouth of potato, heading north for the great river.

Pastor Melksop nodded: So did I. Once. He thought for a moment while P.T. George took draughts of wine, chewed, swallowed, helped himself to more. It's bad out there, he said eventually. Men without God, animals without fear, a hostile land. It needs a missionary, it needs God's everlasting kingdom.

Maybe, said P.T. George, but I want to see it wild.

Years ago I prayed for the Lord to send me to savage parts, sighed Pastor Melksop as if P.T. George hadn't spoken. But He always knows best. The priest drank from a stray glass of wine. I suppose He knew I was too weak for work like that.

The dancers on the square billowed and swayed. There was laughter everywhere. Even Nick the Herd, still pale as a ghost, joked with Augustus Niemand. In his pocket the knifeman ran his finger down the blade. Ha ha. Too much sweet wine, ha ha, they sniggered. Only Maria watched Augustus with a sharp eye. At the head of the table Fat Eddie regaled his adoring wife and audience with battles, colonel's daughters and love-struck enemy soldiers, endless tales of fantasy, of magic. The night was only just beginning.

Pastor Melksop put his head in his hands: It will take a hard man to bring the Lord our Saviour to the hordes and waywards. A man obsessed. A man without fear. A true leader whom people will look to and follow.

I've yet to come across a man like that, said P.T. George.

But if you ever do, you'll know the power of God's will. Pastor Melksop stood up. It's a power no one can resist. He looked at the dancers. It is time I took evening prayers, he said. Even in such God-blessed times as weddings we must not forget our worship. Will you join us, friend?

Thank you, pastor, replied P.T. George, eyeing a leg of mutton, but I am not a religious man.

An atheist?

No. A scientist.

The priest shook his head. There is no greater scientist than God, he said. Then added: Should you wish for a comfortable bed, my house is there beside the church.

P.T. George acknowledged the generosity with a nod, his mouth too full for speech.

The wind had stopped now but the night was still warm. The bluegum trees stood sprayed against the heavens like water and on the square the dancers went down, exhausted, love-struck, drunk.

Such a beautiful wedding, dreamed the old lady, Mrs Hemelswerd, such a beautiful wedding, Ox, God preserve you. Such a lovely daughter.

Tell me more. Tell me more, demanded Ma-Fatsoen as Fat Eddie snuggled against her in their first-night bed. Tell me more, there's plenty of time for that other business. She fluffed up pillows, buttoned the lace to her neck. Tell me more, the candle's not even half down yet, and there's another and another and another when they're finished. So Fat Eddie told stories until they stopped in sleep and Ma-Fatsoen blew out the candle with a smile.

Outside dogs scavenged among bones and discarded plates, licked the bodies of drunken men, gave a wide berth to the sobbing woman whose husband lay in the reeds with a young girl.

As Pastor Melksop had foretold, it rained the next morning. P.T. George woke to bells, drips, and the tramp of the new wife Ma-Fatsoen's boots as she saw to the mission.

Doesn't that woman know about honeymoons? grumbled the men in the factory and the women in the fields bogged down in mud. Doesn't she know about wine heads?

But Ma-Fatsoen, dressed to the nines, was thinking neither of honeymoons nor of wine heads as she crossed the square, waved to Fat Eddie on the verandah dunking dough cakes into his coffee, and, hair shining with rain, disappeared towards the long-drops carrying a sheep's head. She was thinking of large pillows and clean sheets, the warmth of Fat Eddie and the wonder of his tales; she was thinking of the old lady, her mother. The old lady, who, grinning gums, twinkling eyes, had sniffed about her at the wash-tub like a dog.

You'd better, was all she'd said to her newly married daughter when the sniffing stopped, because I'm not going to set foot outside this house until you have. Not even to empty my pail.

Hypocrite, Ma-Fatsoen said inwardly, considering how you said the Ox treated you.

Hypocrite, she said again, dropping the sheep's head into the latrine pit.

Some time later the sheep's head stared malignantly up at P.T. George's English arse as he made himself comfortable on the wooden seat. It stared balefully up at the voiding of leg of lamb, mutton chop, mint sauce, spare-rib. Not once did it blare or blink an eye. Above it, a now relieved P.T. George, feeling he was being watched, kicked closed the door he'd left open to the wet fields. But the feeling persisted, disturbed those precious first moments of his day when he liked to think. Increasingly uneasy, he stared down through the smell into the pit. The sheep's head glared back.

Fat Eddie was still at breakfast on the verandah when P.T. George, wearing only a shirt and boots, clutching his trousers, came running among the mission cottages, causing children to giggle, men to forget their hangovers, women to shut their eyes, raced across the square and disappeared like a white bob-tail into Pastor Melksop's house, shouting about a dead man in the privy. No it's not, everyone laughed. But no amount of persuading – It's just there for the worms – would take him back to the long-drops, and three days later he left the mission as constipated as a pregnant cat.

May the Lord go with you, said Pastor Melksop, as the scientist swung on to his horse. We all need faith in the badlands.

P.T. George smiled weakly, tapped the reins against his horse's neck, and rode into the veld.

Bedtime Stories

The mission settled down to cold, snow, shrivelled vegetables,
lost lambs, the admonitions of Pastor Melksop and the memories of a beautiful wedding. In Mrs Naald's window the dress
went on display, in some cottages hearts that had been broken
were mended, husbands proclaimed undying love to their wives,
wives promised servility to their husbands, everything returned to
normal except for Nick the Herd's wound, which festered despite
Maria's tears through all the bad weather. If there was gossip in the
early winter it was nothing out of the ordinary: the smell of an old
woman, the bed-wetting of an uncle, or the eager anticipation of a
pregnancy. Each long night, the villagers noted, candles burned in
Ma-Fatsoen's bedroom where she sat propped among pillows, her
feet warmed by a hot brick, listening to Fat Eddie's stories until
they stopped in mid-sentence. Each morning she was first up,
emptied her mother's pail, collected eggs, pulled milk, prepared
dough cakes, got on with the business of running the mission.
But there was no sign of a swelling stomach, morning nausea,
or the old lady.

It was the old lady's absence which first loosened tongues. They
could see her in the depths of rooms, sometimes peering out from
behind the drapes, often framed in the kitchen window like a ghost.
They knew from Pastor Melksop that she was not ill and, as the
months passed, they suspected, in part, the vow she had taken.

If the womb's empty, it's God's will, said Mrs Naald. No hiding
in rooms is going to change that.

But maybe it's him, said Mrs Zimri, from eating all those dough
cakes.

Bedtime Stories

No marriage is a marriage without a child, added Mrs Naald. I can understand Mrs Hemelswerd's shame.

Month followed month, winter spring summer, Christmas, New Year's Eve, the night when the laughter started and everyone and the old lady heaved a sigh of relief. It had happened at last.

How it happened surprised the lustful Fat Eddie even more than his virginal wife. Despite seven months of demanding, coaxing, pleading, despite threats to stop telling stories, despite occasional glimpses of tender lamb-brown flesh which drove him crazy and brought anemones, marshes, sludge, fingers, sticks, probing, prodding into his stories, despite kisses that sometimes started upwards from her ankles or othertimes downwards from her neck, which she had to wriggle out of like a child, despite all those days of emptying the old lady's stinking pail, Ma-Fatsoen was indifferent to her husband's lovemaking.

Please, begged Fat Eddie.

One day, promised Ma-Fatsoen.

But when? he pressed.

The time will come, she said.

In the kitchen her mother sniffed with disdain and shat more foully and copiously each night. On the distant farms thick-lipped sons sniggered, watched their fathers lift disgraced heads and smile for the first time in months.

There was a smell of revenge in the summer air. The Lord in His infinite wisdom was merciful. Until the eve of New Year.

Perhaps it was the wine of celebrations, or the good food, or the curtains rustling at the window, or maybe Fat Eddie's connivance with a soothsayer had at last produced a spell which broke the hex – whatever it was, the candles went out in Ma-Fatsoen's bedroom earlier than they had done in seven months and Fat Eddie found himself flat on his back with his sniggering moaning chuckling wife, nightdress hitched about her thighs, riding him the way she rode her horse, hard, tight-eyed, laughing. And no matter how he bucked, shied, tried to throw her off, even more humiliated than in the days of abstinence, she rode him with all the exuberance of an old hand, wild at the delight. Out of the paddock into the hard veld she galloped leaning forward over Fat Eddie's head, her hair lashing his cheeks. Galloped through the pounding of Pastor

Melksop's concern, raced over streams, rivers, torrents, laughing louder and louder urged on by her grinning mother in the hallway. High in the mountains where her laughter echoed without ceasing, Fat Eddie neighed and was spent. But not even that final tumble could dislodge his rider, heaving squint-eyed over him.

It's just like storytelling, she gasped, dismounting, falling asleep.

I am milked, thought Fat Eddie. Milked and shamed.

In the hallway, the old lady, nine months off being a grand-mother, sighed, remembered how her husband the Ox, Lord judge him fairly, had covered her roughly, rudely, night after night until the birth of their daughter.

Beast, she spat. Be just, oh Lord.

When, in the middle of the next morning, Ma-Fatsoen, cool in cotton print dress, a smile fluttering about her mouth, and, slightly behind her, Fat Eddie, sheepish, grinning weakly, stepped on to the verandah, everyone clapped. The Zimris came out of their store, Mrs Naald and her ladies lined the shopfront, the bootmakers put down last and leather, even in the furthest fields the women rested on their spades to applaud.

At first Pastor Melksop, still pondering the old lady's enigmatic statements, kept his arms folded, completely at a loss.

Clap, whispered Maria, for some it's a happy day.

Why especially? he queried. In God's eyes every day is a happy one.

Because the mission is saved, said Mrs Zimri.

Pastor Melksop shook his head, wondering why her world, the world of everyone on the mission, was so different from his. He sighed and began to clap.

The applause wasn't heard on distant plains, vleis and mountains but as Ma-Fatsoen's stomach put new demands on Mrs Naald's ladies for more dresses, so it also brought shame back to those parts. Once again fathers hung their heads and their ungainly sons, biting lower lips, went out to herd sheep in far-flung camps.

But on the mission, each day was a cause for celebration. Never had the men drunk so much wine. Evening after evening they sat under the bluegum trees passing the flagon from mouth to mouth. Never had the women been so talkative, worse than mouse-birds in the vines, or the shuffling in church been so irritating to Pastor

Melksop. Inevitably Augustus Niemand's blade slashed across someone's chest and would have cut again had Nick the Herd not smashed the knifeman's wrist with his staff. At least once a week Pastor Melksop was called to put an end to their quarrels, their gambling, their good moods soured by sweet wine. His congregation shrank, he had to go among the cottages waking sodden men still in their boots for Sunday worship.

What is happening to everyone? he complained to Maria, as she laid the table and set his dinner before him.

The people are happy, she replied. Now they believe there'll be a boy with Hemelswerd blood.

Or a daughter, said Pastor Melksop. Any child is a joy.

Not here, said Maria. Remember the last words of Enoch the Ox.

Blah, exclaimed Pastor Melksop, that's pure fabrication.

Still it puzzled the churchman, who sent a string of urgent prayers to heaven that evening asking for guidance, asking God the Father to strengthen his soul, God the Son not to let his life have been in vain, and God the Holy Ghost to help him bring these sinners to the everlasting kingdom. Also he went to seek Ma-Fatsoen's help.

These people know not what they do, he told her.

She offered him her famous syrupy dough cakes. He took one and licked his fingers.

They are poor wanderers in the desert. We – he looked at her – we must take them out of the wilderness.

We shall, said Ma-Fatsoen. The time will come.

Later, at prayer below the Blessed Martyr, Pastor Melksop sighed and thought of the virtue that is patience. How could one life, he wondered, be so completely misunderstood? Why did God punish him with such weakness? Each night he asked hard questions, but each night the Lord his God remained mute.

As, month by month, Ma-Fatsoen swelled, Fat Eddie's grin got broader, pushing to some back field of his mind the wild dangerous ride into the mountains. She was his girl, his wife, the expectant mother of his child, that unseen son who bumped against him at night while he was telling stories. How could he ever have known that those constrained kicks were trying to get him to keep quiet? And what would he have done if he had known that his tiny daughter, usually content in her warm balloon of water, raised half-formed hands to half-formed ears each time she heard his voice come booming through the depths about once upon a time there lived . . .

Fat Eddie was too pleased with himself even to suspect those gentle knocks might be malicious. I'm going to be a father, he thought to himself. I'm going to tell marvellous tales to my children.

But although, when the time came, he fussed about his wife like a meercat, fluffed up the pillows, swabbed her brow, ran for the midwife, paced up and down the verandah, as soon as she started cursing, Fat Eddie hid under the altar cloth. And there he stayed even when Pastor Melksop crawled in to beg him: Please go and talk to your wife, she mustn't say these things. But Fat Eddie only shook his head and wouldn't take his fingers out of his ears.

Perhaps, thought Pastor Melksop, standing before the picture of the Blessed Martyr, dusting his knees, praying to God to forgive the weakness of the flesh, this was the way of women, Benedictus qui venit in nomine Domini.

In Ma-Fatsoen's bedroom the old lady smiled her pink gum smile at the midwife who was measuring the opening with her fingers.

Damn you, damn you, Fat Eddie, hissed Ma-Fatsoen biting the rag, panting, straining. Geld him, Ma, stamp out the worm. Oh Jesus, oh Christ, damn God for this pain.

Almost there, said the midwife taking her finger from the dike, letting the waters break.

Male bastard, screamed Ma-Fatsoen, why can't he have children? Him and God too for making women go through this.

Dear Lord forgive her, she knows not what she says, prayed Pastor Melksop.

She's right, whispered Mrs Naald. If God was a woman He'd have made it fifty-fifty. The dressmakers nodded but didn't look up.

Oh Jesus, Fat Eddie, I'm going to cut it off. No more of your serpent's temptation, you snake in the grass, you toad in the hole, you . . . you . . . spermbag.

Bedtime Stories

All through the afternoon Ma-Fatsoen cursed and screamed while inside her Martha, pleading with her mother to be quiet for just one moment, got the cord wound tightly round her neck, almost panicked, then saw light at the end of the tunnel and dived out. There were the hands of the midwife to catch her, pull out umbilical cord, placenta, while Martha gasped: Give me air, give me air. But it was too long in coming. Hands fumbled with the noose around her neck, cut her free, spanked her again and again until she broke into sobs, spat up the blood on her lungs. Too late, her one eye rolled loosely and never found a home.

It's a girl, whispered Pastor Melksop to Fat Eddie lifting an edge of the altar cloth.

It's a girl, said Mrs Naald, Mrs Zimri and the rest of them in disbelief. It can't be. Dear Lord, what are we going to do now?

It's only the first one, reminded Mrs Zimri.

But look how long that took, said Mrs Naald. If a womb's reluctant it could be the last.

And Ox Hemelswerd had seed only for a daughter.

Oh Lord help us. Lord don't forsake us, they prayed.

He won't. There'll be a boy one day, said Maria tight-lipped.

Hah, scoffed distant farmers. Is that all he's got in him? She should've married a man, they joked with their sons.

Sissy. Ma-Fatsoen breathed a sigh of relief holding up little Martha, giving her a breast. Thank God it's a girl. Don't let me ever bring one of those other monsters into this world.

A girl, exclaimed Fat Eddie dusting off his pants. What's the use of a girl?

We are all God's creations, said Pastor Melksop. We must give thanks for a life.

A life! What sort of life is that? thought Fat Eddie looking down at his daughter, still blue, tiny-eared, rolling her eye. And little Martha smiled back thinking she was beyond the reach of her father.

If she's going to have any chance in life I've got to fill her head with more stories than a sponge has holes, reasoned Fat Eddie submerging a dough cake in his coffee until the liquid overflowed. I've got to tell her about everything because there'll be no moonlit nights for her with boys staring into her eye.

When he'd slurped the coffee from the saucer, licked syrup from his fingers, Fat Eddie went indoors and sat down at Martha's cot. He told her about fairies and gnomes and horses with one horn; he told her about ancient empires, pharaohs, pyramids; about continents of ice, mountains that coughed fire, about piranhas, pirates and pirouetting ballerinas until Ma-Fatsoen said: That's enough, Fat Eddie, let the poor child sleep.

But even when she slept he wouldn't stop.

This child needs all the help I can give her, he told his wife, interrupting the passage of dinosaurs or the bellows of the minotaur, surely you can see that?

So awake, asleep, feeding, little Martha heard the history of nations, the story of the world, the world's stories: a long sad rush of noise that came whistling in her tiny ears, drove her to tears, to tantrums, to wishing the midwife hadn't cut her free so soon. In her cot, on the verandah, being walked about the mission, among Mrs Naald's clothes, the Zimris' preserves, through the sheds of tanned leather, the boot factory, out into the fields where women leant on their hoes to ooh and aah at her grimacing face with its drifting eye, little Martha never stopped hearing about elephants, rhinoceroses, giraffes. Until . . . until right at the end of a Zulu battle, just when she didn't want to hear any more, ever, the noise stopped and the world was perfectly still. For the second time she looked up at her father and smiled.

Such encouragement was all Fat Eddie needed. He turned to physics, gravity, the laws of motion. He spoke of apples, feathers, lead and eureka. In the cot beside him little Martha gurgled and spluttered, let her eye circle its socket.

Isn't he a happy father? remarked Mrs to Mr Zimri at the store. So doting.

But aren't they going to try again? said Mr Zimri. We need a boy.

And, as these things will, in Ma-Fatsoen the worm had turned. She forgot her threats of gelding, stamping out, cutting off; she remembered an exciting gallop into the mountains and thought of riding out bareback once more. Which again she did on New Year's Eve, sliding a leg across Fat Eddie, hefting herself up, lashing him, taking off with a giggle that turned to laughter. The only one in that whole mission who didn't hear her was Martha lying an arm's length away, her face at rest in a beatific smile.

And, come the end of winter after the last frost, Ma-Fatsoen, once again sending Fat Eddie to cower under the altar cloth, cursed him, his father, her father, all fathers including those most high. The old lady, her mother and the midwife added their bit like a chorus, grinning at one another across the swollen stomach. In his room at the back of the mission, Pastor Melksop, hands clapped to his ears, stared fixedly at the picture of the Blessed Martyr intoning over and over again: Benedictus qui venit in nomine Domini. But it didn't help. At the end of the blasphemous malediction Ma-Fatsoen gave birth to another daughter. And, as the years passed, another and another and another and another, repeating with only one variation – Pastor Melksop on the bells – the pattern that Martha had established. With each girl the people on the mission grew more cowed, more unhappy. On distant plains, vleis and mountains fathers laughed out loud at a man who could produce only daughters. It is God's justice, they said to their sons, who knew nothing of women, who cared only for sheep. The man himself, ridden every New Year to exhaustion, sent scurrying under the altar every spring, told stories to Martha alone, and those were insipid tales of romance. Even his appetite for dough cakes shrank; Fat Eddie hung on his skeleton like old clothes.

It's our revenge, cackled the old lady to the midwife, at the birth of the last daughter. In the church Pastor Melksop, sweat pouring down his face, pulled and pulled at the bell rope. Have mercy, oh Lord.

But the Lord was not being merciful. Martha's first summer saw the end of rivers that not even the winter could revive. Martha's second summer saw springs dry up that had not been dry in living memory. During her third summer the locusts came. Pastor Melksop looked at his flock, thinner, hungry, festering with sores, and vowed once more to talk to Fat Eddie.

It is written, he told him, thumbing through a Bible where the words often disappeared beneath grime, that husbands shall rule their wives. And not only that, he said, but that women will desire their men and give birth to children in sorrow.

Pastor Melksop sat back. Fat Eddie watched the wasps bringing mud to their nest under the eaves and pictured Ma-Fatsoen astride him – hair flying about her face, great rhythmic leaps crushing him beneath her thighs. He sighed.

Pastor Melksop looked at Ma-Fatsoen's husband closely: at sweat clinging to stubble, at fear twitching the corners of his mouth.

All these things are written, he said lamely. They are rules.

Rules, said Fat Eddie, thinking of how he'd once seen a man do it to a woman, spread out on top of her, thrusting with all the force of a knifeman. Again and again. Hadn't the woman cried out? Rules.

God always punishes people who break the rules, Pastor Melksop was saying when Fat Eddie came out of his daydream. The men stared at one another: the priest seeing a scarecrow; the husband seeing nothing but the bright light of the square. I will pray for you, said Pastor Melksop getting up.

Once, after the birth of Hendrina, the third child, the priest considered threatening Ma-Fatsoen with hellfire if she did not show more respect for the Lord his (and her) God. A week he spent praying, asking for strength, begging for courage, pleading for nerve. But in the end, when he saw Ma-Fatsoen with little Martha on her hip, striding through hens and chickens, though he tried to step forward, he instead cringed further into the church's shadow.

I know what, he said, relief filling his chest, next time I'll ring the bells.

Which he did. But the drought kept on burning, searing, evaporating, wilting, killing sheep and even goats.

I told you, said Maria. I told you she shouldn't marry in a hot wind.

Hide, Hide He's Got the Flu

But Ma-Fatsoen didn't care. About her the mission crumbled as cracks opened in scorched dry walls, bricks turned to dust and thatch caught fire spontaneously. With the rest of the congregation Ma-Fatsoen went down on her knees to pray for rain but they were merely words she mouthed without thinking. Even after the birth of Augustina (the fourth), when there hadn't been so much as a shower of rain for two years, Ma-Fatsoen gave no thought to the drought. In truth, since the birth of Martha she'd given little thought to anyone or anything.

She had Sissy, simple deaf Martha, who seemed to need no one, who sat contentedly in her quietness drawing pictures of dragonflies. Ma-Fatsoen had first taken her to see the dragonflies on her second birthday when the reservoir was still almost full. They fascinated Martha; she liked especially the blue ones that dived and swooped and sometimes hovered, stacked four high. Getting Ma-Fatsoen to take her to the reservoir was the only demand she ever made: a short cry followed by a sharp tug on her mother's latest fashionable skirt. They spent whole afternoons there: Ma-Fatsoen lying on the grass bank, her daughter, flat on her stomach, staring across the surface at algae rafts and beautiful dragonflies vibrating their wings into silver. But each year the water level dropped and sometimes there would be days without dragonflies. Then Martha cried, not like a normal child, but slow tears that would take all afternoon to roll down her cheeks. When that happened, Ma-Fatsoen wanted to castrate Fat Eddie with the knife she used for gutting chickens.

At about the same time Fat Eddie's stories dried up like the mountain springs and Ma-Fatsoen moved into another room with Sissy, leaving her mother and a succession of wetnurses to care for Paulina, Hendrina, Augustina, and eventually Wilhelmina and Justina. Only on New Year's Eve did she use her husband's bed, and then on ever wilder, briefer charges. Not that Fat Eddie encouraged it. Despite his loss of weight, his shrinking form, he put up greater resistance as the epidemic got closer: first by locking himself in his room before the conception of Wilhelmina, then by trying to flee before the procreation of Justina. But Ma-Fatsoen guessed his intentions even before he thought of them and kept him manacled to the bed with a length of her father's chain from Christmas to New Year.

It's unnatural, Pastor Melksop complained both to the picture of the Blessed Martyr and to Maria. The woman should stop having children if she's not going to care for them.

Neither the Blessed Martyr nor Maria replied. Maria, at least, felt that she had nothing more to say on the matter. All she and the other villagers could do was endure the hardships and pray that, like everything else, they would eventually end. As long as Ma-Fatsoen kept on producing children there was hope, of a sort. One day it had to be a boy. A boy would be their salvation.

Then, not long after the birth of Justina, in the days when Martha spent afternoons alone at the reservoir, now a mere mud-hole with a single dragonfly passing again and again over the stagnant water where soon she'd find it dead, the epidemic was brought to the mission by a man on a donkey cart carrying a load of salted fish. He arrived one Wednesday as he usually did with all the other donkey-cart traders bringing stores for the Zimris and great barrels of water from the only spring in the district. Even when he was at the top of the pass, even when there was a noise in the square of braying donkeys, cracking whips, people, children, the bootmakers haggling prices, greetings and Pastor Melksop ringing the bells for morning prayers, even then everyone heard him, blessed him, counted one two three four five sneezes, marvelled, laughed, waited impatiently for the arrival of the bokoms' man. Down the pass he came in a shower of stones and mucus, eyes inflamed, nose streaming, crystallised snot trails on the back of his hand. But, as always, neither his fish nor his price was to be sneezed at. An hour later, the monger rolled up his hessian bags thick with salt, blew his nose a nostril at a time in expert runs at a passing goose, and went back up the pass sucking loudly on his congestion. That night almost everyone ate bokoms except a handful of people too poor to buy them and Pastor Melksop, who loathed the taste of fish oil, and the Zimris, who ate only from tins, and Maria, Mrs Naald and her sewing ladies, Jonathan the chief bootmaker and David his assistant, Augustus Niemand, Nick, Ma-Fatsoen and five-year-old Martha. Of everyone, Fat Eddie, by then only a shadow of his former self, ate the most. Which is maybe why he was the first to die.

By the Saturday morning Fat Eddie was dead, but nobody realised it until the Sunday service when the old lady, Ma-Fatsoen, four daughters and two others being suckled slid into their pew but Fat Eddie did not. All through an October Saturday afternoon filled with motes in sunlight he had lain curled up like a foetus because he'd been shivering with cold, dead to the world. And now Pastor Melksop waited and waited. His congregation, sniffing, snorting, sneezing with sore throats and the start of coughs, shifted restlessly in their seats wanting nothing more than to go home to bed.

Dammit, said Ma-Fatsoen eventually. The lout's still asleep – and swished out of the church with a rustle of starched petticoats. Martha followed her. Five minutes later Ma-Fatsoen returned to whisper in Pastor Melksop's ear: Fat Eddie's dead.

Let us pray for the souls of the dear departed, intoned the priest while Ma-Fatsoen asked Mrs Naald to make a shroud and Mr Zimri to sell her a coffin. By lunchtime Fat Eddie lay beneath six feet of earth. Four days later, the old lady, Ma-Fatsoen's mother, in a blaze of mucus and high temperature, also died.

See, said Maria to Pastor Melksop, this is the evil of hot winds.

And so it seemed when first baby Justina, then Wilhelmina, Augustina, Hendrina, Paulina all succumbed to the influenza: gave up, withered, passed on.

Just not my Sissy, please, prayed Ma-Fatsoen at each funeral, but Martha neither sniffed nor coughed nor spat the grey globs that so many hawked up in the streets.

Returning from the burial of Paulina, Mrs Naald looked at her diminished racks of calico and wondered if she should order more. In his store, Mr Zimri counted four coffins left and gambled that there would be other deaths.

No, said his wife. Be thrifty, God has punished us enough. The mission is finished anyhow.

But they'll always be used, said Mr Zimri filling in an order for ten. No matter what.

He was right. In fourteen days each box was bespoke: mothers shared with daughters, fathers with sons. Mrs Naald ran out of calico for shrouds, suggested linen until it too was finished, gingham, worsted, silk, but who could pay such prices for their dead?

Is there no end to the dying? wondered Pastor Melksop as his congregation shrank from Sunday to Sunday and he came to know the burial service by heart.

The Lord is just, said fathers to sons on distant plains, vleis and mountains, see how His wrath is now brought down upon the sinners.

But in the months to come neither they nor those in ports, towns or desert outposts were spared. The influenza got them all.

On the mission there was no time for winding sheets, coffins, separate ceremonies, separate graves. No time really to hate Ma-Fatsoen for bringing all this on their heads, as some truly believed, no time to gossip on corners, to spread rumours in Mr Zimri's store, or confide secrets to Mrs Naald, no time to think of anything but tending the sick, dying, dead, and to wonder which was going to be the last sneeze. Those who were strong enough to lift a spade dug a trench knowing that, in the end, they too would probably fall into it. And many did, even before a day's work was done. Those bereft of family helped neighbours, took in orphans, widows, widowers, consoled the bereaved. Only Ma-Fatsoen kept to herself, would not let Martha out of the house, threatened to shoot anyone who set foot on the verandah, tried to still the itch gnawing between her thighs. Pastor Melksop went among his flock with holy water and scripture readings offering the comfort of the Everlasting Kingdom to those a short distance from the edge of the trench. He even tried to talk to Ma-Fatsoen until she fired a warning round into the dust at his feet.

Some time between Christmas and New Year, when no one had died for three weeks and most of the trench was filled in, a man rode on to the mission. A man slumped forward in the saddle, arms tied round the animal's neck, feet lashed to the stirrups, the mucus of deadly flu streaming from ears, eyes, nose, mouth.

Turn the horse in another direction, Maria told Nick the Herd when he came to tell her what he'd seen coming across the veld. We don't want any more of that plague. There's hardly any of us left to die.

No, shouted Pastor Melksop, suspecting what was in Maria's whisperings. It is God's will.

But none of the villagers came out to help the man when the horse walked into the square. Even Pastor Melksop, on his knees praying for the Lord's word to send him out there to cut the man free, watched from the sanctuary of the church. On the hot square without shadows, the horse neighed, stamped its feet, wandered, pausing to pluck a few shoots of grass, or to drink from a bucket someone had left in a hurry. It looked around, then stood with bent head, tail flicking at flies, muscles rippling where ticks irritated the skin. The man hung on the horse, more dead than alive. Behind their windows the villagers waited. They all knew something was going to happen.

For a long time Ma-Fatsoen watched the man on the horse. Shadows from the church crept over him but he never moved. Only when the shadow reached her did she go outside and cut him down. The man just fell, he didn't even open his eyes. Ma-Fatsoen dragged him into her house, ignoring the voices that started as room whispers, became corner chat, gathered in the square to demand: Get him out of here, we're tired of all this dying.

Show Christian mercy, pleaded Pastor Melksop. God works in mysterious ways.

Inside, Ma-Fatsoen ignored them all: unbuttoned shirt and trousers, wiped away mucus, boiled herbs, sprinkled lavender, bathed saddle-sores, applied compresses, cleaned him up. Not even when Martha came to the bedroom to look at the tall man, so unlike her nearly forgotten father, lying there on her mother's bed between starched sheets where even now there were flecks of phlegm, spots of spittle, did Ma-Fatsoen stir from her absorption with the prostrate form to chase the child away. Instead she bent over to wet cracked lips, wipe a damp cloth across fevered brow and only smiled vaguely when Martha stroked the man's long hair. So did mother and daughter keep vigil for two nights and a day while the man sweated and coughed, groaned and choked, raved of bandits and cattle thieves, rapists and murderers, went sometimes so black he seemed to have died, sometimes so red they could feel the heat, until on New Year's Day he sat up and opened his eyes. Eyes that were the colour of a mud-hole. Then and only then did Ma-Fatsoen look at her daughter sitting on the floor beside her.

Sissy, the dragonflies are calling you, she said.

Without a sound Martha left the house, went out across the field, up through the eucalyptus trees to the dried-up reservoir where she knew there would be no dragonflies. Ma-Fatsoen bolted the bedroom door behind her.

All afternoon Martha sat beside the reservoir with its one dark patch where the last dragonfly had died. All afternoon she sat pulling at bits of grass, breaking twigs, throwing them out on to the jigsaw of dry mudflakes. She wasn't waiting for a chance dragonfly, she was waiting for her mother to finish.

In her bedroom Ma-Fatsoen stripped the bed of its stained sheets, fed them one by one into the stove. She dressed the man in his washed, ironed, darned clothes and pulled an old blanket underneath him, shuddering when his body rolled against her.

To Mrs Naald she said: Make a shroud of this, and gave her a wedding dress no one had seen for seven years.

In the store Mr Zimri said: You know I haven't had a coffin here in four months. Besides, there's still room in the trench.

From the quiet at the back of the church, Pastor Melksop heard her say: Pastor, he's dead.

The Lord is merciful, replied the priest.

Martha left the reservoir when she heard the bells. At the side of the trench she clutched at her mother's dress and listened to the sounds of her own body: blood and air and crusts of bread dissolving in her stomach. Nick the Herd shovelled earth on to the white sack that was still covered with bits of lace and dead flowers. When he finished the trench was completely filled in.

At least now there won't be any more deaths, said Mrs Zimri watching from the store window, saying, amen, amen, when she saw Pastor Melksop turn away.

And she was right. But not only were there no more deaths, there were winter rains. Great rains that came down in sheets, in blankets, in curtains that closed the view on hills and distant mountains, that brought the survivors out on their knees, hallelujah, hosannah to the highest, that slashed down between the church and Ma-Fatsoen's house turning the square into an ankle-deep, slippery, no man's land where no one but she, ever swelling, ventured come hell or high water to give praises and thanks for a conception that was untainted by laughter or mad bells. And the reservoir filled up higher than it had been when Ma-Fatsoen first took Sissy by the hand and went up there to see the dragonflies. With all the rivers running, with the wells and dams full, with hearts singing, Ma-Fatsoen, panting on a bright day, arms clasped over the extra weight which kicked against her, went back with Sissy to the reservoir hoping that as she'd known a miracle there'd at least be the miracle of dragonflies.

See, Sissy, said Ma-Fatsoen, I told you the dragonflies were calling.

One was the brightest Martha had ever seen. Not large, but double-winged red and blue: now hovering perfectly still in the middle of a wing-blur; then darting across the water up out of Martha's squinting sight to reappear everywhere here there until she realised there were not one but three. She gurgled joy, grunted, squealed, forced sounds out of her untrained throat that made Ma-Fatsoen want to weep.

Damn you, Fat Eddie and your stories, she cursed, forgetting the many fabulous nights of tales. Damn you for not knowing when to shut up.

But Martha was happy, careless in an afternoon of warmth and water when there wasn't a sour thought on the mission, when everyone who'd had colds and sniffles, who'd watched potatoes wither and sheep die of dry tongue, was grateful just to be alive.

And of course there was Ma-Fatsoen's pregnancy: perhaps, as Maria predicted, this time it would be a son.

If anyone knows, Maria does, said Mrs Zimri. She's got the eye. She was right about the hot winds, she was right about all the daughters, let's hope she's right again.

It'll be a boy, said Maria, looking at a long hair caught by a splinter of wood in the back of the pew where Ma-Fatsoen and Martha sat every Sunday. She put down the broom. Careful not to break it she pulled free the hair, held it up to the light, drew it between index finger and thumb from one split end to the white, slightly bulbous root at the other. In her mouth the saliva dried and a cold ached inside as she played with the almost colourless strand, drawing it again and again across her palm.

He'll live, she said grimly, feeling nausea at the back of her tongue.

Maria took to her bed, the cold pain in her muscles and joints relieved neither by blankets nor by warm bricks wrapped in sacks. Only fire eased the ache but she nearly burnt herself crawling ever closer to the grate.

It's rheumatism, said Mrs Naald, come to comfort her with roses.

It's the inevitable, said Maria. There's no mistaking it.

But when the mission heard she had predicted a boy they gave thanks in toasts many and long, in church glory be to God on high, in presents of wine, cheese, cakes, meat, bread, a posy of peacock feathers, two chickens and, from Maria, a Bible, all left on the stoep for Ma-Fatsoen to find in the morning.

We are saved, they rejoiced. Praise the Lord.

Only Mrs Zimri, pessimist to the end, wouldn't believe it.

There's nothing to give praises for, she declared. A womb that's known six girls won't suddenly change.

Who to believe? Oh who to believe?

The men took bets. An axe for a sjambok, two jugs of wine for a skin of brandy, until Nick the Herd, fed up with low stakes, put a month of goat's milk to a crop of Mr Zimri's yellow-cling peaches that it was a boy – after all hadn't Maria said it was! Never, said Mr Zimri, Mrs Zimri was never wrong on matters like these, hadn't she foretold the six girls as well? Maybe, said Nick, but Maria knew.

Even Pastor Melksop, dreading the blasphemies he thought were inevitable, praying to the Blessed Martyr to ease Ma-Fatsoen's labour, found himself engrossed in the anticipation, listening for kitchen gossip, wondering why Maria was so glum.

Isn't this what you've wanted? he asked in exasperation.

But Maria, a strand of hair knotted tightly about her finger, didn't hear him for the pain.

Is it the ague again? he wanted to know, pausing to watch the kitchen woman.

It's the cold, pastor, said Maria, and she disappeared into the scullery.

Pastor Melksop shook his head in bewilderment, put on hat and jacket, went out into the winter sun. Across the square, stepping between puddles came Ma-Fatsoen and Martha. He raised his hat.

Just five more frosts, Pastor Melksop, said Ma-Fatsoen, laughing.

I will pray, replied the priest, wondering what it was he would be praying for.

Nevertheless he prayed. Sometimes to the Blessed Martyr, sometimes to whoever was listening, but always to prepare them for the coming irreverence and to beg their forgiveness. He counted the frosts one two three four, waited for the next clear night when the ice would set in hard across his marigolds. It came. Pastor Melksop lay awake until the early hours dreading the curses.

That night the whole mission kept vigil over bitter coffee. Opened their ears for any sound that wasn't the howl of jackals, an owl, baboons or a laughing donkey, said: Ssh, wait, what's that? – but it was never anything more than a leopard coughing in the hills.

Double it, goatherd, teased Mr Zimri. Last night my wife dreamed of fur: it's going to be a girl. Go on, double it. What's a man like you got to lose?

But the goatherd wouldn't. He stared into the fire and wondered why Maria just kept to her bed with the secret inside her. Maybe it was a girl after all.

It's a boy, isn't it? he had wanted to know that morning. Tell me it's a boy and I'll have the shopkeeper's whole orchard.

I've told you once already, said Maria, and lay with the frost black within her.

But still Nick wouldn't believe it, went out slamming doors, scowling worse than a goat.

On the morning of the fifth frost, Ma-Fatsoen's waters broke like a river in spate reaching even to the square where, steaming, it refused to freeze. In her room behind the pastor's house Maria groaned.

Sissy, sighed Ma-Fatsoen, nightdress hitched up, squatting wide-thighed, hands ready to catch what kicked inside her: fetch Mrs Naald.

And Martha ran off through clouds of breath down the square, passed the church over the bridge between the cottages where people called out: Is it happening, Simple Martha? Is he born? Ran to the house with lace curtains and blue bootees in the window.

Come quickly, she wanted to say, it's him, it's my brother at last.

Tugging, pulling, grunting, Martha drove Mrs Naald back through all the curious faces now crowding behind her, following silently, hopefully, to stand outside the house. And there they waited while inside, without shouts, without curses, without blasphemies, a boy fell into his mother's ready hands.

He's born, said Maria, grim with pain, to Pastor Melksop. You can ring the bells.

Show him at the window, Sissy, said Ma-Fatsoen. It's him they've all been waiting for.

A boy, Nick the Herd shouted.

Our saviour, echoed the rest.

We'll baptise him Enoch Mistas after his father and my father the Ox, said Ma-Fatsoen. Bury his cord in the churchyard. That'll keep his feet on the ground.

A Tall Story

Once there was a boy whose umbilical cord lay buried in the churchyard, who was pampered and molly-coddled, given breast whenever he squalled, who was adored, who was worshipped, who spent those first years strapped to his mother's back as she went from kitchen to fields to factory, to this one to that one to show him off, such a happy contented child.

Isn't he just, cooed Mrs Zimri offering syrup of figs and cod-liver oil. Just look at him, Maria. Just look at the depth in those eyes and the set of that mouth – but if anything Maria drew back, couldn't bring herself to adore with all the rest. Not that anyone noticed in the crush and press to see this baby boy.

Oh you've got a strong one there, Ma-Fatsoen, said Mrs Naald. Keep him fat, keep him healthy, he's the only sign that the mission has a future.

To which everyone agreed: thank heaven it's happened at last. We must give thanks, we must give praise.

And even more: the best goat's milk, the ripest cheese, fruit in season, melon preserve and later shoes, jackets, Sunday suits because people felt if they sacrificed now they'd get back a hundredfold later although their own children went cold or hungry or even curled up to die. But never mind, they consoled themselves and the grieving parents, it'll be worth it, you'll see. One child's not too great a price to pay if he'll save us all. After the hardship we've had to bear, one more death on the way to freedom is neither here nor there. Above everything we've got to keep him with us.

So, children treat him properly, mothers warned their boys and girls before they went out to play. Enoch Mistas's special, he's better than any of us. We're relying on him.

Why all this fuss? queried Pastor Melksop. He's just a boy, though he's growing faster than most I've seen. But that's all. Being so tall doesn't make him anything extraordinary.

Not that you can see, said Maria. Yet the time's not too far off.

Of course he's special, pastor, added Mr Zimri. Nobody springing up that quickly couldn't but be headed for lofty things.

And despite himself Pastor Melksop was taken in.

I think, he said to Ma-Fatsoen, it's time the boy learnt to read. Just see the way he's always at that Bible staring at the pictures until they'll fade from all the looking.

It's better for him to work in the fields, replied Ma-Fatsoen. It's not readers we want but someone to look after the sheep and goats.

At night, then, persisted Pastor Melksop. Just for a few hours.

At night I need him here, said Ma-Fatsoen. There are things to be done about the house that need a boy's hand.

But Pastor Melksop won out in the end. Told Enoch about floods and arks, and lions and many-coloured coats, and giants and slings and battles, and burning bushes and plagues and slaves and pillars of salt until Enoch wanted to know: Where do you get all those stories from, pastor? And in triumph Pastor Melksop held up his Bible and said: It's all in here, my son.

Young Enoch took the book, rubbed its cover, fingered its pages, looked at the print strung with rivers.

Tell me again, he said. In the book's words.

All right, agreed Pastor Melksop holding his hand out for the Bible – but Enoch kept it back. Come on, he insisted, how am I to read otherwise?

Young Enoch bent towards him, whispered: I don't want her listening too – and he pointed at Maria sitting in the warmth of the kitchen stove.

Of course she can, replied Pastor Melksop. They're her stories as well. They belong to all of us.

No, said Enoch.

But she's always listened before. Why not now?

A Tall Story

Enoch Mistas kept his eyes down, said nothing.

You're not frightened of her are you?

Enoch Mistas shook his head.

What then? What's this all about?

But young Enoch wouldn't say.

From the kitchen Maria said: Let the boy have his way. It's no good arguing with him – and she went out to her room at the back.

Never again did Maria sit in the kitchen when Enoch Mistas came to listen to the stories, and later on was taught to read. At first Pastor Melksop tried to reason with his pupil that it wasn't right to treat people so, but humane logic was useless against a tightlipped silence so he soon gave up, thinking that when children took to strange ideas it was probably best to wait until the nonsense wore off.

It's just a passing phase, he told Maria. He'll get over it quickly enough.

Maria made no comment; tried to keep out of the boy's way.

Which was easy enough because first during the evenings, then during the days while the other children were drawing water, tending flocks, beating dough, opening furrows to flood the vegetable patches, or hunting dassies among the rocks, Enoch Mistas sat furrow-browed as the words unlocked: The Lord will take vengeance on His adversaries, and He reserveth wrath for His enemies . . . Woe to the bloody city! It is full of lies and robbery . . . Thy people is scattered . . . Thy wound is grievous; there is no healing of Thy bruise.

I thought you said evenings only, Ma-Fatsoen chided Pastor Melksop. The boy's useless if all he's got is a head full of stories. We've had one of those types already.

Give him time, said Pastor Melksop, you'll see this is different – and he raised a hand to bless mother and son walking home across the square, then went in to his supper.

Teach him carefully, pastor, said Maria as the priest mumbled grace. That may be God's learning you're putting into his head but if he wants to he'll turn it back to front. There's a goat in him: he can do dangerous things.

Bah. That's nonsense talk. Scaremongering.

I've seen it. I know what he can do, said Maria, drawing into her coat but not stoking up the fire.

Pastor Melksop put down his fork: He's just a boy, Maria. A boy like all the rest.

Maria said nothing, stirred the kettle of soup, stifled a gasp as the shivers of ice ran through her.

Then why does he hate me so?

It's not hate, it's just some childishness, protested Pastor Melksop.

Oh yes, said Maria, then why does he spit at me in the streets, try to kick me in church, call me bad names when he's with the other children?

To which Pastor Melksop had no answer, could only shrug, raise his eyebrows, lift his hands in bafflement.

And if it's just some childishness, why is it going on so long? It's been months and months since he started this business.

He'll get over it, sighed the priest, mopping up gravy from his plate with a chunk of bread, wondering why life always had these problems.

No he won't, said Maria. Because I know what he's going to do, I know the deaths he'll be guilty of.

No, stormed Pastor Melksop almost choking on the bread. No, I won't have this. It's blasphemy to say you know God's plan for human lives. It's sinning against His will.

Maria hung her head and there was a silence in the house.

These are hard times, pastor, she said eventually, and in hard times people will listen to anything or anyone who'll give them cause for hope.

It was ten years on from the birth of Enoch Mistas and things had gone from bad to worse. Where were full employment, full stomachs and a full box of coins under the bed as some had once known? Where were the good times everyone had predicted? Where travelling salesmen? Wandering vendors? Hawkers? Auctioneers? The commercial touts? Where the smous with his buttons and brass? Maybe the mission wasn't all crumbling walls and ruins, yet there were children who had never worn shoes, young men who had never sold a pair of boots. And without that incentive, who was willing to work, even though Ma-Fatsoen railed that unless you lazy-lot stick to your lasts there'll be no stock worth a wholesaler's second glance and you-all heard him say without supply to meet his demand we could forget it, that he'd be taking his custom elsewhere. Or words to that effect, who can remember exactly, it was so long ago?

Without a doubt, after a slide and slither to the mission down the pass which was little better than a goat track and the mere thought of having to walk back up bringing out a sweat on the chandler's brow, because no horse would make it carrying a lump like him, the sight of only three pairs of boots being offered for purchase had the merchant chastising each and every one: If you think that after all this distance I've come to bring commerce and trade to your backward corner you can sell a line as measly as this which isn't worth the horse's feed I paid to get here, let alone my precious time and diet, you've got another think coming. Not me, not any miserable trafficker cutting his margins is going to be doing all this hell way of heat and heights for no boots. If you want to do business again flag me down on the main roads but, people, you'd better have stock, supplies, goods, a whole warehouse full. Got it!

They had. But what to do about it?

Argue: You can't do that. How are we going to make a living? How are we going to pay taxes? You're not the only dealer, we'll just take our custom elsewhere – which raised a snort from the salesman.

Plead: If you don't buy boots we're gone. We may as well all have died of the influenza. Where's your mercy, Mr Regrater?

Explain: Can't you see we're down to not enough hands? It's all we can do to plough plant harvest let alone make boots.

Wheedle: Just give us one more chance. Come back in a month, we'll work overtime and raw fingers to fill your order. Even take a bigger discount, only please no sanctions, no boycott, no economic blockade.

And being a profiteer, convinced that market forces ruled, that greed for capital drove every human heart, he said: All right, I'll be back in a month. But travelling salesmen don't live on promises, you'd better make it worth my while.

Oh we will, they chorused. Now we've got the boy, you'll see things will get better. We'll sell shoes again.

But, of course, they didn't. With sods to be turned, crops to be sown, sheep and goats to be looked after on the veld, who had the energy to work long nights by candlelight? They tried. Shoes piled up, but not enough to fill a corner of the warehouse let alone corner the market. And then the leather ran out without spare cows for slaughtering.

What to do? What to do?

Buy it in.

With what? The cash had dried up like a stream in summer.

And with no money, how could they do business with the snoekman, who held up his hands, said: No, no, I don't want carrots, potatoes, even your best red wine. That's no good to me, I can't put that in the bank. I need coins. The hard stuff with the president's head. It's that or nothing. Bartering's for primitives. Nowadays we're living in a cash economy. When you've got that again, flag me down and I'll sell you fish.

That's it, said Ma-Fatsoen. We're on our own.

I thought the boy was going to be our saviour, muttered this one and that.

Don't doubt it, he is.

Well it's not showing yet, they grumbled.

We need God's strength, said Pastor Melksop. He'll get us through.

It's all very well for you, his flock responded. You've got the Church to pay your pension. We've got nothing.

You've got God, said Pastor Melksop.

And the boy, reminded Maria, grimacing at the words, but compelled to utter them anyhow. He'll deliver you. Give him time, he's just waiting for the word.

But how long's that going to take?

Another few inches. Keep measuring him. He's not yet tall enough for things to start changing. Thank God.

But nobody heard that last whispered sigh as Maria pulled tight her shawls because they had Enoch Mistas backed up against a tree and Nick the Herd was notching his height in the bark.

How tall, Maria? How tall? they all demanded, and where

she pointed above the scowling boy's head they nicked another mark.

Then each week they measured him. Made him stand against the tree after Sunday service, shoes off, back straight, head up, only to find he was growing so slowly that week by week by week it seemed to be no growth at all.

It'll take as long as it takes, Maria said to their groans. It's no good your feeding him up or making him lie down each afternoon to grow. He'll get there when he does. In the meantime don't wish time past.

Easier said than done, of course, especially in the first weeks when everyone thought this was it, by next summer autumn winter there'd be traders and money and books to balance and the taxman off their backs. So they stopped young Enoch in the street to listen, ears jammed against femur, spine, rib-cage, to the grind and crackle of expanding bone. At least they could hear it, at least deep down in the flesh things were getting bigger, even if against the tree there were no signs of sprouting.

But it was hard. These were tough times more bitter than the drought, almost as fearful as the influenza years, and what else if it wasn't sins that brought this persecution? But who was guilty? Who who who was bringing down such wrath on them? Who was the transgressor, who the wicked one keeping them suppressed?

There's talk, Mrs Zimri, that one among us has the evil eye.

I've heard it, Mrs Naald, and had bad dreams these nights. What do you think?

They're sure signs. D'you think . . .? D'you think it could be . . .?

Shh. Don't say it, she'll hear you even if you whisper.

It's why he's not growing, isn't it. He's been bewitched.

Maybe. Who knows. But have faith, he's got the spirit.

Not that Enoch Mistas knew anything of it as he ran in the fields, chased dragonflies, watched sheep. Maybe he could read, maybe he got the best of everything, maybe growing pains ached in his hips and knees worse than in the other children, but that was the way it was. No one questioned it, least of all him. And didn't everyone – especially the children – listen to him anyhow? They were already his band, his disciples, who played his games,

sat enraptured by his stories, who bared their wrists when he said:
This is our secret, don't let anyone know, we're brothers and sisters
– and slit their skin until they had all mixed enough blood for him
to draw a cross on each forehead, starting with Allermann and
Simple Martha down to tiny Goodwill, the way he'd read. And
you mustn't wash it off, he commanded, which none of them
did despite furious mothers shouting: What is this? What are you
children playing at? They were told: Enoch Mistas did it. That
got them off the hook. Then it was a matter of children would
be children, although it worried mothers, fathers: What was he
up to? To think they did it with their blood.

What else? said Maria. It's the way it's always been done; it's the
way it always will be. But don't worry, it's to your advantage.

If they'd only known it, there had already been a sign that
would have set tongues wagging but they didn't have the eyes
for it, because you needed the vision of a child. Or of Maria.

Simple Martha saw it first on the evening of Enoch's eleventh
birthday: a tiny flame like a glow worm above her brother's
head. She stopped at the sight of it, squinting with concentration,
forgetting the lambs, creeping towards him as quietly as she crept
towards dragonflies until she could touch what didn't burn, what
was there to only a few eyes. Again she put out her hand, and in
its cup a fire shimmered weakly. Simple Martha sat back content
to watch the flame playing now lighter, now brighter an inch from
her brother's dark hair until about them the veld was in shadow
and it was time to take the flocks down. Yet even as they walked
it didn't go out, moved with him after straying sheep, glowed
the way bushes sometimes came alight in spring.

The other children could see it; Allermann, ever the faithful
young lieutenant, walked ahead as guard, but no adults noticed.

It wasn't there for Nick the Herd when they brought the sheep
in, nor for Pastor Melksop waving from the church doorway,
nor the Zimris or Mrs Naald, neither for Augustus Niemand nor
Ma-Fatsoen preparing her annual commemoration to birthdays
and things past. Only Maria, wrapped in shawls despite the mild
weather, gasped at the sight of it and fled indoors.

At home, Simple Martha, her free eye rolling with delight,
dribble-laughing, pulled Enoch Mistas towards the old mirror

in their mother's bedroom, but even he could not see the blue tongue darting from his head, could hardly see himself for all the vague figures crowded in the glass.

What is it, Sissy? What is it?

But as always, Sissy couldn't say. Could only point and grunt, saliva welling in her mouth from the excitement.

Especially when all evening, all through the presents and the homage and the food, the flame flickered, pale iridescence, so beautiful it made her cry.

And what are the tears for, Sissy? asked Ma-Fatsoen, Pastor Melksop, Mrs Zimri at different times, each brushing them away with warm fingers.

For the wonder of all these things, said Mrs Naald, weaving the small hook of a crochet needle in and out of intricate designs, looking up to flourish it at the heap of gifts – leather sandals, sheepskin jackets, shirts, knives, dried meat, sable horns and a brass crucifix. For the wonder of all these things.

For what's to come, you mean, mumbled Maria, pulling the shawl tighter across her shoulders, shrinking even further into the darkness beyond the candles, beyond the birthday boy who sneered and taunted her.

Don't, commanded Ma-Fatsoen taking her son by the arms. Leave her be.

But Enoch Mistas would not. Behind his mother's back he pricked Maria with pins, pinched her, pulled at her hair until she could take it no longer, fled weeping to her room.

Won't you listen to me? cried Ma-Fatsoen making for the boy. What's got into you? I said to leave the woman alone – but before she could put a hand to him young Enoch was gone like a shadow.

What's got into him? lamented Ma-Fatsoen.

I've seen him scare her in the street, added Mrs Zimri.

I've heard him use God's curses on her, said Mrs Naald.

He'll get over it, counselled Pastor Melksop. It's just one of those things.

Will he? sighed Ma-Fatsoen, clearing up the plates, sweeping cake crumbs, doughnut crumbs from the floor. It's when he's like this I blame my weakness and his father's sad eyes.

No, no, said Mrs Zimri.

Never, said Mrs Naald. Without a boy this mission would be weeds and crumbling now.

A thought which later shivered in each and everyone because on that celebratory turned uneasy night all they were clinging to was children's make-believe, which had it that Ma-Fatsoen's son would see them right despite internal revenue impounding, seizing, attaching, sequestrating without any concern for personal circumstances, let alone the general depression, the bear market, or sheer hard times.

It's criminal, said Mr Zimri in bed, what the state can get away with. It's nothing but theft with a government seal.

The Lord's got his own ways, replied his wife, buttoning up her nightdress, blowing out the candle, and this boy's got the marks on him, you'll see. No matter his strange ways. Things will get better.

The Trouble Men Make

And then . . . and then . . . and then . . . years later, heaven only
knows why but for no rhyme or reason, inexplicably, Simple
Martha took it into her head to live with the sheep and goats.
Just like that. One morning she kissed Ma-Fatsoen goodbye, as
she always did when she and Enoch left to drive the sheep to the
hills, which they always did, and in the evening when they brought
them back, that was it, she wasn't budging from the paddock, she
made it quite plain with cries and whines, with arms that pushed
her brother away, with feet that kicked Nick the Herd's ankles,
that she was going nowhere, from now on she'd be staying here.
With that she lay down among the sheep and buried her head in
their wool.

Fetch your mother, said Nick the Herd to Enoch. I'm not
having this sort of nonsense.

Ma-Fatsoen and the whole mission came streaming. But neither
she nor any one of them could get Simple Martha to leave. No
matter how much they cajoled, threatened, pushed until she bit,
scratched, clawed even her mother, she would not relent. Then
they begged: in the light of candles and lamps, against the tinkle
of goats' bells and the occasional bleat, they begged: Please, Sissy,
come inside. Out here is no place for you with the coming frosts
and sometimes jackals howling close. You'll catch your death,
you'll die of the flu we've all survived. We love you, don't you
understand? Life's bad enough for you without this too.

Oh it's no use, said Ma-Fatsoen, close to tears, spurned by
her determined daughter. She's only got ears for what she wants
to hear.

But. But but but, spluttered Pastor Melksop, we can't have her living with sheep and goats! It's unheard of. She's got a home, she's not a vagabond. She's not a common wild man.

Then you change her mind, snapped Ma-Fatsoen. It's your doing this anyhow. It's all the stuff you've talked into Enoch's head about saviours and second comings and prophecies and dire revelations, all those stories which work on young minds because why else do you think they drew crosses in blood or call dragonflies angels if it's not your strange ideas? And now this happens as if we weren't struggling enough, oh God what trouble you men make – and she broke into sobs that shook her viciously, more deeply than grief.

Come, my child, said Pastor Melksop, laying a hand on her wrist, encircling her shoulders with an arm, you're overwrought.

That did it. That was all it took. Afterwards Ma-Fatsoen was never the same again. She went mad: ranted at the men who had fouled up her life from Father the Ox to Fat Eddie after him, cursed the man Mistas dying of the influenza who could still make her mouth water, wept at her weakness, tore her hair, swore to high heaven until Pastor Melksop scuttled off to ring his bells in alarm, then vowed to kill young Enoch – You devil's sperm, you vile fanatic – as she fell on him in a rage quite out of control that took Nick the Herd, Augustus Niemand and Mrs Naald to pull her off, but by then she was gone, she'd had it. She was laughing, not crying. Shrieking, not weeping.

Let's get her back to the house, said Nick, lifting her up, starting off at a run. First things first. There's no telling what she'll do next.

Which they did, and strapped her to the bed with Fat Eddie's old belts.

Now get Pastor Melksop to stop the bells, said Mrs Zimri, before he drives us all crazy. Dear God, what is the world coming to?

While she bathed Ma-Fatsoen's brow and calmed her down with mushroom soup, the others hurried back to where Enoch Mistas and Simple Martha sat dry-eyed and determined among the sheep.

If this is where she wants to stay, let her stay, said Enoch.

The Trouble Men Make

The boy's right, said Mrs Naald, it doesn't matter whose doing this is. She's taken it into her head and that's the way it's going to be. There's nothing to be gained by ranting, just accept it, give her blankets and food. It's not the end of the world.

Maybe not, but they all spent a restless night. In the paddock, Enoch and Allermann curled up among the sheep with Simple Martha; in her house, Ma-Fatsoen, still strapped to the bed, strained at the belts, sweated and cursed, broke into the wild laughter they'd heard six times before, and wouldn't be calmed by Maria's potions. In the church knelt Pastor Melksop beseeching God the Father, Son and Holy Ghost: What have I done wrong? What unpardonable sins have all or one among us committed? Forgive each of us our moments of weakness, spare us this, have mercy on poor lives. In her kitchen Mrs Naald stirred a spoon of honey into her hot milk and echoed Pastor Melksop's thoughts but lacked his charity: It's her blasphemies. We're being punished for her blasphemies. In their bed the Zimris prayed that it was only a nightmare, that tomorrow they'd draw their curtains and see Ma-Fatsoen feeding the chickens, stamping out to the latrines with a fresh sheep's head. All over the mission, in each hut and cottage, people whispered: What now?

What now?

This: uneasy days, troubled nights. Long faces, subdued spirits. And gossip.

I've heard she foams at the mouth.

Wets her bed.

Bit clean through Fat Eddie's belts to free herself.

Wears only her old coat.

Doesn't wash or clean the house.

Laughs to herself.

Yet through it went Simple Martha with quiet content. She was up before Nick the Herd, played midwife to the lambing ewes, chased off jackals, smiled as if her mouth could be no other way, neither begged for food nor looked sickly when the frosts came on. Not that she was neglected. Everyone saw to it that she had blankets, canvas, a serving from all their tables which did for Enoch and Ma-Fatsoen as well.

Time passed. In the hands of Enoch Mistas sores erupted and

bled for a week, but he hid his hurt in gloves. Only Maria guessed what festered there: imagined black centres as if iron nails tore the skin, and blood, partly flowing, partly congealed, about them. On the first day he left off the gloves she risked his temper, had no option but to cross his path and provoke his angry gestures. Yet even in that moment's scuffle she saw new scars: dark flesh in his palms and on the backs of his hands. In her a cold welled up – a cold that was of deep waters where now a current moved. Maria kept her fear to herself, knew she was powerless before him.

Time passed. No one dared measure Enoch Mistas, nor ask after Ma-Fatsoen. Mrs Zimri left cakes on the stoep of the shuttered house, Mrs Naald sent shawls, others brought jam, dried figs, or fruit for Enoch to find at the back door. Even Pastor Melksop gave up his heavenly ministrations to the male-cursing woman. What was the use in offering communion when it was scorned, smashed from his hand, when the woman was clearly bent on heaping sacrilege on top of blasphemy? Only Maria went each midday to be briefly housemaid, doctor, nurse. It's a wonderful thing she's doing, people said, but if Enoch finds out anything could happen. You know how he's always at her. But as month followed month it became the way of things – until the day Enoch left his sister with the sheep on the veld and slunk back behind the cottages so that no one saw him, though they all heard his howl when Maria, laden with herbs and sweet water, let herself in at the front door as she always did only to be thrust back by Enoch Mistas shouting: Away. Away, witch. You're stealing my mother's soul.

Maria went down in a heap of coats and packets and Ma-Fatsoen's cackle ringing through the house.

Away, yelled Enoch Mistas. Be gone, be gone, be gone – and he was kicking at bunches of buchu and bottles of water before Maria had a chance to pick herself up from the dirt.

It's you who are the devil, Master Enoch, she cried then, the cold turning to ice within her, her breath misty even in the sunshine. You're the one who's bringing all the trouble. You'll see. You'll see. There's no way out of it. You can do what you want to a woman like me but nothing's going to change. There'll be blood on your conscience; people will die in your name.

Witch, he hissed, pushing at her, driving her backwards across the square. Witch. Witch. Witch.

In God's holy name, please stop, please stop, begged Pastor Melksop, trying to intervene, himself being thrust aside.

It's all right, pastor, said Maria taking shelter behind him. Master Enoch can't help himself. He's just doing what he has to do.

But he did stop. There in the middle of the square with Pastor Melksop and Maria cowering before him, with Allermann on his right, with the others from the mission huddled outside Mr Zimri's store, with Ma-Fatsoen's laughter shifting from room to room as she ran about the house, he raised a threatening hand: Be warned, witch, he said, and turned away. That was where it ended except now the word was out.

Could it be? wondered Mrs Naald.

She's always been a strange one, added Mrs Zimri, what with her coats and shawls even in summer.

And she brews herbs.

And she predicts.

Could it be? Could it be?

No one could say for sure because Maria kept to Pastor Melksop's kitchen, dusted his rooms, or lay huddled on her bed growing colder by the day. Each Sunday she crept into church before everybody else and sat out the service on a chair below the altar. She spoke to no one and no one spoke to her, not even Nick the Herd. They didn't dare to, in case it was true what Enoch said, and then he'd be after them for harbouring witches. They all remembered how he'd raised his hand; they all remembered what he'd said as if he spoke to each one personally.

From his pulpit Pastor Melksop called for prayers and more prayers, preached love and understanding, tolerance and goodwill, the boundless mercy of almighty God. People heard him and bowed their heads: But what can we do now the children have turned against her? It's no use, we can't talk to them. It's not like when we were young and listened to our mothers, fathers. These days things are different. The youngsters want a better world and who can blame them? They've no time for what we've got to say.

What some of the children were saying when they talked at the dragonfly pool was: Let's stone the witch, ja. It's what people have always done, urged Allermann.

Stone the witch, stone the witch, echoed the brothers and sisters.

Or burn her, ja, as they used to do.

Burn her, burn her, echoed the brothers and sisters.

No, said Enoch Mistas, our time will come. I know it.

But how could he be so sure? Simply because that's what he'd been told one bitter winter's day when he sat with Simple Martha among the sheep.

What the Voices Said

There was snow on the high peaks and an ice-sharp wind coming out of the blue when the voices spoke using Sissy's tongue.

My son, said the first voice, take comfort. These are harsh days but we promise salvation.

Hear us, said the second voice, we've come to tell you about certain things that aren't quite right here, that need some . . . ah . . .

. . . Divine intervention, added the third voice.

Yes, said the second voice irritably, we think it's time we took a hand in affairs.

They paused as the wind gusted loudly across the plain, raking up tumbleweeds, tearing off the litter of final demands and tax notices pinned on doors, trees and fences around the mission.

My son, said the first voice, don't be afraid. We're not here to strike a pact with you, we're here to tell you what we've got planned . . . the way we see things working out.

It's like this, put in number two, you're not being treated fairly, you and a thousand others, a thousand thousand others, millions in fact.

That's right, said the third voice, you're being beaten down, oppressed, suppressed, victimised, enslaved, exploited . . .

. . . Marginalised by state bureaucracy, an expendable resource to capital, industry and the captains of mines . . .

. . . Discriminated against, cynically stripped of all dignity, dehumanised . . .

. . . In short, my son, made to be less than men . . . and women.

The problem is, people don't always see it this way, explained voice number three. They accept it as their natural lot, they bow down to officialdom and millionaires, they wear their fingers to the bone so that others can sit back eating langoustines with sparkling wine.

Now obviously that's not right. We're talking about gross iniquities here, stressed number two. Especially when there's such abundance. Enough land for food for every belly. Enough gold for everyone. It just needs redistribution, less greed, less money-grubbing, less bathing in milk when there are children starving. What's happened here is quite beyond the pale. So it's time we redressed old wrongs, revolutionised, nationalised, turned out the corrupt order for something new.

Think, Enoch, added voice number three, how people have suffered. How they have been dispossessed, relocated, turfed from their houses by government decree, paid next to nothing for a full day's work, made to live in swamps, marshes, deserts, fallen prey to every travelling disease, eaten bark because there was no meat and all so that the privileged could swan off to the ballet.

And, said number two, remember those who disappeared, who were tortured, murdered, hunted, massacred in their hundreds until whole nations were wiped out. These are debts that have to be accounted for. The guilty must be punished. Both those who signed the orders and those who let them do it.

What it amounts to, my son, is the day of judgement, the end of the world, the coming of the kingdom, blood across the land, tears in the firmament, weeping, wailing, gnashing of teeth . . .

. . . In other words, just deserts . . .

. . . In other words, comeuppance.

It's nothing new, of course, added number two: history abounds with precedents. But these things don't just happen. Revolutions aren't that simple. Like any recipe you need the right ingredients. A pinch of economic deprivation, a heap of social ills, a cup full of political grievances and you're in business.

Not to mention the will of the people, if you'll let me break the metaphor, put in number three. A will which, I must tell you, it takes some doing to stir up.

What the Voices Said

Which is why the most important thing, my son, is a leader. A man with the courage of his convictions, a man with vision, a man who can rise above it all.

As I've said before, went on number two, history's made up of them . . .

. . . Heroes and martyrs . . .

. . . Saints and paragons.

And we think, summed up voice number three, that you've got what it takes.

But it won't be easy, my son, said the first voice.

You'll be reviled . . .

. . . Cursed . . .

. . . Hated, spat at . . .

. . . Misunderstood, hounded . . .

. . . Incarcerated . . .

. . . Cast out as a subversive, as a traitor, even an impostor . . .

All this you will have to bear, my son, but your cause is the righteous one, your liberation inspires us all, your struggle is our struggle.

As it has always been, said number three.

Believe me, chipped in number two, we have stood behind every man, and woman, who has said: This is wrong. Who has raised a fist, thrown a stone, fired to kill because there was no other way to see justice done.

And fear not, you're on the side of the angels, you've got history, international opinion, bishops, prelates, the whole bag of tricks rooting for you. You've got a good cause. You're in a state of grace.

To put it briefly, nothing can go wrong.

It's foolproof, concluded number three.

Having said that, my son, continued the first voice, we now need to brief you for this mission.

So listen well, quipped the second voice, this is the struggle we're talking about, the act of liberation . . .

. . . Your freedom, your chance to rule . . .

. . . This is power we're dishing out.

The way we see it, my son, you're the liberator. People will follow you, you've got the touch . . .

. . . The personality . . .

. . . A word from you will set their hearts alight.

Therefore, leave all this, get out, spread the word, care for the old, heal the sick, give hope to the young. From every corner gather them, from the farms where they labour with bare hands, from the towns where they are abused and maltreated, instil the new kingdom in their hearts, take them to a place where they will be their own bosses . . .

. . . Where they won't have to beg . . .

. . . Where they can shout the odds.

We have a dream, my son, a dream of equality, of love and common kindness, of concern and caring. The kingdom is our dream, the new country where men – and women – will rule with a sense of justice and fair play in a land without petty jealousy or the plots and plans of power-mad politicians . . .

. . . Call it a one-party unitary state . . .

. . . Call it heaven.

This is our dream, my son. Think on it carefully.

As you can understand, said the second voice, it needs a selfless man who'll sacrifice for his people.

In short, who won't let matters go to his head.

Because if in your heart you lust after gold baths, luxury cars or the comfort of large houses, my son, then be warned, these things are signs and portents which we know well . . .

. . . And we'll not tolerate that . . .

. . . Remember we are not to be trifled with.

Go now, my son, cleanse your people's hearts, purge their ranks, set their souls on the path to salvation.

Waiting for the Word

Enoch Mistas bided his time. Told neither his right-hand man nor any of the brothers and sisters about the voices. Went each day to herd the sheep with Simple Martha, sat quietly in church on Sundays, wandered alone by the dragonfly pool and kept his counsel.

Ah, said Pastor Melksop, things are returning to normal.

Never, said the well-wrapped Maria. Things are as they are. Don't be deceived.

For you it's just doom, doom, doom, exclaimed the pastor, putting down his pencil, looking up from his next sermon. You expect the worst of everything.

I expect what's going to happen and nothing more, replied Maria, finishing her dusting, quietly leaving the room to Pastor Melksop and his thoughts of God's love for mankind. The churchman stared through the open window at the crumbling mission: the derelict houses where the influenza had spared no one; at Mr Zimri sunning himself because his store was empty; at the young men with nothing to do, the thin dogs, the threadbare washing. Surely, he pondered, even in these hard times God's love was manifest. Surely they had suffered, they had come to know the lot of downtrodden men . . . And now, weren't things returning to normal? He picked up his pen: Because our faith was strong, he wrote, we have been led like the chosen people through adversity into the divine light of the coming kingdom.

Can it be? questioned Mrs Zimri after his service. Is that what the signs say?

Why not? replied her husband. The signs are there for everybody. Make of them what you will.

But who ever heard of a churchman getting them right? put
in Mrs Naald. Let alone Pastor Melksop.

One day he has to be right, said Mr Zimri, but for now it's
good to see the children being children again.

Children who darted about them as the congregation made their
way home. Children who raced between the mission houses as
if the plague were after them. Or, in the quiet afternoon hours,
fashioned clay figures at the river, or sat beside the dragonfly pool
listening to Enoch Mistas telling stories.

He's got a natural way with them, remarked Mrs Naald as they
watched the children flock around the boy. It must be his mother
coming out.

And just see how he's getting taller by the day, added Mrs Zimri.
He's got an inch on most of us already.

Umm, said Mr Zimri, and they thought of Maria's prophecy
and the notch Nick the Herd had made in the tree. But nobody
dared mention it.

Yet whenever he had a chance and there was no one in the
streets, Enoch Mistas stood at the tree, placed the palm of his
hand flat against his head, and measured his height. Each time he
was closer to the notch. Enoch Mistas began to walk taller and
taller: he commanded Allermann to accompany him everywhere,
even when, each day, he and Sissy grazed the herds and flocks.

Our time has almost come, he told Allermann. We must be
prepared. Any day now we'll get the word.

Enoch Mistas never left his sister's side. At night after he'd fed
the wretched Ma-Fatsoen, he locked her into the house and took
his blankets to the paddock where Simple Martha slept. But the
voices kept silent.

Enoch Mistas grew impatient. He had Allermann call the
brothers and sisters to the dragonfly pool. There he told them
of someone on the mission who was keeping them all in bondage.
Someone who spied on them, who told their secrets to the taxman,
who cast spells to keep them in chains.

Who? Who? demanded the brothers and sisters.

You know her, said Enoch Mistas. She gives you fruit and

cakes with one hand, she smiles and puts her cold hands on your heads to bless you. You know her, you think she is a friend but all the time she's stealing your souls. She's trapping you little by little because that's what she's been paid to do.

Who is she? Who is she? his followers screamed.

You know her, replied Enoch Mistas, speaking so softly that his voice sounded like wind catching in tall trees. You know her. Each day you see her. She walks among you and you hold her hands as if there is nothing wrong. But she is evil. She came here alone in the night. She came here as traitors do, slinking in when no one was around.

Then, so loudly the smallest among them shrieked, he roared: Until she is gone we cannot be free.

Who is she? Who is she? howled the brothers and sisters.

She is the devil, returned Enoch Mistas. A witch. A collaborator.

Find the witch, yelled Allermann.

Find the witch, find the witch, chanted the brothers and sisters, rising to their feet, swaying forward, singing, Ay e ay a ee, ay e ay o oo, as Enoch Mistas led them down through the trees towards the mission.

They stopped outside the church.

At the noise Mr Zimri woke from his doze in the sun muttering: Oh Lord, what now? and called to Mrs Zimri to shut the shop. From their sewing machines and needles, Mrs Naald and her ladies came running, as did all the other mothers, fathers, even Nick the Herd and Augustus Niemand.

What's going on?

What's happening?

What's got into the children this time?

Shh! There's Pastor Melksop. What's he going to do?

Pastor Melksop held up his hands: What's all this about, my children?

Give us the witch, give us the witch, chanted the brothers and sisters.

What witch? Who do you . . .

But his words were lost because behind him in the doorway

appeared Maria in coat and shawls, and Enoch Mistas screamed: Her. It's her we want – and he pointed with his Bible.

Don't you dare . . . shouted Pastor Melksop, for the first time in his life seeing red. Don't you dare use the Bible for such base means – and he knocked it from Enoch Mistas's hand into a silence deeper than the sea.

As the boy – because wasn't he still a boy? – bent to pick up the book, Pastor Melksop knew the fear that follows sudden anger. He sweated, stammered, turned for help to everyone, even Maria, but found no comfort in the watching eyes.

Enoch Mistas straightened up, blew dust from the covers, smoothed out the crumpled pages: Never again will this book be beaten from my hand, he vowed. Never again. And to Pastor Melksop, said: Beware, missionary. You are giving shelter to a servant of Satan. Then he spoke to the brothers and sisters: Go home, he said, now you have seen her. Let my words not be forgotten – and he and Allermann turned away.

Never again could Maria walk about the mission. When the children found her in Mr Zimri's store they beat her out with sticks and switches. If they heard she was collecting eggs they howled around the fowl runs until she fled, discarding basket and smashed shells. Nor could anyone, neither Nick the Herd nor Augustus Niemand, come to her help, because the brothers and sisters would torment them too. Leave the witch, warned Allermann, she is against us, ja. This is our time, because look everywhere around to see how you have failed.

Why are you doing this? demanded a despairing Pastor Melksop of his former pupil. The poor woman's terrified to go out.

If you don't know why, replied Enoch Mistas, you don't share our burden. She knows what she has done.

Oh Lord do not forsake us, prayed Pastor Melksop, looking up at a picture of the Blessed Martyr: Benedictus qui venit in nomine Domini. And when Maria brought in his supper he confessed: They won't listen to me, Maria. I have given learning to a maniac. Let us just hope this will blow over quickly.

It won't, pastor, said Maria. There is worse to come.

Somehow, although the brothers and sisters were out in the fields and on the veld, they got to hear that Mrs Naald had called for Maria to cure an ache in her stomach. Even as the herbs brought the first relief she'd known in days, the children began gathering outside her house. First they shouted slogans Enoch Mistas had taught them, then they threw stones against the door.

Give us the witch. Give us the witch, they chanted.

I must go, said Maria, collecting her concoctions, buttoning her coat. Now you are in danger too – and she went out into the taunting horde.

Leave her, cried Mrs Naald. Please leave her. She has cured my pain.

But her words were as weak as an earth wall against flooding waters. Laughing, whistling, the children pursued Maria, hitting at her legs with sticks, pulling at her coat until in that rushing chase that was almost a game, a stone struck. Maria collapsed, blood opening above her eye like a flower. Silently, startled by their power, the brothers and sisters stood about her where she lay curled up and terrified against the church wall.

Leave her, said Enoch Mistas. Get away before her witch's blood poisons all your hearts with shame. She deserved your stones, don't let her turn them into tears.

Quickly he and Allermann sent the children back to their tasks. And only when they had gone, when the street was deserted, did Pastor Melksop hurry out to help the fallen woman.

Now what's to be done? asked Mr Zimri moving back from the window, cracking his knuckles in his worry.

Maybe it's true, whispered Mrs Zimri. There's things she knows which no ordinary person could.

She's not a witch, said Mrs Naald slipping in. Her fingers have the healing touch, just as mine can cut a dress.

But they always say a child knows a witch, said another joining in.

We've always said Ma-Fatsoen's son would put things right, added a third.

Yes, they all agreed as more sneaked through the back door like thieves.

And who is to say the pastor's not in cahoots?

Or she's bought his soul?

Or bewitched him?

Or . . . or . . . or . . .

Shh! There's thoughts that shouldn't ever be spoken.

But you won't see me in church again.

Nor us.

Nor I.

What's the good of that? We can't all forsake the Lord.

Oh who to believe? On the one hand. On the other hand. According to this. According to that. But either way, come the next Sunday, only a few pensive faces stared up from the pews no matter how long and hard Pastor Melksop pulled at the bells.

Good, said Enoch Mistas to Allermann. Measure me.

The time had come. Enoch Mistas was as tall as Nick the Herd's notch. But the word he awaited came not through Simple Martha but from a stranger.

It came on a day when Enoch Mistas sat among the trees behind the mission, frustrated by the waiting and the inactivity, impatient to begin what was ordained. Here he mused, and here he was approached by a stranger carrying no worldly goods, who stepped from the bushes with the stealth of a leopard.

I'm Dead Das, the man said. I've come to tell you the way it will be because in my death I saw the burning of witches and oxen, the slaughter of sheep and goats, the fire of houses and temples, great flames, smoke, until there was nothing left but blackened carcasses, charred ruins. Only then can we be free. Hear me, I saw it in my death. My short death when God spoke.

Enoch Mistas scratched the red circles in his palms, weighed the chain that now bound the Bible to his wrist, looked at the man with the tie of death, nodded. Tell me, he said.

A Man of Purpose

And Dead Das confessed dreadful deeds, said he was a bandit, a robber who had murdered on a night when he with three others crossed the veld, more silent than snakes, clutching knives, heading for the small circle of light where a man and his family read from the Bible. In the darkness they stood looking at the two children nearly asleep on their chairs, the mother with bowed head, hair falling loose, the father, bearded, squinting against the candle at the tiny words: Behold a people is coming from the north country, and they ride upon horses. Go not forth into the field, make mourning, make most bitter lamentations, for suddenly the destroyer will come upon us. And he prayed for the souls of his family: eyes closed in reverence, face raised, his words breaking inside their heads like stones. No dogs barked; there was no warning tread, no timber creak, no sixth sense. Just the sudden hands of violent men, as if from nowhere, bunched in the children's hair, pulling back their heads for a quick knife to be drawn across their throats. And he, the father, felt the cold roundness of a barrel in his ear, opened his eyes on a moment of terror but heard only the sing of lead before his head exploded the way melons burst in the heat. The woman screamed even though they beat her mouth until it filled with blood and teeth. All through the night she screamed, each time they took her, helpless, bound with thong, the smell of their meat and ferment solid in her nostrils. All through the night they drank and ate, hardly talking, hearing her sobs and about them the tick of insects, until in the grey light before dawn they slashed her wrists and left, taking rifle, salt, strips of dried meat. And by the time they had crossed the plain and gone into the mountains she had bled to death in the quiet house, flies at her blood, the last sight in her eyes a child's leg, red with veld scabs, bright in a shaft of sun. So the house held its corpses for the day a farmer and his son rode up, wondered at the open door and found this murder.

By then, Saunders, the man who would become Dead Das, who would be born again, had held that same rifle to a banker's face and fired. And in the spit of bullets one among them went down wounded in the leg, screaming at the sight of his blood.

They ran out of that town, the one called Cob holding up the wounded youth, and Saunders and the other known as Bushy behind them to make sure no one followed. The youth's wound looked bad but they washed it out and tied it up and the bleeding soon stopped.

Bloody Jesus! That bloody Jesus, Saunders cursed the banker. The damn fool, if only he hadn't played the hero he wouldn't have got it.

For three days they were on the run through the hills and thick growth but they weren't too worried about being chased, knowing it would take time to get a platoon up there because the railway stopped a hundred miles off on the other side of the mountains. But they kept on the move anyhow, despite the youth's complaints. Perhaps they should have left him because those couple of days were crucial and they didn't get as far as they should have done. They needed horses but the farmers were all down on the plains and none of them wanted to risk the open lands. Then they came across a house built high up in a kloof and knew there would be horses there because they'd seen dung and hoof-prints on some of the paths. They stopped on the rocks above the house to get the lie. It was simple, the horses were in a paddock to one side, and there was only the farmer, his wife and an old man under a tree, who didn't move all the hours they watched.

Let's get them before dark, said Saunders.

He could see the others didn't like that but they needed to find their way out of the kloof and that couldn't be done at night. Sitting around was wasting time.

It would be better tonight, said Cob. Maybe they won't even hear us. Saunders shook his head.

A Man of Purpose

Now, he said. We need the light.

They got the horses without any trouble. Cob and Saunders walked right up behind the farmer where he was plucking fowls and he didn't know anything about them until Saunders stuck the rifle barrel in his back. Then he just put down the knife and turned round to them with a face of sadness as if he'd been robbed a hundred times before. He didn't say anything, just did what they told him. Bushy brought out the farmer's wife who started crying and begged not to be raped. That made Saunders mad and he shouted at her that they weren't rapists, they weren't bloody thugs. He stuck the rifle in her face until the smiles came back to him.

Come on, said Bushy, let's stop playing games.

So they tied them up in the yard, back to back, lying down, and left one of the kitchen knives a few paces off. They figured it would be about an hour before they got free. The old man under the tree was no bother either because he'd been dead for days, probably weeks.

They rode out and a week later a platoon sent to get them picked up their trail on the stone plateau and kept after them for many days because the lieutenant – a man named Trotter – was in no hurry. Each morning through his telescope he measured the distance separating them, nodded with satisfaction at the closing miles, and went back to his breakfast, knowing the bandits would have only dried meat and a little water. Some days he chased them hard, stretching his men and their horses, gaining, gaining, coming within rifle-shot then slackening off to a steady trot, relentless, determined, confident.

They're going to get us, said Cob, taking the last of his water, looking back at the platoon's fires on the veld. They can do it any time they want to.

Shut up your fucking mouth, Cob, snapped Saunders.

Shut up your own fucking mouth, arsehole. Just look at the youth, he's exhausted, he's bleeding again, he's so weak he can't ride unless he's tied to the horse.

So, we'll leave him.

Nobody gets left, said Bushy.

Oh no! If I say he gets left, he gets left.

Then the youth spoke. He had said nothing since the day they'd ridden out from the hills and seen Trotter's platoon like a mirage at the end of their horizon. He could hear Cob breathing at his side but it was too dark to see either Bushy or Saunders.

You can leave me, he said. It doesn't matter.

Neither Cob nor Bushy responded. Saunders got up to pee; they could hear his water splashing into the ground, long and hard. The youth shivered, he wanted to clasp Cob's arm and stop being frightened. Saunders finished. They heard him fumble with his flies in the dark and turn back towards them. Then came the thud of a blow and Saunders groaned. It all went very still. Bushy drew his knife, wishing Saunders wouldn't always carry the rifle.

Saunders, he called, inching forward, listening, as good as blind and deaf.

It's not the soldiers, whispered Cob. Come back, Bushy. It's not the goddamned soldiers. You got to be back to back to fight off these little bastards.

The three of them drew into a knot.

Jesus. Jesus, Cob, what're we going to do?

Shut up. You got to listen for them. You got to listen.

They kept quiet, straining over their hearts, over the rush of blood for whatever was hostile in the night. Suddenly, not far off, a man laughed, low, strangely, the way a hyena does when it smells meat. Hee hee ja. He stopped.

I've heard of you-lot, a voice said. I've heard about what you-lot did to the farmer woman and about the bankman too. You-lot are a nasty bunch – and again the laugh came loudly before pitching down into a giggle – a nasty bunch heading straight for the rope if the soldiers get you. Hee hee ja.

Who are you? shouted Bushy.

Oh maybe you-lot haven't heard of me. Maybe you-lot haven't yet been where Mximba's name is king. Except Mister Saunders, here. He's heard of me from the old days. Not so, Mister Saunders?

Silence.

Ah, Mister Saunders isn't talking yet, but he will soon enough, said the man, laughing. His giggles trailed off into the night that was thick and locked around them.

A Man of Purpose

Eventually, wire-tight, breaking, the youth cried out: Christ Jesus. Christ Jesus what'd you want? His voice was strangled, barely a whisper.

The man considered: Not much. Not your coins. You can keep all that. All I want are your horses and this rifle of Mister Saunders's here. You-lot have any objections?

Mximba didn't wait for a reply: But I'll do you-lot one favour. I'll show you-lot a cave that the soldiers won't find before the coming of the prophet. I owe Saunders one.

Because years ago in a hole of a prison that had more rats than a pit latrine, that stank of urine, where lice and bedbugs and the whole host that lives on man bred in cells dripping semen, spit and slime mucus, where the regiment of the hills recruited its warriors and wives, where men died of a sharp wire under the ribs for nothing more than a too curious look, where Mximba should have been for ever, Mister Saunders became warder, second class. He moved in, a mongoose, a meercat, slipping along the corridors without the jangle of keys, cunning, listening, seeing all with a knowledgeable eye that knew what was what. Knew who was king, who queen, who ran strong drink, who stocked dagga, who guided the wire spoke, who ordered its use. Yet he said nothing: didn't tell of midnight courts, initiations, secret tattoos, blood marks, mysterious signs, beatings, revenge, rape, plots and plans, the exchange of coins, the passage of orders to wild men in the hills. Even when a warder fell, bludgeoned on morning patrol in broad daylight before every prisoner and Saunders so that all eyes were on him when the commandant demanded culprits, even then he kept his witness. Who is this man? asked Mximba, fingering his necklace, counting the teeth. Who is this snake in the grass? Give him rewards. Small things at first: copper rings, carved handles, shoes, then European liquor, a boy he couldn't use, a woman he did, but they got no thanks, just his silence, more precious now, worth soap with embedded diamonds, a pat of butter and gold. And for these favours? Nothing. Not less time in the quarries, not soft jobs in the kitchens, no good reports, no allowances. Only an all-seeing blind eye.

Until a boy who was still a child, long abandoned, chased off, shot at, assaulted, left more than once for dogs, who scavenged the edge of towns and markets, was finally caught with both hands in the rice bag, and marched to that fetid jail of murderers, bandits, maniacs, there to be love-pet and doll, a comfort for bad types. Mximba first, of course. Come here, my beauty, come here, my lovely, come to my warm bed. Not a bad deal for the unloved, some might argue. Here now was care, concern and status, a chance to strut about untouched, cock of the walk, following wherever his master's business called: a shadow that couldn't be trodden on. And Mximba loved this one. Even at the end of lust, despite complaints and taunts, he wouldn't share him. Lay off, he warned, this one is mine. Men mumbled but they kept their distance. Grumbled even more when he sucked on other flesh while this one didn't leave his bed. Until one day the boy made eyes and hooked a desperate man. Lured him in to Mximba's bed while the king was breaking rocks. Nothing sacred, nothing decent: the reward was fruit. Mximba knew. Maybe he heard it in the whispers, maybe he saw it in the way others looked at him. Maybe he sensed it on the unchanged air. Maybe he smelt apple on the boy's breath. Anyway, he knew, and everyone could see it except the boy. The boy played more than good wife that night. Washed his clothes, washed him, fetched food and coffee, offered himself without reserve. It saddened Mximba; it didn't stop the knife. Good night, said Saunders, grinning, turning the key without a sound.

But what to do with the body?

Blood can be mopped up and flushed away, but a corpse attracting flies with a faint sweetness in the air is another matter. All night Saunders puzzled out how to solve this one: considered sawing it up, boiling it, sinking it in the flooded quarry pit, dumping, reporting an escape or saying nothing so that justice could take its course. Just what to do? A stiff question. Because there was no way to walk the dead boy past the eyes of all warders and the commandant. No chance of slipping out with a bundle of death thrown over his shoulder. Little guarantee that an informer after meat or marrow bones wouldn't drop a word. Absolutely no possibility of sweeping this one under the carpet. Maybe the living can escape, he thought, but the dead haven't a chance. Which left only one option robbing him of sleep: how much could he demand? Three-quarters? Half? A quarter? He settled on half. Most men would save their lives for half their fortunes, he reasoned, and half Mximba's wealth would leave them both rich men. He fell asleep with dreams of gold beds and ostrich-feather fans. And so the deal was done with the boy's body still slumped in the corner and blood gone hard on the floor.

Before morning call Saunders put something like this to a grieving Mximba: for half your gold coins I'll get you out this evening after lock-up. I know you've got them in the hills so don't play innocent. Think about it, for this murder you'll hang without a trial. I'm offering salvation. Mximba nodded, too heartsore to argue. Good. Good. Just leave the boy in your bed, as if asleep, no one will disturb him. Oh, and a word of warning, don't take this any further. For two corpses I'd need three-quarters which is not worth your while.

Hee hee ja, sniggered Mximba, coming out of the dark, walking Saunders before him. Oh yes, your Mister Saunders knows how to organise and for that we must all be most grateful. But he's got you-lot in a mess here, boys, and you need Mximba to get you out. So follow me.

He led them to a cave and left them there, taking the horses. In parting he shouted: Where's the money I paid you now, Mister Saunders? Gone. Gone on cards, and women, and too much liquor. Hee hee ja. What a type. I knew you, Saunders, right from the start, great big silences couldn't hide the weakness in your cheeks. Oh no. Now you-lot just stay here and in some days you'll be as free as ever men are – and he faced the horse into the rising sun, rode away.

From the cave mouth the bandits watched the soldiers searching in confusion for the lost trail and laughed with relief. When the platoon headed off, they, too, went out and continued on foot.

Escaped, Trotter! shouted Major Hedley Goodman, shifting from buttock to buttock, longing for a cool and soothing cream. Nobody escapes, Trotter. Nobody escapes proof just like that. They've gone underground, goddammit man, can't you see that? Underground. Into a cave. Into a ruddy aardvark's hole. It doesn't matter, but just don't say that they've escaped. And then, calming down: I don't care how long it takes you to find them, Trotter. I don't care whether you spend the winter out there. I don't care whether you ride on ostriches or zebras when your horses drop, just do not come back here without them. That's my order, it's the CO's command, and the president's desire. Do you hear that, Trotter, shouted the major springing up from the seat of his pain with a quick grimace: the president's desire. He wants it to be as safe as a picnic out there. Fluffy clouds and woolly sheep. No more lawlessness, Trotter. No more murder, rape and pillage. No more anarchy. No more renegades.

Out on the plains, heading away from the mountains, Lieutenant Trotter and his platoon found the tracks of four men without horses: two walking close together, one dragging his foot. Tracks that were three days old.

A morning later he surprised them naked on a river sandbank, their clothes scattered about, the bags of money heaped carelessly, a fire died to embers: the youth swimming; the one called Cob face down asleep; in the shallows, squatting, the man known as Bushy; only Saunders about, slapping at flies. No rifle visible unless rolled in a jacket. Through sweat he watched the youth limp on to the sand, lie down beside Cob as Bushy got up to wade towards the bank.

Saunders called: Bring some tobacco.

And Bushy waved in acknowledgement.

Get them, yelled Lieutenant Trotter, standing up, firing two revolver shots, unleashing his frustrated, straining platoon in a wild gallop down the banks into showers of water and laughter at this sudden capture. They took the youth first, although he hadn't moved. Then Cob, blinded by sand, staggering around in circles; and at the same time Bushy, his hands above his head, grinning a welcome. Only Saunders ran off the sandbank, beat up against the tug of the river, looked back at the charging horses and pushed out harder into the deep water. The soldiers whooped, dug in their heels at the chase, gaining with each surge. The river-bed fell away, Saunders flailed out of his depth as the tow curled around him like pythons. He came up coughing, spitting beneath a horse's belly, heard the shouts and went down again, drawn to where the river was muscle, was sinew, where it moved with the strength of snakes. Get him, yelled Lieutenant Trotter, seeing Saunders whirling in the brown, disappearing, rising, slipping from his grasp. Get him for two guineas. And a soldier did, striking out for where the body lay on the river's back, not struggling now, content to be pulled towards the shore and life.

In court Saunders smiled. He did not bow his head, did not look down, as Cob did, as Bushy did. He heard the youth weeping and the magistrate's grave tones: For such heinous wrong-doing against society, for such blatant disregard for the sanctity of human life, for such violation of lives and property, for such crimes there is only one appropriate response, one just end demanded by God, the president and society; and that is death. I sentence you, Roderick Matthew Saunders, and you, Bushy Mathebula, and you, Cob Afrikander, and you, Vasco Manuel, to be taken to a public place and there to be hanged, your bodies to be cut down at sunset. May the Lord have mercy on your souls.

They were strung up together, all four of them on a special platform outside the jail. It was hot, even in the early morning. Saunders could remember standing on a stool, the noose around his neck, the slack against his shoulder, looking down the street at some pigs snuffling in the gutter. It was a hot town that stank of rotten vegetables. The youth was sobbing, Cob kept saying: Jesus, oh Jesus, over and over again. Bushy and Saunders kept their mouths shut.

The official executioner had travelled up from the Cape to hang them, but he'd brought only one rope and was surprised to see four condemned led out of prison chained ankle to wrist. That upset him. He shouted at the sergeant, saying he hadn't been told there were four, that he hadn't come equipped, and couldn't they get a simple thing like a message straight? The sergeant shrugged, said messages were none of his business, and went off to buy more rope leaving the condemned to wait around in the shadow of the gallows. And a thin shade it gave in that heat. The crowd got noisy. They wanted them to be hanged one at a time but the executioner said that wouldn't be fair. He kept looking at his watch and pacing up and down. Once he even went over and said: Sorry, boys.

Bushy and Cob kept their heads during that wait, but the youth, who'd been crying most of the night, howling so badly sometimes that they couldn't sleep, now started fouling himself. He stank and they couldn't move away from him because the chains were short.

Do something, Cob, Saunders said, he's your bride.

Cob glared at him and Bushy sniggered.

It was as well there wasn't enough rope because the priest came late. Or maybe he was hoping to bless the dear departed so that he didn't have to look into their living eyes. He sidled up in his black suit, one of those thin types with hands cold as vulture's claws, coughed, mumbled something about the Lord giving and the Lord taking away. But they could tell his heart wasn't in it. He just wanted to do his duty and get back to holy silences. And no one could blame him for that. Priests have no place at a hanging: it's men's work, not God's. Then the sergeant came back with three ropes, all there was left in the town, he said, and the priest took off in long strides back to his church at the other end of the street.

They had to stand on stools under the gallows. The youth got the official rope, then came Cob and Bushy and Saunders with the town stock. The stools were all tied by thin rope to a frisky horse. The executioner said: Ready, boys, and lashed the horse. It took off down the street dragging the stools. Cob and Bushy and Saunders fell on the platform: those ropes were rotten with maggots and wouldn't have stood the weight of a child. Only the youth hung there, broken-necked, choking to death.

God's mercy, Saunders shouted, struggling up. God's hand.

The executioner was spitting angry, screaming at the sergeant for incompetence, for interfering with the ends of justice, for showing no compassion to sentenced men.

What'd'you think it's like for them? he shouted, pointing at the crumpled three, dazed, not believing their luck. They came out prepared to die like the magistrate decided and we can't even hang them right. For days they've been dreading this moment, living each minute closer to their deaths, right up to this last day when they saw the sun come up and knew they wouldn't see it set. That we'd all be here to eat dinner when they were facing God's judgement. Just think of their feelings, sergeant. Just think of how these boys feel now.

God's mercy, Saunders shouted again. God's hand.

But the executioner couldn't hear him above his own thunderings: I don't care what they've done. I don't care who they killed or how or what mayhem they caused. This is justice, this isn't retribution. It's bad enough for a man to hang, but to hang like this is no just death at all. You hear me, sergeant? I'll see that this . . . this . . . insubordination gets back to where it should.

Then quietly, turning to them, he said: Sorry, boys. Accept the president's apologies.

God's mercy, Saunders yelled. There's God's hand in this.

Sorry, boys, he said again. I've not got any power to pardon you.

When the youth was dead the sergeant took him down and the good rope was put round Cob's neck. Again the horse was lashed, the stool ripped out from under Cob's feet and he died slowly with blood filling up his eyes. Bushy went the same way. As they took him down Saunders vomited what he hadn't already shat behind the platform.

When he got up on that stool the second time he saw the pigs had gone. All the townspeople were at his feet, even children. Some women cried. The executioner sjamboked the horse and again Saunders fell on the platform.

God's mercy, he croaked. God's hand.

Saunders could see the sergeant was grinning at this official failure. The executioner didn't look at him, just fashioned another noose.

Before he slipped the new knot over Saunders's head, he said: Have some water. It'll make you feel better. And then: If it breaks again you've got the president's pardon. Saunders nodded and tried to drink, but nothing would go down.

On the third time Saunders hung there for what some men said were five full minutes, just barely breathing, keeping his neck muscles tight as bark while the crowd looked up to see if God was with him. Even the priest stood alone and behind them, black in the empty road. That was all he saw before this world died for him. And then he was born again on that platform, the noose still round his neck, the rope broken, the hangman splashing water in his face, from that time on men called him Dead Das.

Since then he had become a man of purpose.

The First Notes of Freedom

Far off, as if from a world that once was, came the sound of Pastor Melksop's church bells drifting through the trees with the twilight. And in response the brothers and sisters sang: By the waters of Babylon, there we sat down, yet we wept when we remembered Zion. But neither Maria scuttling through the church doors to take her lonely seat beneath the pulpit, nor the Zimris, nor Mrs Naald, nor any of the few others who heeded the pastor's calling, nor those still in their houses – the man who sat alone or the woman, or two friends, or a wife and her husband who looked at one another like strangers – heard this singing. Although they listened to every sound on that raw August wind, it was at first the congregation's small hymn that gripped their hearts with anguish: Oh Lord our help in ages past, our hope for years to come; and in their dark homes they chewed the words like sour figs. Only later, when the church fell silent as Pastor Melksop ran out of prayers and for a moment the wind held its breath, did that other distant singing swell briefly, alarmingly discordant. What's that? What's that? But it was gone. Outside there was only the wind and the scratching of branches.

At the dragonfly pool the brothers and sisters took up brands and followed Enoch Mistas down the narrow path to the mission. He walked slowly between the trees, the Bible clasped against his chest, the chain tolling at each step. Then came Allermann and Dead Das side by side, holding high their torches, beginning the chant that stirred the first notes of freedom in all their throats: Ay e ay a ee – and its echo: Ay e ay o oo. Enoch Mistas lengthened his stride. Behind him, surging and ebbing, snaking with impatience, the brothers and sisters linked arms, became one. Running now, screaming – Ay e ay a ee, ay e ay o oo – they saw the church, white, with a flickering yellowness at the windows, which shattered as the song gathered force, as the stones . . . as the hands . . . as the fire consumed.

THREE

Mentioned in Dispatches

Communiqué Q248/34

To:	Officer Commanding, North Western Territories
From:	Major Hedley Goodman, Cape Royal Fusiliers, Sector Five, North Western Territories
Classification:	Secret
Subject:	General conditions, third quarter
Date:	18 September

Morale

It is my pleasure to report that despite an exceptionally harsh winter which tested the men's resourcefulness and dedication beyond the call of duty, and some minor matters that have necessitated sending patrols to remote areas where they operated under extreme provocation, often losing immediate communication with senior officers owing to the difficult terrain, but nevertheless acquitting themselves with discipline and valour, morale among the men is, as always, a credit to the good name of the regiment.

Casualties

Regrettably, in the course of obeying orders and ensuring the peace and security of ordinary citizens, I must report the sad loss of five men killed, a suicide possibly due to one of the aforementioned mortalities, and nineteen natural deaths due to typhoid, syphilis, dysentery, snakebite, and unknown causes. Also thirty-five men suffered serious wounds during engagements, of which twelve suffered the amputation of limbs to avoid the spreading of gangrenous infestations. Currently forty-two men are incapacitated in the sickbay, including the wounded and those suffering natural ailments such as pneumonia and one who has contracted a strange delirium. It is my experience of these parts that not only does a savagery lurk in the hearts of the natives, but the very land is plagued with diseases never before encountered by modern science.

Operations
As you will have noted from my previous interim communiqués (Q579/90, Q68/AW3, and Q44/3) in the last quarter, the need to maintain law and order required our intervention in, and I itemise:

Twenty-four (24) cases of stock theft
Eighty-one (81) instances of receiving stolen goods
Six (6) murders
Fifteen (15) allegations of rape
Thirty-three (33) unrest related incidents, including stone-throwing, looting, and burning
Five (5) punitive expeditions
One (1) negotiated settlement.

In all operations justice prevailed and it gives me pleasure to report that the division's image in the eyes of the common citizens and the natives is one of efficiency and fair play. Not only have we performed as civic law enforcers but we have kept the peace in what were at times extremely volatile situations that, without the division's timely and incisive mediation, may ultimately have endangered the good government of the state.

Costs
A detailed account of expenditure arising from the performance of duties is attached. As you will appreciate the uncertain mood in recent months has necessitated a greater expenditure than budgeted.

Mentioned in Dispatches

Special mentions

As briefly detailed in my communiqué Q68/AW3 a patrol under the command of Lieutenant Trotter, who has considerable experience in these regions, was sent to investigate a farmer's complaints that vagrants were establishing a village on his farm. As recorded (in Q68/AW3), the patrol was overpowered in a surprise attack and held captive for eight days by the said vagrants. Here follows a full account of the incident and my recommendation that Lieutenant Trotter, who distinguished himself as a leader and a soldier, be accorded an honour in recognition of his conduct. You will also note the meritorious actions of his corporal, a man named Bloodstock.

To enlarge on my earlier communiqué: When the patrol entered the village – which comprised some fifteen mud and grass huts – they were at first cordially greeted by these people who give their allegiance to a man referred to as the 'redeemer'. It would appear that he is obeyed without question and is virtually worshipped by his followers. While Lieutenant Trotter was awaiting an audience with this 'redeemer', he noticed some extremely dangerous and notorious men in the crowd which had gathered around them. He ordered Bloodstock to arrest these men but the crowd grew so restive that the corporal was unable to carry out his duty. At this point the 'redeemer' – also known as the prophet of the people – a tall, thin man who wears a Bible chained to his wrist, made his appearance and order was restored. Lieutenant Trotter then explained that he had come to serve notice on the group because they were occupying the land illegally. (Please refer to my remarks in General Observations below for further details about this issue.) He also mentioned that he would be forced to arrest certain dangerous characters among the crowd. At this the 'redeemer' raised his hand and the soldiers were set upon by the mob – both men and women – and disarmed. Such was the swiftness and ferocity of the attack that the patrol was caught completely unawares. The men were then chained in such a way that they were forced to squat on their haunches, and left in the centre of the village for the remainder of that day and night without food or water.

THIS DAY AND AGE

On the afternoon of the following day Lieutenant Trotter was brought before the 'redeemer' who told him that as the land had been illegally taken away from the people who had always lived on it, he and his followers had no recourse but to break the law because they had no place to go to. Lieutenant Trotter explained that the people had not been illegally dispossessed as a special act of parliament had rendered them ineligible to own such land. At this the 'redeemer' flew into a rage and sentenced Lieutenant Trotter and his men to death. That night and on the following four days the patrol was given food and water, but Lieutenant Trotter now feared for the safety of his men as there were signs of increasing hostility all about them.

On the sixth day, he requested to see the 'redeemer', and pleaded for the lives of his men. In the end the 'redeemer' agreed to this on condition that he and his followers were granted a concession to winter in that place. Lieutenant Trotter conceded to negotiate such an arrangement with the farmer and undertook that, provided there were no further reports of unlawful harassment, the authorities would abide by the conditions. I realise he was not empowered to make such a declaration, but in the circumstances he clearly had little alternative. Despite the lieutenant's word on this matter, the 'redeemer' refused to free the men until his terms were agreed to by the farmer. So it was decided that Bloodstock, in the company of two men renowned for their nefarious deeds, would travel to the farmer's house to secure his consent. It must be noted that Bloodstock's life was in considerable danger during this period, and especially when the consent had been given, as those accompanying him – wanted criminals commonly known as Dead Das and Jabulani Mximba – have records of gratuitous murder. (See my General Observations below.)

However, once they had returned safely to this makeshift village, the 'redeemer' honoured his promise and released the patrol although he kept their rifles and ammunition. (See my General Observations below.)

Given these facts it is my opinion that Lieutenant Trotter acted in a wise and honourable way to prevent what could so easily have turned into a nasty incident of considerable bloodshed. Likewise it has been my honour to congratulate Corporal Bloodstock on his selfless bravery.

General Observations

1) The Vagrant Question:

It is indicative of these times that, in my humble opinion, due, in part, to the wars on the eastern frontier and the marauding bands at large in the north, and also to the recently promulgated Native Lands Act, there is now an increase in vagrancy in the hinterland. This has given rise to the unstable conditions we are currently experiencing, which in turn have put considerable demands on the division.

It is a common sight these days to see families, or small groups (sometimes they even have sheep, goats and cows with them), wandering aimlessly along the roads. We have done our best to escort these people out of the North Western Territories towards the resettlement areas, but the problem grows daily to such proportions as to render our efforts futile. In my opinion, a policy of impounding these vagrants prior to controlled relocations by train would perhaps go some way towards alleviating the situation.

The formation of groups of vagrants, such as that controlled by the above-mentioned 'redeemer', is becoming common-place, although in my experience they are usually smaller than his band, which, I am told, is daily being enlarged to unacceptable proportions. In the near future we will have to take special measures to ensure these groups do not pose a threat.

2) Vagrant Bands:

I wish here to comment specifically on that group headed by the man known as the 'redeemer'. As I have already mentioned, it is larger than the others and appears to be more controlled and disciplined. A most worrying factor is its attraction for other groups of vagrants and criminal elements. Apart from the incident mentioned above and one or two reported cases of harassment from local farmers we, admittedly, have not been called upon to deal with any instance of armed conflict concerning this group. However, as already stated, we know there are unsavoury men among its ranks and they may have power to influence the leadership. In addition the band is armed which makes it a potential threat.

There is little I can discover about this 'redeemer' except that his prophecies of impending freedom from what he apparently calls, and I quote, 'the chains of the oppressor' are what draw his followers. He claims, too, the imminent end of the world and the coming of the day of judgement when all unjust men will be called upon to atone for their sins. He is also not above lacing these biblical predictions with demands for the vote, or for the redistribution of wealth. He has been heard to proclaim that none of his followers pay tax, which alone ensures him an enthusiastic audience.

If this information is scant, then my informers are equally uncertain about his origins. There is some talk that many years ago, and I am referring here to perhaps a decade back, he was involved in the burning of a witch and the subsequent razing of a mission station in which a priest died. But this is at best speculation.

Although the following is unconfirmed, I believe it would be safe to assume the maxim, where there is smoke there is fire, so that in all probability there is a large degree of truth in what I have been told. It has been brought to my attention that this 'redeemer' has a penchant for young women – sometimes, I am informed, they are hardly pubescent – whom he is in the habit of sampling and discarding at will. There are even reports of occasions when he has women paraded before him while he inspects their merits as if he were choosing a horse. It is my contention that this licentiousness, apart from reflecting directly on this 'redeemer's' degeneracy, is indicative of a general moral torpidity that is common amongst this plague of vagrants currently infesting the land.

All this notwithstanding, it is clear that this 'redeemer' has set himself above the law and believes he can act with impunity. I would like to sound a warning note here, because this man is a potential threat.

3) Felons:
As I have constantly pointed out it is the presence of undesirable types which makes the vagrant question particularly worrisome.

The man identified (see above) as Dead Das, alias Roderick Matthew Saunders, was once sentenced to death for his part in some brutal murders but escaped in rather dubious circumstances. Since then whatever grim deeds he has committed have been well hidden. He is believed to be the 'redeemer's' right-hand man, along with another known simply as Allermann. This latter individual has no criminal record.

The man identified as Jabulani Mximba, alias the King, alias Two-boy Sevenpence, alias John Satwa, is an extremely dangerous felon who has served long prison sentences for a variety of petty and heinous crimes. He has a reputation as a cold-blooded, ruthless gangleader who, according to my information, made his men renounce all intercourse with women and confine themselves to the buggery of boys. He is said to be totally loyal to this 'redeemer' although I can establish no reason for this.

Although these were the only two men positively identified, it is Lieutenant Trotter's conviction that other villains are harboured among this group.

I must reiterate that the presence of this group in the North Western Territories is a cause for grave concern.

Leave Benefits
Attached is a list of leave benefits owing to various privates, non-commissioned officers, and officers. As this tour of duty is now in its third year, considerable leave benefits have accrued. I would appreciate some guidance on how this matter will be handled as there are mutterings among the ranks because no leave has thus far been granted.

Extra-ordinary Medical Supplies
Owing to the harshness of the winter diet a large number of conscripts are suffering from haemorrhoids. It is the medical officer's request that appropriate salve be dispatched with the next consignment of medicines.

(Signed)
Captain Hedley Goodman
2nd Division, Cape Royal Fusiliers
Officer-in-chief, Sector Five, North Western Territories

Fairy Tales

Once there was a young girl whose birth killed her mother and whose father stole a horse and ran away at the time of the Spanish influenza. She lived with her stepmother in a shack on the farm of a man known for his hard and demanding ways. The man had a wife and two sons of his own but every night he would visit the stepmother's shanty and stay until long after the young girl was fast asleep. The farmer was good to her. He gave her milk and porridge and occasionally brought a comb of honey for her to suck. The young girl liked the farmer and would often sit in his lap while he stroked her hair with his large hands that were as rough as the desert. The farmer seldom spoke. When he did, his voice sounded like rocks crashing down a ravine. The young girl couldn't understand a word he said and cowered in the darkest corner of the shack. It always frightened her when he spoke because his voice was so loud and threatening. More often than not the farmer was angry. Although he never lifted a hand to the young girl, he would hit at her stepmother's face until her teeth broke or blood poured from her nose. Afterwards, in the mornings, the farmer's wife would squeeze a yellow paste into her stepmother's eyes and tell her that God was just in His mercy. The young girl's stepmother never thanked the farmer's wife for the ointment, nor did she ever help the wife in the kitchen as did the other women who lived in the shacks. But her stepmother never complained about the beatings because at least there was always meat and they had a bigger piece of ground than the others in which to grow potatoes and the corn that usually withered in the heat before the cobs were ripe. Then one night the farmer didn't come to them. The young girl, who was sitting outside the shack waiting for him, watched him leave the house where his wife stood boiling fat for candles and his sons stared sullenly into the kitchen fire, but instead of smiling at her when he reached the shack he kept his face turned away and went in at the door of the woman Malan. The young girl didn't know what to do. She waited to see if the farmer would come out again but he didn't and soon the smell of lamb chops being cooked drifted out of the woman Malan's chimney. The young girl felt very sad and lonely. Although she was hungry she dared not ask her stepmother for food. That night her stepmother beat her even more badly than she had the night her father had run away. The young girl sobbed and sobbed until at last she fell asleep. The next morning the farmer was very cross. He shouted at the young girl's stepmother that she was not to hit the child, that the child was beautiful, that she was pure and should be cared for properly. After the young girl's first blood he said he would come back to them but until then he had no use for a hag like her stepmother. Then he struck the stepmother with his sjambok and for the first time the woman hit back. But that just made him even angrier.

A young girl once lived with her stepmother who treated her very badly. She had all sorts of tasks to do morning, noon and night, and if it wasn't for the farmer's gifts she would never have known about kindness. In winter the young girl was the first to break the ice on the pools of water that welled up in the river-bed. In summer she spent hours and hours digging holes to find some seepage. In winter, even though she wrapped cloths round her feet, her toes turned raw with chilblains; and in summer nothing could protect her from the sun which blistered her skin. The young girl never complained. Every morning she fetched water for the kettle, water for the potatoes and corn, water for the farmer's kitchen. Sometimes the children from the other shanties pushed her from the holes she'd dug and filled their buckets first, and when she fought back they made her swallow sand. You're nobody, they taunted. Your mother's dead, your father's gone. You don't belong. And once, when it was so hot she had taken a whole day to draw hardly enough water for the kettle, one of

the farmer's sons snatched her bucket and poured it over his head.
She went home empty-handed. Where's the water? demanded her
stepmother, slapping her face again and again, even though she'd
seen what the farmer's boy had done. You'd better go back and
fetch some more. All alone the young girl sat at the hole waiting
for the bucket to fill. Even when the sun went down and the jackals
howled across the desert she had to sit there while water seeped
slowly out of the earth. But fetching water wasn't her only task.
When she'd done that she had to pick up the fowl droppings from
the yard – even those that were still wet – and sprinkle them over
the potato patch. Come on, hurry, her stepmother would shout
as she struggled back with the last bucket of water. Make sure
you get there before the other children do. Oh, if only you were
my child you wouldn't be so useless. And the young girl would
run into the yard where some of the other children were already
squabbling over the pickings. Let me see, let me see, how much
did you get? Her stepmother always wanted to know when the
job was done, but never said good, or well done, just grumbled
that it wasn't enough, or complained she was too slow and beat her
knuckles with a stick. But there was one task which the young girl
enjoyed even though it was hard work, much harder than drawing
water, or collecting droppings, or sweeping out the shack. And
that was chopping wood. Because they lived in a desert where
trees couldn't grow, they had to journey to the mountains for
firewood. It was always a great adventure. The farmer would
inspan the wagon with three oxen and for two days they trekked
towards the mountains that were quite invisible from the farm.
The young girl loved the mountains. In the ravine there was a
waterfall and a pool where they swam after a long day sawing
trees, chopping branches, or gathering kindling from the lower
slopes. Also there was so much colour there, green and soft yellow
flowers, beautiful birds with flashes of scarlet, lizards with bodies
that shimmered red blue purple as they sunned themselves on the
rocks. But most of all she liked it because in the mountains there
she felt free: she could laugh with the children and join in their
games, even her stepmother didn't scold her or beat her if she ran
off to splash in the pool before the day was done. At night they sat
around a fire while the sharecroppers told stories from their fathers'

time. Stories about the stars which walk the sky unsleeping, or the ash which a woman threw high up on the wind until it settled against the night and became the Milky Way. But the story the young girl liked most was the sad one about the full moon riding across the sky, her belly round with children. All night she would shine. From the moment the sun went down in the west, there she was growing bigger and brighter as she travelled among the stars until at daybreak she still hung above the earth, huge and full. Then she would call out to the sun whose long arms were reaching over the horizon: Your knife is killing my children, she would call out, your blade is stabbing them to death. Let me live, let me shine. But each morning he brought out his sharp knives no matter how the moon cried, a cry so painful it broke the heart of anyone who heard it. Tears stung the eyes of the young girl when the sharecropper told this story but she was always careful to make sure no one saw her unhappiness. Yet on those nights she sobbed herself to sleep because she was alone in all the world. And come morning when she woke she blocked her ears until the sun struck the top of the trees and she knew the moon had cried the cry that could break her heart. In the daylight with all the work to be done it was easy to forget about the moon and her children, just as it was easy to forget how strict and horrible her stepmother would be when they left the magic of the mountains. The day when the wagon was full of logs and faggots always came too quickly for the young girl. She hated the moment the axes stopped ringing through the trees and there was a hush without even the call of birds. It was such a sad time. Then the farmer cracked his sjambok and they started walking away from the mountain. No one spoke, no one said anything until they stopped to camp for the first night. By then the mountains were so far away they were almost as blue as the sky. Back on the farm the old life took up where it had left off. There was water to be fetched, droppings to be collected, the shack to be swept and always her stepmother's moaning voice driving her on. The only peaceful moments were when the farmer gave her honey comb to suck or allowed her to sit on his lap but eventually these times too had come to an end. For years and years things went on this way until one day the stepmother made the young girl take off her dress so that she stood completely naked shivering in the cold. Turn slowly, said the stepmother, I want to see what you look like. The young girl obeyed her stepmother because she was afraid of being beaten, although to be stared at by the ugly woman frightened her as well. She turned and turned until she was giddy, then the stepmother said: Get dressed. Your time is coming. The young girl gasped in alarm. What time, stepmother? What time? Oh please tell me. But her stepmother just laughed. Not a happy laugh, but a hard, cruel cackle. You'll find out, she shrieked. For the rest of your life you'll find out.

A long time ago, when what happened actually happened, said the sharecropper's wife to the young girl who had been made to live in the cold stone hut at the far end of the field, there lived a girl just like you in a place that was far far away. In this place there were lions and big eland as once there were all sorts of animals here, too. The people lived a very peaceful life: they hunted when they were hungry and afterwards smoked until the dreams and visions came. The men were wise and the women were glad they had such thoughtful men. Because of this wisdom it was seldom that anyone was angry. Nor did they fight wars because the men had brought them to live a long way from the people who made trouble. One day when the men were smoking they heard the Eland telling them that if they wanted to continue living such happy lives then they should put right the thing they had neglected to do. And what is that? asked the men. The Eland replied that in future, when the blood came to the young girls, they should be sent off to live in a hut by themselves until they were cleansed. This time of the blood is an evil time when there is great danger, warned the Eland. And beware, too, that they never leave the hut and that they see no man, for who can say what will happen then. The men told the women the story and the women built a special hut for the young girls. For years and years this ritual was observed, and the Eland told the men that because they obeyed him they would be rewarded with buck for the pot and sweet water where others saw only sand. The people grew fat and were most content. And then a young girl, who had been taken by her mother to the hut and warned that she was to stay inside until the bleeding that reminded all women of their sin had stopped, broke the Eland's laws. After a few days all alone in the dark hut she went to sit in the sun that shone through the doorway. While she was sitting there, two young men, great hunters who were bringing home buck and hares and delicious porcupines, passed a short distance from the hut. The young girl heard their voices and, forgetting what her mother had told her, looked up to watch them go by. When she saw them they were turned into lions. All the women, especially the hunters' wives, wailed and rolled in hot ashes when that night the Eland told the men what had happened. Those hunters will never see their women again, the Eland said. And now you mustn't kill lions any more because you might be killing one of your kind. The men became angry for the first time ever and said they would beat the young girl when she was clean. But in the meantime they commanded the young girl's mother to tell her daughter that she must stay in the dark of the hut. The next day the young girl forgot everything she had been told when she saw a cloud covering the sky. It got darker and darker until the day was as dim as night. In all her life the young girl had never seen a storm and when it started to rain she was so frightened she ran out of the hut to search for her mother. First the lightning slashed at the earth where she ran until it struck her and she changed into a frog. Then the wind came in a rush and caught up the frog blowing it higher and higher until it turned into dust. That night, when the storm had gone, the Eland told the men what had happened. The men told the women, who wailed and rolled in hot ashes, especially the young girl's mother. So you see, said the sharecropper's wife to the young girl sitting on a mattress in the cold stone hut, you must stay here until the blood has come and gone because nobody wants bad things to happen.

There was once a young girl called Tasmaine, who lived for years and years and years in the cold stone hut at the end of the field waiting for the blood her stepmother kept telling the farmer would start today, tomorrow or the next day. But each night when the stepmother took the rag from between Tasmaine's legs she could see the girl wasn't even spotting. What's wrong with you, yelled the stepmother, you slut, you evil cow? What am I supposed to say this time? And each night the stepmother had to tell the farmer it hadn't started yet and show him the still warm unsoiled rag as proof. Each night the farmer roared like an avalanche and struck the stepmother before she had time to get away. It'd better happen soon, he warned, or else . . . But it didn't. No matter what herbs her stepmother squeezed into concoctions for the young girl to drink, or sniff, or rub on to her stomach, no matter how many hours she made Tasmaine stand legs-wide over the smouldering ashes of sheep turds and porcupine quills, no matter what chants the sharecropper's wife recited, the young girl refused to bleed. Why are you doing this? shouted the stepmother. Can't you see how he beats me? Oh why didn't I have a daughter of my own instead of being stuck with you, you useless orphan of no-good parents? Then she would beat Tasmaine so hard that the sharecroppers in their huts shook their heads sadly and sighed. If the blood doesn't come soon, they whispered together, that woman's going to beat her to death, that is if the farmer doesn't kill the stepmother first. For more than two years things went on like this. Other young girls from the sharecroppers' shacks came to stay in the hut but the longest they ever remained was a few weeks. Tasmaine was always pleased to see them because apart from her stepmother and the old woman who told her the menstruation story, they were the only people she saw in all that time. When each new girl came, Tasmaine prayed: Please let her be my friend, please let me have just one friend – but each and everyone spurned her. If they didn't spit in her face, then they cringed away as if she were more loathsome than a frog. But Tasmaine did not give up. She offered them food she said she couldn't eat; she even slept without her blanket if they complained of the cold. The girls took her goodness, but gave nothing in return, not even when she brought cool cloths to wipe their brows, or hot rocks wrapped in rags to warm their beds. How she longed to comfort them when they groaned with pain, or shrieked in terror at the first blood trickling down their thighs. But none of them wanted her soft words or caring hands. They all squirmed away from her into the furthest corner of the hut, called her every name under the sun, made it perfectly clear they needed neither her nursing nor her kindness. We're women now, they hissed, what'd you know about that? You're still just a girl. And Tasmaine had to slink back to her mattress where she hid her shame and her sorrow beneath the blankets. When she was alone in the hut – which was most of the time – Tasmaine stood at the small window that looked over the plains towards the mountains which were too far away to see. She watched with tears in her eyes whenever the farmer inspanned the wagon and set off with the sharecroppers and their families to collect fuel. She imagined the cool water where they swam, or the thud of their axes striking home in a shower of white chips, or the birds among the trees; she imagined the mornings when the shadows were dark and the evenings when the rocks blazed like fire; she imagined the mountains until her heart ached with memories. But why can't I go? she pleaded with the sharecropper's wife each time the firewood expedition set off. Oh please, oh please, oh please. But the sharecropper's wife shook her head and said: I've already told you why not. Just be pleased they've gone, and you can get some sun for a few days. At least when everyone was off collecting wood, Tasmaine didn't have to face the wrath of her stepmother or the daily inspection for the faintest trace of menstrual blood. At least now she had a friend: someone to lie in bed with, someone to share a day of life. So although Tasmaine longed for the mountains she also enjoyed her freedom with the sharecropper's wife. All the tasks she'd hated doing for her stepmother – fetching water, picking droppings, sweeping – she now did with a song as if they were no trouble at all. And they weren't, because the old lady always thanked her, brewed tea, or baked cornflour biscuits as a special treat. You're a good girl, said the sharecropper's wife one night while they sewed skins into a kaross, your day will come. But until then it's no good complaining. Not that Tasmaine ever did. She may have suffered inside or fought back tears whenever people hurt her, yet she never learnt to hate, nor ever thought of revenge. Now it happened eventually, as it was sure to, that the farmer wouldn't put up with any more excuses about Tasmaine's condition. You're lying, he screamed, knocking the unspotted rag from the stepmother's hand. I've waited long enough. If there's not been blood yet, there will be when I'm finished – and he beat the stepmother black and blue. Now get out of my way, hag, he ordered, there's men's work to be done. And while she whimpered in a corner, the farmer and his sons snatched up a lantern and set off for the cold stone hut at the end of the field. On the way they met the sharecropper's wife, who asked them where they were going. To the girl, shouted the farmer, knocking her aside. I'm not having any more of this nonsense. Oh but you can't, cried the sharecropper's wife running after them. If any man sees her before she's bled he'll catch the plague and surely die. Rubbish, spat the farmer. That's kaffir superstition and this is a Christian land. Be off. But the sharecropper's wife wouldn't leave them. No, no you can't, you mustn't, she wailed, dragging first this one back and then the other. It's not worth the risk, oh help me please, someone, don't let this happen. But the other sharecroppers were too afraid to lift a finger. They'd seen the farmer kill a man before and leave his body where it fell. So now they kept inside their huts. Only the stepmother, already so battered another blow was neither here nor there, came limping up. She's my stepdaughter, she told the men, barring the door to the shack, you'll touch her over my dead body. The farmer raised his fist to smash her down but the woman said: No, just wait one moment, then you can have your way. And with that the stepmother disappeared into the hut where Tasmaine crouched on her mattress like a frightened animal. Come, said the stepmother, pinning down the young girl, let's see what's the matter between your legs – and she groped there with desperate fingers.

One winter's night, when the jackals howled in the distance and a moon full of children hung over the veld, the ugly stepmother died of laughter in the cold stone hut at the end of the field. But before she died, the farmer, who turned red with anger at her laughter, kicked open the door and was about to strike the life from her when the stepmother said: The girl's not got one. She's not a woman with any use for men. Your thing's got no place here. And then she laughed and laughed until she died. The farmer was so angry at being scorned by the stepmother and cheated by Tasmaine that he ordered her to leave the farm and never return. But where shall I go? she cried, I don't know anywhere else but here. Don't worry, whispered the sharecropper's wife. Just walk towards the mountains. And so it came about that while Tasmaine was walking towards the mountains, carrying nothing but a crust of stale bread and a small pot of water and feeling very sorry for herself, she saw, on the second day, a dustdevil moving slowly across the plains towards her. At first she was frightened and looked for an aardvark's hole in which to hide. But the aardvarks were all at home trying to sleep and snapped at her when she disturbed their dreams. Oh what am I to do? What am I to do? she cried because there are so few places in the desert to hide. By now the dustdevil was getting closer and closer, so close she could even see its legs swishing over the ground. It had long scaly legs and three-toed feet with big claws. Tasmaine crouched down and pretended she was a rock. Maybe then it won't see me, she thought. She covered her head with her hands and held her breath to keep absolutely still. About her the dust whirled and the three-toed feet beat on the ground louder and louder until suddenly they stopped. Then there was a roar like the roar of a lion and Tasmaine, so frightened she couldn't help herself, looked up to see a man sitting on an ostrich. What are you doing there? asked the strange-looking man, who wore a necklace of teeth. He bent down to get a closer look at her. The middle of nowhere is no place for a young woman like you, he said. There are bandits out here, and restless spirits seeking revenge. Oh please, pleaded Tasmaine struggling to hold back her tears, won't you help me? I'm all alone in the world because my stepmother's dead and the angry farmer doesn't want me any more. The strange-looking man took off his top hat and wiped his brow. Then he laughed, not a wicked laugh, but a kindly one that made Tasmaine feel better. We're each of us all alone, he said mysteriously, and there's no changing that. But come on, jump up, you can come with me. The strange-looking man lifted Tasmaine on to the ostrich. She sat behind him with her arms clutched tightly round his waist. Hold fast, he called out, and with that the ostrich roared and they were off at a gallop.

The Sickness of Unrequited Love

When, three days later, the ostrich bearing Jabulani Mximba with the outcast Tasmaine still clutching round his waist in terror came high-stepping in from the karoo, Enoch Mistas caught the merest glimpse of the young woman as she was lifted from the feathers by people gathered round to see what the redeemer's messenger had brought back this time, but even that was enough to lodge an ache in his heart and a desperation in his loins.

Allermann, commanded Enoch Mistas, shifting on his stool, flicking through the Bible at his wrist, call Jabulani. I want to see him now. I believe he's found my bride.

Maybe, said Jabulani Mximba with a smile. There is no telling what's meant to be.

It is ordained that I will know her at first sight, scowled Enoch Mistas. Have her washed and brought before me.

Which was done, and Enoch Mistas was enraptured as she stood there in his rough stone temple, lovely in a way he'd never seen a woman's beauty before. So sad, so gentle, her head bowed, her hands clasped before her. All his. He touched her hair, ran a hand across her skin leaving a faint smear of blood from the bleeding in his palms, lifted her chin and searched deeply in the eyes that looked back in alarm.

Do not be afraid, he murmured, leaning forward to kiss lips that had never felt other lips before.

Behind him Allermann smirked and Dead Das longed to touch the young woman's breasts. Behind him Ma-Fatsoen suddenly rose from her mat in the darkest corner, gave a cackle more hideous than a hyena's, and came flying across the room like a bat.

Sissy, she shrieked. Sissy – and clasped the fainting Tasmaine in her arms.

Enoch Mistas fumed, shouted: It's not Sissy, you mad fool – as he tried to pry the girl free. But there was no undoing his mother's logic. Sissy, she crooned. Sissy, Sissy – cradling Tasmaine, rocking her the way she'd rocked each child.

Fetch my sister, ordered Enoch Mistas. But even when Dead Das and Allermann returned with the startled Simple Martha, there was no convincing Ma-Fatsoen.

Sissy, Sissy, she droned over the collapsed Tasmaine, stroking the girl's hair, brushing rough fingers over silky cheeks, oblivious of her raging son and cowering daughter.

Get them out of here, snapped the redeemer, stricken by the ache and desperation that would not now be stilled.

Not then, not in the winters and summers that followed. It drove him mad, he was so angry, impossible to pacify. He herded his flock from the mountains in the east to the cold ocean in the west and back again. Only on the Sabbath did they rest from wandering, glad of this brief respite while their prophet paced about the scrub reciting psalms through clenched teeth.

Beat me, he instructed Allermann, handing over a whip, exposing his back. And when Allermann hesitated he cursed him for a coward and turned to Dead Das. Do it, he said.

But what good was a flogging? What was raw flesh rubbed with salt compared with the pain in his heart? A pain that lacerated him each morning when he saw her loveliness stirring beside his mother; and flayed him each evening when he watched her lie down to sleep.

She's yours, whispered Dead Das in his ear. Take her.

Yet still Enoch Mistas couldn't bring himself to give that final order. Instead he fasted: took only stiff porridge and water in penance until his cheeks sank against his skull and the skin hung loose on his bones.

I am being punished, he told Allermann and Dead Das in a voice as cracked as a frog's. This is my lot for the sins of our submission. For those who bow down to the boot and the law there can be only suffering, only more hardship. We will not know freedom.

No, prophet. You have been sent, hissed Dead Das, striking heat from the fire's coals, lifting a thin gruel to his leader's lips. You have been awaited. See how people follow you. How they seek you out. You are their saviour. You are their freedom. It is what the voices foretold. Do not desert them now.

I am just a man, Dead Das, as weak as other men.

You are the redeemer. There is no changing that. Should we lose everything for the sake of a woman? Bah! It is unthinkable.

Look at her, Dead Das. In her shines a light. In her there is a purity no others possess. See what she does for Ma-Fatsoen. The care, the love, the goodness of her heart. She has that for an old lady who gives her nothing, who is a burden . . . Yet she spurns me as if I were a rabid beast.

Take her, insisted Dead Das. Before this thing destroys us all. Just command and I will fetch her.

But the redeemer, the prophet of the people, the man who promised sanctuary for all refugees, who spoke of the country that was soon to come and the time when all would live as equals, who now lay wasted upon a pallet, who could no longer walk where they were forced to travel, feebly shook his head.

No, shouted Dead Das, springing to his feet, spilling soup into the ashes. I did not bear the rope for this weakness. I did not die for this humility. Our vision will not be so easily crushed – and he was off to haul Tasmaine from the kaross where Ma-Fatsoen lay curled in the young woman's warmth.

Sissy, shrieked Ma-Fatsoen, clawing up at the struggling forms, burying long nails in Dead Das, holding on to her precious friend. Sissy. Sissy. Sissy.

But she was too frail for Dead Das's virulence and boots. He kicked her aside, left her howling as he dragged Tasmaine to where Enoch Mistas lay supine.

Get done with it, he yelled, throwing Tasmaine to the ground, stamping off with Allermann into the night.

Why do you not love me? groaned Enoch Mistas across the

young woman's sobs. I am the redeemer, the prophet of the people
. . . you follow me and yet you show no love. He reached out for
the soapy skin, the perfume of her sweat and body. Come to me,
come.

But Tasmaine pulled away, like a mouse crouched trapped and
shivering.

If you would give me love, whispered Enoch Mistas so softly
he might not have spoken, I could grow strong to lead my people.
Here, feel the bones, the flaccid skin, the sickness of my unrequited
love – and he clamped her hand about his shrivelled arm. I am
dying because of you.

Her fingers let go of his arm. She cried, but wouldn't answer
him.

Leave me, he said at last. Go. Get away.

When she had gone, and the howling Ma-Fatsoen was quiet,
Jabulani Mximba, in top hat and long coat, stepped out of the
darkness into the fire's small light.

Woo her, he whispered in the redeemer's ear. Once I had a love
like that. A love that needed kindness, presents, soft words, the
comfort of gentleness. There is no other way.

Perhaps you're right, sighed Enoch Mistas, leaning on one thin
elbow, succumbing to melancholy. But how?

Leave it to me, said Jabulani Mximba. I know the words
that do it.

Even so he had to wait his moment. Enoch Mistas looked on and
grew weaker. Each day they travelled less, rested longer where the
ground was rich. When farmers drove them off they went without
protest. When soldiers approached they hid among rocks. Only
Dead Das and Allermann plotted a dark conspiracy to force the
bitch's love: because if the redeemer goes, this lot will fall apart,
our struggle will be for nothing.

Don't, warned Jabulani Mximba, this calls for subtlety.

Huh! scoffed Dead Das. It demands strength and resolution.

I have a plan, grinned the ostrich rider, fingering his necklace,
flicking dust from his hat: Just wait and see.

And so, whenever Ma-Fatsoen squatted far off at her business
behind a bush, or fell asleep after the day's long road; whenever
Tasmaine, for the briefest moment, was alone as she boiled

early-morning water or sat with tears before her dying embers at nightfall, the love-songs of Jabulani Mximba rose through the chirk of insects and crept into her heart.

Eventually he told Enoch Mistas: I have sung the magic. Now all we can do is wait.

The Love-Songs of Jabulani Mximba

Without You

Without you I can
See no blue sky
Hear no birds call
Feel no warm wind
On my skin.

Without you there's
No laughter
And no music
No songs that I can sing.

So won't you stay with me
Live with me
Be my love
Through thick and thin.

Without you I am nothing
I am no one
Can't you see the state I'm in:
I am sad
And I am empty
All my days are bleak and dim.

Without you life is aimless
There's no meaning
It's a game we cannot win . . .

The Love-Songs of Jabulani Mximba

So be my fantasy
You are my destiny
Let me be with you
Let me lie with you
As night draws in.

Pretty Bird

When I was a young boy I listened to the story
About a starling brave and bright
Oh he was true
His songs were true.
He lived in a cage of thorn
Couldn't stretch his wings in the morn
But even so he flew
Oh yes he flew.

For he sang of a brilliant morning
When the air was clean and warming
And the world would be new
It would be new.
But when his songs rang out clearest
When he sang of love and his dearest
Oh then he cried
His heart broke inside:

   Come to me my beautiful
   Come to me on your wings of glory
   Sing for me my lovely one
   Sing of hope and of ringing reaches
   Sing of dancing on sun-struck beaches
   Sing for me.

And then he cried
His heart broke inside.

One day as he sang of freedom
In a voice without hope or reason
His love came by
She heard his cry:

THIS DAY AND AGE

Come to me my beautiful
Come to me on your wings of glory
Set me free my pretty bird
Set me free on this brilliant morning.

And she opened his cage of longing;
Took him out of his age of longing:
She set him free.

Lovers
Sometimes the world is full of tears
And it takes lovers
To find the joy that's gone
It takes lovers
Who know what's going wrong
And face the day.

Lovers, we have to tell the world
That we are lovers
With hope and care and faith
Truly lovers who want to show the world
A better way.

Because as lovers
We have a kingdom to be built
Because as lovers
We have rivers to be crossed
Because as lovers
We have dreams and stars and yearnings
For a day . . .

When only lovers
Will fill the world with laughter
Only lovers
Will sing and praise each other
Only lovers
Without hate and spite and anger
Walk this way.

The Love-Songs of Jabulani Mximba

Sometimes when the world is full of tears
It takes lovers
To find the joy that's gone
It takes lovers
Who know what's going wrong
And face the day.

A Summer Romance

There was no helping it, nothing Tasmaine could do. Not even when Ma-Fatsoen, woken by an insect bite, heard the songs and screamed and swore until she'd chased away Jabulani Mximba, and made Tasmaine plug her ears with wool, was there a chance things could have turned out differently. The songs were sung. No matter how closely Ma-Fatsoen now stuck to Tasmaine, never letting her out of sight, sleeping with her hand in hand, attentive to every sigh, to every brooding look at where the redeemer lay thin and red-eyed, there was nothing she could do. The songs were in Tasmaine: their tunes lilted on her tongue, their words formed on her lips: Lovers, we have to tell the world that we are lovers. Ma-Fatsoen shook her head and wailed: Sissy. Sissy.

What, Ma? begged Tasmaine. Tell me, please tell me . . . But the old woman only lamented louder: No, Sissy. No, no, no.

No what? pleaded Tasmaine, helping Ma-Fatsoen through bushes, steadying her on steep paths. What is it you're trying to tell?

Then the anguished woman would point at her son, propped up on his pallet being carried over the difficult ground, and tear out her hair, keening. Tasmaine followed the finger to the sight that sharpened the ache in her heart. Mournfully, Ma-Fatsoen sank into herself.

Little by little Tasmaine was drawn to Enoch Mistas. First she brought birds' eggs, wild honey, then food from her pot, a breast of francolin, a leg of hare – all offered quickly, shyly, with a blush, before she fled back to where Ma-Fatsoen hummed old rhymes and talked to her dead children.

A Summer Romance

Your songs are working, smiled Enoch Mistas at Jabulani Mximba. I can feel her love already.

Food isn't love, grumbled Dead Das. We'll see how long this lasts.

For ever, said Jabulani Mximba. At least for her.

And then at night, when Ma-Fatsoen lay snoring, Tasmaine stayed up on one pretext or another: patching clothes, tending the ill, but never asleep until the flames of the redeemer's fire were down. At the end of each day's journey she chose her resting place closer and closer to his pallet until she could hear his voice intoning prayers and lamentations. There Tasmaine was most content. There she could forget the hard ground and the next day's painful distance. There were moments of happiness before sleep. And for a time that was sufficient.

But only for a time, because love is not so easily appeased. Now it demanded attention, acknowledgement, soft words, touches, laughter and passion. Now it was stirred up, agitated, getting desperate. Proximity was not good enough, it wanted the same fire.

And yet . . .

I am not worthy of him, she told herself again and again as the prophet's people traversed plains and mountains moved on by harsh words from one brief camp to another.

Nonsense, said Mrs Naald limping up, resting on her stick. I've known him all his life; there's no difference between you. Ask them, or those, or him, all mission people, who follow him to salvation.

There is, groaned Tasmaine. He could not love someone like me. I am nothing. No one. Invisible to him although once he felt my skin.

A thought which gave her hope. So each evening she took him what food could be spared, laid it beside his pallet, hardly looked at him, hardly dared to hope he would unhood his eyes and ask her name. But the eyelids never flickered. She drew back tormented: Oh, redeemer, my redeemer – but the words were locked within her like starlings.

Now she denied herself, gave her plate, lived off little more than seeds and water. All of which Enoch Mistas saw. As did others.

Bring her here, he said one night when his heart ached sorely and his loins were more desperate than ever. This pretence has gone on long enough, it's time I got to know her.

Not yet, said Jabulani Mximba, restraining Allermann with a firm hand. She'll break when she can't bear it any more, but it's weakness to give in.

Bring her, muttered Enoch Mistas, her love is clear.

That's not love, spat Dead Das. That's woman's wiles.

It's love, said Jabulani Mximba. Just wait and see.

Which they did. And not long after that, when the band was camped on the edge of the diamond desert where it was said lived the restless spirits of a massacred people, they saw the young woman coming towards them, more lovely in Mrs Naald's last handiwork than even she had imagined possible, bearing a meal of roast pigeon, wild onions, sweet berries which she placed before the redeemer, but this time did not retreat, stood her ground until Dead Das and Allermann turned away in disgust, until Jabulani Mximba disappeared with a grin, until Enoch Mistas, heart aching, pulse racing, said: Sit, share this food with me – the only words either spoke, although they ate mouthful for mouthful, never taking their eyes off one another: he allowing her the choicest flesh, she giving him the sweetest onions. And afterwards they sat together until there was no brushwood left to feed the fire. Only the coals remained, glowing in the breezes that are said to be the grief of wronged souls.

What did I tell you? said Mrs Naald next morning. A good dress sets everything straight. It's just as well love's nothing new. It's just as well I saw your plight.

How his strength came back now that she fed him, now that she cooked at his fire and slept within his circle. His bones disappeared into the thickness of flesh, his eyes stopped their retreat, the ulcers of his languishing healed; he got back on his feet to lead them out of the desert into a land of vleis pink with flamingos and pans loud with geese. Here they built shelters of mud and stone in the shade of old trees where the children collected figs or caught the roosting guinea fowl. Here they rested. On the sweet vleigrass Simple Martha and Nick the Herd fattened their sheep; among the wild spinach women found the tendrils of pumpkin and the seeds of gem squash. From the pans men brought mudfish and mullet until the pots were too full to stir and later there wasn't a belly that didn't belch replete. In the summer romance of Enoch Mistas and Tasmaine the people of the prophet forgot days of hunger and suffering when they had been hounded, chased, driven on like harbingers of plague. They grew content and worshipped Enoch Mistas as their saviour.

It is what we always foretold, said Mrs Naald, sunning her gammy leg, moving imaginary needles with her hands. If only Mrs Zimri were here to share it.

And Mr Zimri, whose wife had died on her feet during the aimless years, nodded because his words were too thick with remembrance to be spoken.

They say all things come to pass, sighed Mrs Naald, heavy with the weight of other times, then brightening at the sight of Enoch Mistas and Tasmaine going arm in arm between the huts. Ah, there was joy, there was promise, surely there must be a marriage soon.

Surely, because each day they were together: hand in hand among flamingos; silent before the sweep of flowers that appeared after rain; laughing with the children; bringing luck to the fishing men and kind words to those gathering spinach. Only at night were they separated. Even though their kisses grew longer beneath fondling hands and the desperation in his loins drove Enoch Mistas to distraction, still he would not take her under his kaross. Instead he prayed for strength of will even as his tongue explored her mouth; for an end to carnal lust as he crushed her breasts against him in desire. And when they sat alone on warm nights with the people asleep in the tiny shelters, Tasmaine was happy in his arms, ran her fingers across his skin, nuzzled closer like a small animal, biting gently at his neck, turning her lips up, parted, eager, searching for his mouth that came down to her trembling with prayers.

This is pure love, proclaimed Enoch Mistas. Pure love unsullied by carnal knowledge.

It's too much petting and cooing, muttered Dead Das. Just get on with it, we're wasting time.

He's only human, said Jabulani Mximba. Let the man have his fling.

There's no time for that when others are dying, snorted Dead Das. Love hasn't a place these days.

We'll see, Dead Das, we'll see. Love's not to be ignored.

Dead Das and Allermann chafed at the inaction: cleaned rifles, sharpened knives, wandered listlessly about the pans or disappeared for days into the hinterland returning with refugees who brought wounds and reminders of the president's rule of law. Even in that quiet place of dragonflies, stories were told of soldiers burning homesteads, the young enslaved, the elderly put to death.

You can't ignore it, Dead Das told the redeemer, as they walked among the displaced offering succour and food. You can't just brush this aside.

It's not the time, he replied, comforting a child, laying on hands.

You mean it's her, said Dead Das.

She's a salvation, said Enoch Mistas. Remember that – and they parted: one to his angry brooding, the other to his love.

For Tasmaine, that summer held her as she had once lived in the brief expeditions to the mountains, without past or future, like a feather drifting slowly across the morning's bright laughter. She stirred songs into her cooking and went somnolent through afternoons that ticked with cicadas. These were her days. Here she healed grieving hearts and open wounds, here she baked sweet dough cakes coated in honey. About her skirts children played, and grandmothers beamed toothless smiles at her radiance when she came among them laden with pickles. Tasmaine was wonderful, Tasmaine was queen. She showed them the magic of buchu leaves and told them the legends of the moon. She made pots from river clay and whistles from the reeds. Tasmaine knew their secrets and their plans, heard their fears and the hopes that still possessed them. They were the people of the prophet, but their hearts belonged to her: she was their joy, their song. Where she walked they followed gladly, singing. When the days were longest she led their procession to the distant sea where from a low-tide spit of sand she and they waded waist-deep to be baptised in the name of the Father, the Son and the Holy Ghost by the incanting redeemer who pushed them under with a firm hand into a blue moment Tasmaine never wanted to leave before he brought her and them gasping back to life. Later he took her to slip again beneath the surface and they knelt open-eyed in the liquid light where the ancestors dwell, her heart hard in her ears as if it were the pulse of the ocean. And so they drifted, face down, flying. This was heaven, this was grace: Tasmaine sung through the sea like a whale.

I dream, she told Enoch Mistas afterwards as they lay upon the sand, of you and me alone with our children. No one disturbs our solitude: we plough, we milk the goats, and if strangers chance upon us they say nothing of the world outside, they just eat and go, and tell no one of our lives. That's what I dream: to be lost to everything.

I dream, said Enoch Mistas, of the land we must take back and make our own. I dream of this and feel its strength.

I dream of silent days and warm nights beneath the stars.

I dream of stones, of the angry stone's simple fury.

I dream of love.

I dream of fire, lead, steel. I dream of judgement when neither their women and children are spared, because our women and children were not spared, nor their men reprieved, because our men were always hanged. I dream of punishment. When an innocent child died at the breast because his mother was too starved to give milk, then guilty children ate chocolate. When an innocent child died in the cold, then guilty children had blankets. At these iniquities I rail: cry justice for those women chained to the production line; howl revenge for men who toil in mines.

I dream of dreams.

I dream of the necessary death: the president, the general, the soldier, the banker, the corporate head, the general dealer, killed. Only then will we be cured, no longer lost in apathy and torpor, free to live our lives. Only from the rotting corpse of the settler can we arise as new men.

I dream of a suckling babe and a man coming back from the fields at sunset.

I dream of history, said Enoch Mistas, rising, starting back on the path to the huts and shelters. We can dream of nothing less.

Nor anything else, leered Dead Das at Tasmaine.

It is not my dream, said Tasmaine.

Only your destiny, laughed Jabulani Mximba. As the song goes:

> Let me be with you
> Let me lie with you
> As night draws in.

The Big Night

So much for wooing and a summer romance; now Enoch Mistas wanted the fruit.

You must be my wife, he told Tasmaine. It is the Lord's will.

I shall love you always, she replied. No matter what.

Our love will be every man's inspiration, he said.

I shall honour and obey, she vowed. I shall remain true.

And I will cherish you now and for ever, said Enoch Mistas.

I am yours.

Then prepare for the big night, announced the redeemer, ordaining Dead Das as priest, declaring Allermann best man, appointing Jabulani Mximba master of ceremonies. Let it be made sacrosanct on the full moon.

Oh what a wait, because now the moon was thinner than cold steel in the sky. Oh what doubts and surety, what absolute confusion.

Every day Tasmaine grew sadder remembering her lover's words at the beach and longing even more to live her dream. And though she smiled as much, went laughing with the children to search for watermelons, yet her songs held new notes of melancholy and questions hammered in her head: Could her dream not be? Why could it not be? Wasn't it better than this hell of struggling? Didn't it offer a better peace? Please, she whispered to the waxing moon, can't I have just this? No, came back the answer. We are losers you and I – there is always a greater sun.

Yet, when she and he spent idle moments on the edges of the pan or lay drowsy among dune grass, all doubt disappeared and she wanted no other world than his, where there would be shelter and food, tables and proper beds, new clothes and well-made boots. Where their children could read of great men's ideas, and medicine was not only for the privileged. In the factories and plants of this new land there would be production and industry, a strong economy providing wealth for all. Shops, supermarkets, wholesalers. The ability to purchase.

Such were the invisible cities he built for her as the moon grew round. Cities made of mirrors that shimmered above the highveld, cities of skyscrapers lost in the clouds, and the one she liked best which was approached through the mountains until they saw its lights and its ships and the open boulevards lined with palm trees. There we will live, he said, in a mansion of many rooms with peacocks in the gardens and dragonflies over the rock pools. And she imagined it all in the moonlight.

In the moonlight it was perfect. But in the daylight all she saw were poor shelters and mean lives. His architecture vanished, his buildings crumbled into a rubble of sentences she did not understand, phrases of discarded plastic and glass and tin she did not know, a language of refuse and pollution that frightened her as she wandered alone through his alien words.

And Enoch Mistas? He was restless again, stalking tall and gaunt among his people or sitting grim with Dead Das bent all day at his ear. Only the evening still heard his soft words for Tasmaine, but she knew his thoughts were elsewhere. For there were rumours from the hinterland of dying cattle that foamed yellow at the mouth and men who set fire to pastures and the hills. Here the sun turned soil to stones and the people took knives and anger into their neighbours' homesteads.

It was as the prophets had always foretold. Young girls drawing water saw the ancestors swirling up in the pools and said they rode on long-horned cattle and their eyes shone like coals. Young boys listened in caves and told of the drumming of hooves and the lowing of mighty bulls.

The Lord is with us, said the redeemer. Those who oppress us will come to a dreadful end. He will send pestilence among them and let blood in the streets. The sword is against them on every side, it is sharpened and polished to flash like lightning and they shall be no more. This is the time of the final punishment. These are our days, the power will be ours.

We must fast, said Enoch Mistas to Dead Das and Allermann. We must purge ourselves, and leave this place for one I have been shown. Go and tell the people.

So Dead Das and Allermann, all smiles, triumphant, went among the huts and told the people of the prophet to prepare for what was coming.

But what about the wedding? everyone asked. Surely there is time for that?

Weddings are human affairs, the henchmen replied. True marriages are made in heaven.

But what of everything we've collected? people wanted to know. The ostrich eggs, mussels, limpets, urchins from the distant sea; melons, fish, fowl, wild figs?

And what of everything we've made: bread, cakes, biscuits, to say nothing of flower arrangements, little touches, our hours of preparation?

Times have changed, said Dead Das.

We bring the call, ja, said Allermann.

It's what the prophet ordered, said Jabulani Mximba, coming up, shrugging his shoulders.

So everything was dumped. Tasmaine looked on dry-eyed.

Why? was all she wanted to know of her future husband. A celebration would have made people happy.

It's impossible, said Enoch Mistas. We must show solidarity with the starving.

And the marriage?

That's different. It represents a united front.

Man and wife. He solemn; she smiling. She soft and splendid; he tall and gaunt. Wife and man.

At full moon, thanks to Dead Das, that's what they became. At full moon the people of the prophet left their huts and shelters to gather in the clearing among the trees. They looked down on the pans of mercury and the vleis of molten lead, they heard scavengers rooting through the wedding feast and some mumbled that this was no wedding at all. About them the shadows shrank away.

The moon strode up – a hunter's moon come out of the distant mountains to go walking across the sky. Tasmaine remembered that the sharecroppers had once said it was the light which guided the stars. Stars that were men, women and children, whole clans of people who had long since gone from their lives. And when the moon slipped away, the two stars that were mother and child, that were always awaited, would come out of the mountain. Look on them for good fortune, the sharecroppers had said. Watch how she leads her child even though, now and then, he hides in a cloud, yet she always finds him. Such is her love.

Such is love, said Tasmaine to herself, it doesn't need a song and dance to get it going.

My wife, said Enoch Mistas to his bride when Dead Das was done, this is our night – and he led her off through the silent people to his hut.

It'll come to no good, said Mrs Naald. A marriage isn't a marriage without celebrations. And to think of everything I did for his mother.

Keep your thoughts to yourself, said Dead Das, this is the prophet's way.

Maybe. But think of the girl.

We do, ja, sniggered Allermann.

Without another word the people returned to their shelters. Women lay down with their men as now Enoch Mistas took Tasmaine under his kaross. It was a night for love. They caressed. They sighed. They held each other tightly. The moon walked on. Men slept, their seed spent. Women listened to the night sounds, uncomforted.

Enoch Mistas, for the first time without prayers on his lips, kissed his fair Tasmaine. His free hand went where it had never been before, slipping from her shoulders on to those breasts he'd imagined would be as smooth as melon skins, as soft as tiny birds. In his loins the desperation grew unbearable. Further down went his hand until it met with hair, and there it stroked and rubbed, crawling about her like a spider. Enough. She was his: she was his wife; she was his woman. He heaved on to her and thrust between her thighs – thrust expecting the warmth of acceptance, thrust anticipating the relief of moisture, thrust on the assumption of silky passage, thrust on the presumption of ages. But there was no way in. He was blunted. He was denied. He spat his semen against a wall of skin.

And then he lit a candle and looked.

Nothing.

You lied, he hissed. You cheated me. You witch.

Enoch Mistas rose over her like a spectre: You led me on, you bound me with love, chained me to you, me, the redeemer, the prophet of the people. You are worse than those who persecute us, you are more a devil than the president, more evil than his minions. It would have been better if you had never lived. Whore, get out of my bed.

Tasmaine obeyed, crawling out, naked, frightened, on to the dirt floor.

Your soul is damned, shouted Enoch Mistas, but you will not drag me into your mire, into your hell-hole. You are no lover of men, you harlot, you will destroy us, laugh at our humiliation, reject us who are your masters. We, slut, manage the world. Your place is where we command. Your worth is in bearing children.

The redeemer held the Bible up before him like a shield: Get dressed, you Jezebel, cover your nakedness because you are not a woman. You are of no use to men. You cannot satisfy us, you cannot have our sons. It would have been better if you had no arms, if your leg was lame, or your teeth had rotted to stumps. You would still have been a woman. Men could still have come to you. We could still have offered you shelter, a fire. But what can you give in return? Nothing. You are worthless. A temptress to lead men from their God and damn them for their lust. Get out, Messalina.

Enoch Mistas raised the Bible as if to strike her: Get out, collaborator. You who would conspire with the oppressors to overthrow me, get out. See, I have triumphed, the Lord is with me, He leads me in the paths of righteousness. I shall not be sullied.

And Tasmaine, heavy with sadness, went out into the night which the hunter's moon had left to the stars, to the mother and child, venturing further out from their distant mountain. So many stars: so many clans of people. In their beds the women sighed but the men slept on. Tasmaine lay beside Ma-Fatsoen and looked up at the sky. Tsau, tsau, she heard the stars singing as the sharecroppers had said they did whenever tears overcame them.

From the Diaries of P.T. George

I have seen mass slaughter; I have seen wanton destruction. I have witnessed men being brutally slain. I have had to watch women and children put to horrible deaths. And these atrocities were all for nothing. For imagined wrongs, for a debt of twelve cows, or for trespassing on pasturage, or the refusal to water horses. For such excuses men go to war. It sickens me. How true have become the words of a pastor who once warned me of this hostile land and its savages. Little enough I believed him then; now it is all I see.

This is no place to live; this is no country for decent men. Yet it is a place of such beauty: in all my years of travelling I have forded wide rivers and looked on mountains and great plains thrown beneath the sun with triumph, and yet still I stand in awe at ever grander vistas. Never could I have imagined such splendour in one land. Perhaps this is what has soured the people: perhaps this magnificence has turned them sullen and bloody. I don't know, but I do know I must leave these parts.

Last night again there was a raid. Two men were killed, a woman raped, huts razed. Who by: passing bandits or renegades from the hills? Some say one, some say the other, and all talk of forming a commando to obliterate the faction. But what about the police, I interject, even though I am as unconvinced by my own suggestion as they are sceptical of the authorities' will to end the violence. How many deputations have not been made to the president only to be turned away by his secretary with promises to send special forces or increase patrols? Neither has happened. Instead the police seem to have kept away, or, when present, stir up trouble between the tribes. For no one cares about these people, least of all the president. Their lives are as nothing to him, so why should he mourn their deaths!

When I arrived in this village I was overcome with enthusiasm for the rugged veld and these hardy tribes. Here was man unbowed by nature: sowing crops among stones, drawing water from the sand, grazing his herds wherever scrub grew. Here was a people more generous than I had yet encountered in almost three decades of wandering. Who would have thought they had time for jealousies and bad thoughts when each day was a battle for life? Yet for months I would not see the base side, nor listen to complaints of stock theft or water poisoning. Men were not like that in the desert, I thought. In the desert men were true to name – *Homo sapiens* – the wise men. What wisdom? What wisdom that burnt crops or cut the shanks of cattle or set cobras among the fowls? What wisdom that could not leave another man's world untainted by blood?

My time here has been absolute heartache: witness to poverty and hunger. Witness to a people's suffering and their oppression at the hands of a malevolent regime. But above all, witness to murder and mayhem on an unspeakable scale. How, then, can I feel sorry for these people? How can I share their struggle when in one night they can do this: lay waste to lives; run so savagely amok? All sympathy withers at such time, all understanding crumbles: humanity becomes weeds and ruins. Ruins and weeds. Oh God – if you exist – I have had enough. I must get away from this depravity.

29 January

Where are you going, Mister P.T., they all wanted to know. I shrugged. You can't leave us, they pleaded, we need you. But for what do they need me? What have I given them? A better way of drawing water. To a few the ability to read. In one or two cases their health. But no matter how much I plead and cajole and negotiate I cannot stop the fighting, and before that everything else is inconsequential.

When they saw I was in earnest they fell silent and sullen

while I packed. Only the children laughed about me as is their way when I leave on a painting expedition or a fossicking trip. They clamoured to come with me and would not take no for an answer. I am not coming back, I explained. I am going for good. You will never see me again. Then the truth of my words sank in and I had to confront their dejected faces. This was almost enough to make me recant. It takes a hard heart to disappoint a child.

If the truth be told I felt wretched. Never before so guilty, never before such a traitor. But what option had I? To stay on, irrelevant, useless: at best a recorder of their misery, at worst a voyeur insulting their dignity! No, that was not a solution. A man's first duty is to himself. He who ignores that is of no use to the world, he has no pride, no self-respect, and without that a man is worthless. This is why I left them. They had stripped me of all high thought, they had rendered life meaningless.

When I rode out there were tears on some cheeks. They cast their eyes down the way victims do before their tormentors. I rode on. As I left the kraal one of them threw a rock which struck my back. I did not turn round. I can understand the protest. I can acknowledge the despair.

5 February

There is no escaping one's fate. Even in this vast backveld where I have travelled for days without seeing another soul, even here there is no side-stepping what is in store. The further I went into the desolate fastnesses – this country of black rocks – the closer I came to the inevitable. How foolish to think I was freeing myself from the past, when all the time I was binding myself to the future.

When the two men stepped out of the night into the circle of my fire I was at first alarmed, because I had not heard them approach, but I was not surprised. In a way there was something familiar about the tableau: it was as if I had been expecting these two rough characters, the one a sweet talker, the other hard-eyed and silent. Automatically I reached for my rifle, a stupid gesture, for had they wished me harm they would not have walked in so brazenly from the dark. The one with a scarf around his neck laughed, the other grinned. It's all right, said the first one, we are friends. I laid the gun across my lap as they sat down on the opposite side of the fire. I offered them coffee and the remains of my pot. They accepted and ate hurriedly.

Are you prospectors? I asked when they finished, although they carried no tools. Yet the only men crazy enough to haunt these iron landscapes are diamond diggers driven mad by their dreams. Again the one laughed. No, he said, they were not prospectors, but they were searchers, men looking for a place where they could live in peace and freedom. I was about to say there was no such place but my guest rattled on. I use the word rattled advisedly because he seemed to speak with difficulty, as if sometimes he couldn't shape his words and they clattered among his teeth like stones.

He talked about a redeemer, a man who performed miracles, who could heal the sick, who offered salvation. This individual would lead them out of bondage to a free land where everyone would be equal and none would suffer hunger or misery. He was a great man, this redeemer, said my guest; he inspired, he carried the light of God, he was a man of the people. From all over the country the downtrodden and the outcast were flocking to his side. They sat enraptured at his words, and their stomachs were filled with food from his table. Even now they were planning a city that would be impervious to the president's treachery, rich beyond imagination, glorious beyond dreams.

I heard him out – in truth I had little alternative because once in full spate there was no halting him, despite his affliction. When he eventually stopped he looked at me as if he had asked a question. I dropped his gaze and poked about in the ashes until we had new flames.

Join us, he said at last.

What! I exclaimed. Join you! Why on earth should I join you?

You are one of us, he replied. We can tell.

Oh nonsense, I said. What can you tell? Just because you find a man alone in the desert you think he is a malcontent. But I could be a government agent. I could be a land-owner. I could be anybody.

Here I stopped: they continued to stare at me until I shifted with discomfort. Suddenly, perhaps out of embarrassment at the silence, I confessed: I am a scientist. A man of Newton, a man of Darwin. Perhaps not an atheist but certainly an agnostic. If I cannot believe in God, how can I believe in your redeemer?

You will, they said. Come with us.

I have deliberately travelled out here, I explained, to paint these baked koppies and this landscape of stone. I have come out here to remind myself that mankind, that we, are nothing, that in this adversity not even a succulent can grow. That this is our true estate. I paused, and into the gap he clattered: At least meet the redeemer. There is no harm in that.

I am a weak man; for me it is difficult to say no. I am also a curious man drawn rather helplessly to the unusual and I must admit to being intrigued at this fellow's proselytising. So I agreed. Only then did they introduce themselves: the talker called himself Dead Das, his companion's name was Allermann.

And who is this redeemer? I asked.

A man known as Enoch Mistas, Dead Das replied.

They spent the night at my camp and the next day we went some hours in an easterly direction until we came upon a long, straggling column of people and animals, sleds and carts. It was an impressive sight, this stream of humanity passing through the wilderness. At its head strode a tall man wearing a black frock-coat despite the heat. He had a Bible chained to his wrist. Beside him loped an equally extraordinary individual in a top hat. And behind them came the rag-tag masses driving sheep and goats or carrying fowls tucked under their arms. We joined the column at its head and I dismounted to allow an old woman, who was being half carried by her daughter, to ride. I have subsequently discovered they are the 'redeemer's' mother and his wife. Clearly the mother is mad, and the girl, for she is still very young, seems deeply troubled. I walked with them all through the afternoon, as much to keep the one from falling off the horse as to keep the other from collapsing with fatigue. The girl is in a bad way. There is about her an exhaustion I have seen only in soldiers who have spent days and nights in battle. We did not once exchange a word. Needless to say, my two comrades of the night disappeared as soon as they saw I was thoroughly enmeshed in the column although from time to time they came by to check on me – and to let me know that their lord and master would deign to see me when the march was called to a halt. Otherwise they seemed preoccupied with marshalling the horde. I must admit that in the heat of the afternoon I began to wish I had never let myself be persuaded by these two adventurers to abandon my solitude. I am not the man I once was and my size precludes excessive exercise, so I fared badly and three or four times was pulled up by palpitations of the heart. Fortunately today is the Sabbath – judging by the condition of these people, let alone myself, a much-needed day of rest.

Before I record my discussions last night with Enoch Mistas I wish to make a few observations about the girl, his wife. She intrigues me. She also arouses my sympathy because Mistas rejects her love – in fact he is either downright rude to her or oblivious of her presence. The display of both attitudes while he and I talked caused me considerable embarrassment and seriously marred my otherwise favourable impression of the man. Yet this young woman, although I believe wounded by each encounter, continues to serve him with a devotion that is heartrending in its tenderness. For instance, when we stopped yesterday evening, she, who had been leaning heavily on my arm for many miles, suddenly rushed off to attend her husband. I was left amazed at her reserves of energy, at how quickly she shed the apathy of weariness, for she heated water to bathe his feet, she brewed tea, she prepared his supper. While he ate she was in attendance and afterwards she cleared the site and laid a bed for him. Then she ministered to the old lady, and I am sure that once she was finished there she had no strength left to tend herself. When I returned from my discussions with Mistas I found her lying uncovered beside the fire, as pathetic a sight as ever I have seen. I draped her with one of my blankets but could not get the image of her from my mind. She seemed so helpless, yet clearly she has hidden wells of strength. Today again she was a whirl of activity, beginning before sunrise –

I know, because my mind was abuzz with thoughts last night so that the dawn found me wide awake – and continuing even this moment when the heat is at its most withering and every man and animal has lain down to let it pass. There she is now, not two yards from me, darning his clothes. Between Mistas and his mother the girl is not allowed a spare moment. Hence my belief in her inner strength which, I am willing to wager, is not just physical but emotional as well. How else could she cope with her husband's animosity? But I have other reasons for supposing an inner tenacity. When she returned the blanket this morning she did so with a quiet smile filled with gratitude. I took the opportunity to look into her eyes and she held my enquiry until modesty forced an end. But there was time enough for me to note a resolve – ironically not that different from her husband's – which undoubtedly fuels her love. Or is it a higher belief which keeps her going? Perhaps she is nurtured by a dream? Perhaps all this outward kindliness is merely a sense of duty? Time – and I suspect there will be a fair amount of that – will tell.

But what of Enoch Mistas, the redeemer as his followers know him? Before I say anything more I must preface my remarks by pointing out that he is a considerable man, one of the most forceful I have met in all these years of wandering about the backveld. I cannot but feel he is being propelled by history, and he is every bit able to withstand such taxing demands. Yet even so I am sceptical: not so much of his sincerity as of his ability to realise his schemes. Laudable as they are, I fear they are nothing but ideology. In the end these poor people will be no better off. But those are just my opinions and they count for nothing. To return to last evening. I was summoned after we had all eaten – dined is hardly the right word in these nomadic circumstances. I noticed that Allermann served me from Mistas's table but for some reason I was not asked to sit with the leadership. Obviously he does not observe such niceties, although they are common to most of the people I have come across during my journeys. Or was there some other reason: a pointed reminder that he is a man apart? Perhaps I am too sensitive on this issue, yet I could not help feeling – even during our discussion – that he was testing me, even deliberately trying to unnerve me. Why do I say this? Simply because unexpectedly – one moment he was holding forth on the iniquities of taxation, the next he had grabbed my jacket and thrust his face so close to mine I could feel his spittle – he wanted to know if I was a police informer. You talk like one, he kept saying. You sound like one. And before I could reply he launched into a long diatribe about collaborators and turncoats, not to mention the likes of secret agents who were all set on keeping his people in submission. When he'd finished he said: We do not tolerate spies, Mister P.T. George. For them there is only one fitting punishment: crucifixion. This last was a quick whisper, so unexpected, so gruesome, that for a moment I wondered if I'd heard him correctly. I glanced up, but in that flickering light it was impossible to tell what expressions crossed his face. And then, to further compound my doubts, he began a dissertation on the future of his people that was quite beautiful in its visionary might. By the time he had finished I was captivated. As I have said, he is a considerable man, a remarkable man: a man filled – nay possessed – with a mission. It is impossible not to be moved when he speaks and I can truthfully say he inspired me. Even that one, perhaps understandable, attempt at unsettling me and his attitude towards his wife were forgotten while I listened to him. Then there was only the power of his conviction, a power which stayed with me through most of the night as I lay unsleeping, entranced by images of peace and prosperity.

Reconsidering now his words and the magnitude of his presence one can see why his wife is so besotted with him and why all these people follow him unquestioningly through the desert. To them he is a hero, a modern messiah. As for me, I shall take up his invitation to travel with them, for a while.

26 February

We cover very little distance during a day's march – a man on horseback would take no more than three days to journey what we've done in as many weeks. But for my part this is quite acceptable, especially as the travelling arrangements, although considerably improved, are far from satisfactory. We – mother, wife and I – jolt along now, two of us at a time, in a sort of sled fashioned, by the peculiar man wearing the top hat and necklace of teeth, out of a derelict cart he found abandoned in the veld. My horse seems up to this contraption and may even be relieved not to have my bulk on his back. I have taken up with the two women to ease the burden of travelling for all of us. Although Mistas's wife and I hardly talk there is at least a feeling of companionship. With the mother, Ma-Fatsoen, there is no communication at all as her mind is completely deranged.

I have had no further conversation with Mistas although from time to time he has caught my eye and smiled, which seems to suggest I may have found favour with him, if that is important, which I hardly imagine it is for either of us. As for his henchmen, Dead Das and Allermann, sometimes they are here but more often they seem to be away scouring the countryside for whatever wandering itinerants they can recruit. And of these there are many. Bands of people are continually joining us and hardly a day goes by without some addition to our ranks. But where we are headed is a mystery and I cannot see that when we get there the government would ever countenance Mistas building the kingdom he envisages.

2 March
Should I stay on? Every morning I ask myself that question and each day I procrastinate at the sight of these two women so valiantly pressing forward when everything is against them. So I put aside my restless thoughts to help them through another day. Yet there is nothing for me here, and besides, I sense trouble. We are hearing too many stories of atrocities and ruthless farmers.

5 March
It seems we have a destination. Today I was informed by no less an authority than Enoch Mistas, yes indeed the redeemer

himself, that in a few days' time we should reach a flat mountain as impregnable as a fortress. There he plans to found his refuge, where, and I quote, 'my people will be free'. For most of the afternoon I again listened to him speaking with that utter conviction he has which so enthralls, so captivates, that it is impossible to gainsay him. Yet I am filled with despondency today and not even his fervour can stir me.

6 March

Enoch Mistas puzzles me. All morning I have been pondering why he chose to talk to me yesterday. I cannot arrive at a satisfactory answer.

9 March

Again today he seeks me out. We had stopped for the night: all around people were cooking or preparing rest places. Tasmaine was about her daily duties; the old woman, his mother, lay already asleep; I was resting against my saddlebags, staring without thought at the setting sun, too fatigued even to take in the beauty. Suddenly I felt a tap on my shoulder and turned to see Mistas nudging at me with his walking stick. He indicated that I should join him, which, although not an enticing proposition, was not a summons I could disobey.

We walked in silence down the column of refugees towards the herders minding the sheep and goats at the rear. Eventually he said: I want you to meet the only one who loves me without reservation, as I love her. She turned out to be a deaf mute. A rather simple woman, her face spoilt by the slackness of an eye. Clearly she idolises Mistas because as we approached she ran towards him and fell at his feet burying her head in his frock-coat. After the embrace she stood back and gazed in adoration at a spot just above his head. There was an expression of ecstasy on her face. I think perhaps she has problems with her sight – a stigmatism that leaves her squinting at places where she imagines people to be. It is not a phenomenon I have encountered before. If she regarded Mistas with veneration, then he treated her with extreme gentleness, caressed her hair and her face, all the time speaking softly in an undertone that was too intimate for me to overhear what he said. They remained in this manner for perhaps half an hour. When they parted she had tears in her eyes but I sensed they were not from sorrow.

Again we walked in silence, this time out into the veld. By now it was dark and I could no longer see his face.

That was my sister, he said. Of us all – and he swept his hand towards the myriad of cooking fires jumping in the dusk – she alone deserves neither hurt nor pain. In her simple world there is nothing ugly. Even if she were to witness Armageddon it would be for her a sublime moment: she would see only wonder and magnificence. She is innocent, Mister P.T., innocent in a way we can never be.

It was on my mind to ask: And what of Tasmaine? Was she, too, not innocent? But as always my courage failed me, and I let the moment pass.

Mistas talked on: There are times when I long for her innocence, to have a life that is without right or wrong, that sees no evil in the lure of a flower, that cannot comprehend the hate that hardens in men's hearts. But I have seen too much, Mister P.T. I am not innocent. I have been shown what is to come; I have heard men conspire to commit murder; I know the machinations of wickedness and thievery.

I heard him out in silence; he is, after all, not interested in my opinion. Besides, what I have to say on these matters is neither original nor profound. Then he declared with a new vehemence: There was no alternative, Mister P.T. I was chosen, my way is the way of the righteous, and I, too, am innocent. I have been exonerated.

He took my arm and we headed back to our respective fires: he striding in that long purposeful way he has while I trotted desperately at his side.

What am I to make of all this?

15 March
We are here at last. The days of marching are over. Or at least they are done with for a time, because I fear these people will no more be left in peace here than anywhere else. However,

my pessimism is not shared by Mistas and his henchmen, who are convinced this is their promised land. And indeed it is most beautiful. The mountain plateau is lush and verdant with natural springs and pools of the sweetest water shaded by pepper trees and small date palms. There is grazing aplenty and more than enough space to erect the shelters. If I could only share his dream I, too, would think this nirvana, a haven from suffering, a quiet place away from the noise of violence. And yes, it is an island. An island in a vast and desolate sea of plains that stretch out interminably until they disappear into the watery heat. How can I forget the days we stumbled across those flats towards this chimera, finding strength only in its promise, drawing hope from the coming days of rest? And now we are here, the massif is theirs: people smile again, the children laugh and sing, even the old woman, Ma-Fatsoen, seems to know that a journey has ended. I hope for their sakes it has.

Undoubtedly, Dead Das and Allermann chose this stronghold with care. They will be warned of approaching foreigners days before anyone could reach the mountain's foot. Even a hard-riding patrol could not slip in under cover of night. Yet in the unlikely event that dangerous elements should manage to cross the plain undetected, they would never breach the defences because to reach the summit by any means other than the single gully – or kloof – is impossible, the sides rising bare to a crown of unscalable granite. Truly it is a fortress mountain which half a dozen men could defend without risking life or limb.

My travelling companions have erected a hut – which I share with them – and seem already to have settled into this new way of life. But then, I suppose those whose lot is enforced wandering are quick to adapt to new circumstances. I have noticed that Tasmaine is more than ever drawn into herself, and although she still tends Mistas it is without enthusiasm, rather, I suspect, it is done from a sense of wifely duty or simple habit. Not that this seems to bother him, as I am convinced he no longer notices her presence: she has become a mere servant. Personally I am saddened by this.

Now that these people have reached a destination of sorts I have decided the time has come to move on. There is nothing for me here: I shall paint some of the views but I need – no, crave – the comfort of solitude. However, I think I shall remain until after a baptism service which I believe is planned for a few days hence, and which I am particularly keen to witness. By that time I shall have recuperated from the rigours of our journey to this place, and, equally important, my horse, which was severely strained, will have regained its strength. I do not think this delay will jeopardise my plans although I am anxious to be away before there is any confrontation with the authorities – an inevitability, I fear, but one which will probably not happen for some weeks yet. I have not told Mistas of my intentions; there is surely no need. And he has not sought me out since we arrived here.

21 March

I knew it would come to this but I had not expected it so soon. And now I am once again caught in the middle. It is my own fault. I should have paid heed to my instincts, but no, like a fool too consumed with curiosity for his own good, I continued on my predictable path, perhaps even willing the inevitable. As I have already noted: there is no escaping one's fate. So now I have incurred the wrath of the woolmen, and, I fear, the censure of Dead Das and Allermann. But I have Enoch Mistas's gratitude and the man in the top hat cannot stop grinning at me. More seriously, though, I have made a commitment to this group which is something I had vowed not to do. Leaving will be more difficult, but leave I must before this matter gets out of hand.

The confrontation occurred this afternoon. For many days prior to our arrival we had passed through good sheep country. There were flocks scattered everywhere and I was surprised to note the absence of farmers or their shepherds. I imagined Dead Das and Allermann had charted a careful path to the fortress mountain well clear of the homesteads, but even their stealth could not keep us undetected for ever. Especially as people were feasting on these animals as if they were manna from heaven.

From the Diaries of P.T. George

So it was merely a matter of time before someone picked up the trail of gnawed mutton bones. Of this I warned Dead Das and Allermann but they scornfully dismissed my misgivings on the grounds that no man can deny food to the hungry. Yet I foresaw trouble. Not only because of our own doings but for other reasons as well. Namely, the dispossessed who joined us daily spoke of angry farmers who chased them with sjamboks and rifles. They told of how the farmers rode down the elderly and frail and shot them like jackals. They showed where they had been lacerated by whips or wounded by bullets and I grew increasingly afraid. Then, as I had anticipated, the deputation arrived.

I suppose you could call it a commando – a troop of some fifteen horsemen armed with rifles and slung with bands of ammunition. They stopped at the foot of the mountain. Dead Das and Allermann gathered a group of men and were about to descend when Enoch Mistas called them to a halt. He beckoned to me: I want you to go with them, he said. You understand the mind of these woolmen. I tried to persuade him otherwise but he was of fixed purpose. Go, he commanded. Tell them I have come here so that my people can live in dignity as it has been ordained.

What choice did I have in the matter? Mistas is not a man to be rebutted. Once he has spoken he stares fixedly at you with eyes of fire until you accept there is no other way but his. I went with Dead Das and Allermann, trembling every inch of the descent, my heart leaping and seizing as much from the effort as from fear. The deputation spread out as we drew nearer, each man with a ready rifle. They did not dismount. Our motley collection of weapons was no match for theirs. I knew they could slaughter us at the merest whim, and indeed they looked ready to do so. Their leader, to my consternation, addressed himself to me.

We have come for the boy you kidnapped, he said.

My mouth was as dry as paper, my tongue numb with fright: this was totally unexpected. I had anticipated demands that we pay for butchered or stolen animals, or that we had no right to the land Mistas had annexed – but of this boy I knew nothing. I looked from Dead Das to Allermann seeking some confirmation of the charge. Dead Das merely shrugged; Allermann's face was set in an impenetrable sneer. I had no option but to brazen it out.

No boy has been kidnapped, I said.

Before their leader could respond, one of the woolmen spurred his horse at me, screaming that it was his son who had been abducted, that he had seen the boy dragged away howling for mercy as he was prodded with sticks and thorns. He charged that I lied, that we lied, that we were nothing but scum, filth, that we stank higher than vulture turds. He swung at me with his rifle, and had it not been for the intervention of Dead Das he would probably have smashed my skull. As it was I staggered back and fell over my own feet. Before I could rise, Dead Das was howling his recriminations.

It is you who lie, he shouted. You who make up these accusations. But we will not take your oppression any longer. We have guns. We will fight for what is ours.

Now it was my turn to intervene, although where I got the courage to step before Dead Das's raised rifle – for he was so excited he could easily have blown my head off – I do not know, and am even now overcome with shivers when I think about it. But I did, and it is as well I did. Who knows, Dead Das may otherwise have unleashed a bloodbath.

I have no idea what I shouted, yet it gained a pause long enough for me to wheeze – I could hardly talk coherently – something of a compromise. I suggested that in order to refute this allegation of kidnapping, the father and the leader accompany me up the mountain to talk with the boy – if indeed he was there at all. Grudgingly the woolmen agreed but demanded two hostages in return. I proposed Dead Das and Allermann, who were annoyed by this suggestion but could hardly object.

Naturally the people of the prophet were most reluctant to co-operate with these two woolmen, and for that I cannot blame them. It took some time before I could establish that the man's son was there. I spoke with the boy and he assured me that he had joined the people of his own free will but was either too ashamed or too afraid to confront his father with the fact. This information I relayed to his parent. However, the man stubbornly refused to accept it until he had seen his son. A meeting finally took place well after dark. The son told the father what he had earlier told me. The father, much to my amazement, because I had expected him to fly into a rage, cringed under each word as if he had been struck and seemed to wither into an old man before our eyes. Perhaps this is truly what happens to those who have their beliefs, expectations, their very pride, so suddenly destroyed.

When the boy finished Enoch Mistas stood up and sang out: Praise the Lord, a soul is saved – the cry echoing again and again among his followers.

The two men, defeated, walked away, but they had not gone many paces before the leader turned and, pointing at Mistas, yelled: You have bewitched him! You satan, you have stolen his soul!

That, to all intents and purposes, is where the incident ended. But men like that do not give up so easily. They will be back, either with more of their kind or with the weight of the law. Either way they will not rest until the boy has been reclaimed.

22 March

Today it was my turn to seek out Mistas. I think he was annoyed at my forthright approach but I was convinced there were lives at stake and I could not let personal trivialities interfere with my mission. I told him he and his people were in great danger, that they should leave as quickly as possible, for the woolmen would most certainly be back to cause untold misery. He listened without interjection. When I had finished he asked one simple question: Where should we run to this time? I replied that it was not a matter of running away but of tactically withdrawing to a more suitable location. And where do you propose that to be, Mister P.T. George? he asked. I ignored the sarcasm and told him about the great river that runs through the driest part of the country. On its lush floodplains, I said, could be grown vines and melons, fruit, vegetables and nuts. There whole herds of cattle could graze without ever depleting the grass. But most favourable of all, I argued, in the river were islands where he could establish his kingdom with impunity. No one, least of all the president, would bother him there, I said, because such a place was beyond the interest of government and capitalists. He asked a few more questions and then dismissed me. However, I have reason to believe he will seriously consider my proposal.

25 March
Who should I see this morning slipping away like thieves before dawn but Dead Das and Allermann armed to the teeth. They did not notice me, for I sat among the boulders and no doubt had taken on the shape of the surrounding rocks. By the time the sun came up they were well on to the plain and only the sharpest eye would have picked them out. Perhaps our situation is worse than I imagined.

28 March
Last night I was too tired to record an extraordinary encounter I had with Jabulani Mximba so I enter it now while this makeshift settlement dozes in the noon heat. But first I must note that I feel more than ever that we live on borrowed time, and each day my anxiety increases. I am convinced those woolmen will seek retribution. Is it significant that Dead Das and Allermann have not yet returned?

However, to the purpose of this entry.

Yesterday I was on the south-western buttress, painting a distant mirage as it conjured many and fantastic images, when I felt the presence of someone behind me. I turned to find Jabulani Mximba staring at my efforts. He nodded a greeting, I smiled and continued with my work. Eventually he sat down on a rock some feet away. I have never spoken with Mximba. He keeps himself apart. He is devoted to Enoch Mistas (for what are now obvious reasons), but is ill at ease with Dead Das and Allermann – in fact I would say there is animosity between him and the former.

For some time he sat in silence, occasionally rubbing the bizarre necklace of teeth he wears. I did not venture to break the silence for it was he who had sought me out and I am a firm

172

believer that people will voice their concerns when they feel the moment is right. The moment came after a considerable time. I was about to start my third water-colour when Mximba said: My prophet demands the respect of all men. I was so startled by his voice, let alone the accusation in his utterance, that I dropped the paintbrush.

What in blazes do you mean by that? I asked, trying to flick sand out of the bristles.

It is your intention to betray him, he responded. You are going to leave him in his hour of dire need.

A chill chased down my spine and puckered the skin of my arms into gooseflesh. How could he know my purpose? How could he know my most secret thoughts? But I have been long enough in the backveld to realise that such questions are meaningless.

Am I not my own man? I replied.

He snorted: I thought you were a good man. A man who carried peace in his heart. Not like these others.

I have done my share of killing, I said. Not of men but of animals. And I have seen quite enough of murderous horror. I do not want to see more death.

So you run away?

If you like. But I have no power to change things.

He considered this, his eyes fixed on me. Then he said: You can talk. The woolmen heard you. The magistrates will listen to your words.

Huh! I laughed, turning back to my painting. It is no good their listening to me if the redeemer will not heed my advice.

He hears what you say.

Then why does he not do something! Why do we sit here day after day waiting for the inevitable?

Because we cannot always run. This time we will demand to see the president.

And do you think he will listen to you? Do you think he cares about such as you?

We can make him care.

Nothing will make him care, my friend. Least of all the bleeding heart of a man like me.

My hand was trembling so violently the water-colour lost its delicacy in blobs and splotches. Jabulani Mximba watched unmercifully as I tried to bring my hand under control. Eventually I had to give up. I put the brush into the bottle of water and hunched my shoulders with a moan. I could still feel his relentless gaze.

Do you know this man, the president? Mximba asked.

I shook my head.

But you know the redeemer?

Yes, I know the redeemer, I sighed.

You can see that he is a good man. That he loves his people.

I nodded.

Then why do you desert him? Why do you let all these people suffer from an evil tyrant's decrees?

Because I am not responsible, I shouted. I am not the government. I am not guilty of their ways. I have not caused misery and hardship. Nor did I tell these people to follow the redeemer. I am a traveller here. This is not even my country.

We are all responsible, said Mximba. We are all responsible for everything.

This was no logic I could argue against. I have John Stuart Mill behind my back: but what does Mximba know of him? I have Hume's *Treatise of Human Nature*, I have the metaphysics of Aristotle, the learning of Aquinas, yet here, here under this violent sun, on this mountain, among these rocks, faced with these people and their history, such philosophy can be wiped out in an instant. And after that instant nothing is ever the same again.

Mximba moved closer and leaned towards me. We are all responsible, he whispered. Even when it is not our fault . . . Even then, if one man says we are to blame, his word will have us numbered among the wrongdoers. And we will be guilty, but so will he. Whatever I have done, that man and all the others who twisted my life must stand accused. When I slid the knife into the young boy's lungs their hands held it too.

For a moment his countenance was so contorted with emotion

– hate? anger? it may even have been grief – I could not look at him. I had an urge to gather my paints and flee.

You think I am a savage? he hissed. You think that because I wear these teeth I am nothing other than a wildman? What do you know?

I did not answer, because clearly he was not interested in an answer. He was interested only in goading me into some reaction that would confirm his prejudices. So I held my words.

Now he unleashed all his frustrations on me as if I were that one man responsible for the torrent of evils that have befallen him. When, after what proved as unnerving an ordeal as I have ever been through, the vitriol diluted itself in a pathetic account of his existence, I was consumed with compassion for the man. It appears that as a youngster in some distant part of the country it had been his task to mind the horses of a rich farmer. In this he must have been most efficient, as the farmer placed complete trust in his abilities despite his tender years. However, he was also expected to perform other duties, and it was in the course of fulfilling these – which necessitated his working in the farm's vegetable garden for a day – that one of the horses broke loose and disappeared. The farmer irrationally blamed Mximba for negligence. No matter how earnestly the young Mximba protested his innocence the farmer would not listen, and by way of punishment insisted that Mximba would have to work for him without payment of wages until he – the farmer – considered the debt of the horse had been repaid. The alternative was jail. Mximba soon realised his impotence in this matter and it fostered a deep resentment. Soon after that he absconded for the goldmines. Here he fell in with bandits and highwaymen and was soon forced to live the life of a renegade in the hills. Eventually and inevitably the long arm of the law caught up with him and he then spent a number of years in and out of gaol. Needless to say, gaol did not effect a reform but if anything only went to enhance his stature as a desperate individual who would not stop at murder to achieve his ends. Incarceration and life on the run fuelled his hate for the farmer, for the police, for the judges, for the prison warders, for all those he felt conspired against him. Then, after a particularly saddening experience in prison – upon which he would not elaborate – he resolved to escape. In the attempt he was severely wounded, and although his organisation of desperadoes secreted him away, he was forced to keep moving, which only went to weaken his condition. Before long it became essential for him to leave the goldmining towns and head out for the more inhospitable reaches where there was less chance of being recaptured. Despite his companions soon abandoning him to his own devices he recovered somewhat and even managed, with the aid of a friend's horse, to move ever further westwards out of the clutches of the police. But the wound, which had never properly healed, turned septic and then gangrenous. He told me that one day he was thrown from the horse and lay dying on the veld. It was there, apparently, that Enoch Mistas came to him. While Mximba drifted in and out of consciousness he saw a tall figure striding towards him and he thought it was the shade of death. The figure didn't speak to him, merely bent down, picked him up and, for what Mximba claimed were several days and nights, carried him to where the people of the prophet were gathered. Here Mistas allegedly performed a miracle by laying his hand on the wound and healing it instantly.

As I've said, I listened to this account with great interest, although obviously I am sceptical about the ending. However, Mximba firmly believes it and who am I to question his faith?

When he had finished Mximba got abruptly to his feet and dashed off. Since then I have seen him from a distance but I suspect that, for reasons best known to himself, he may be deliberately keeping clear of me. As for myself, I continued sitting on the buttress until dusk mulling over the pitiful story of his life. I can see now why he insists on this tangle of responsibility. I am intrigued, though, that he feels this does not absolve him from guilt – as so many hard-done-bys believe – but rather implicates society in the sins he has perpetrated. As he would say: We are all responsible. We are all to blame.

1 April
Dead Das and Allermann returned with grave news that there is a force of soldiers and farmers not two days' march away. I

view this with some concern. However, the two cavaliers are elated by this turn of events and even now have a squad of men going through what they imagine to be military manoeuvres. What chance do they stand against trained and experienced troops? I shall try and convince Mistas that it is in his interests to retreat at the earliest possible moment, although I am told he still intends going through with the baptism this afternoon. This is all well and good, but in the face of an impending onslaught it is foolhardy in the extreme. As for myself, I shall be saddled and off at nightfall. I have meddled in other people's business often enough to know that no good comes of it, that one is impotent, unable to exercise any influence and that the only result is personal grief and hardship. Once I have put my views to Mistas my duty will be discharged. Should he choose to follow his own inclinations or the advice of his henchmen, then there is nothing further I can do. The die will have been cast.

FOUR

The State of Affairs

The honorary general, the state president, too hot to sleep one close February night, unable to lie down or sit because of boils on back and backside, was forced to wander the house of colonnades and reception rooms where imperialists had once plotted and schemed to colonise a continent, where the sighs of other presidents still lurked after their unhappy deaths, where he wondered now if he would die of boils, a great man cursed.

Wondered if he would have to lie in state, his face composed, but beneath the dark suit his body still boiling like thick soup. Would the smell of these tiny volcanoes oozing pus and pungency bring tears of nausea rather than grief to the eyes of his mourners?

Dammit, he fumed in the long hall of portraits, pausing before his predecessor, the squanderer, who died slowly, badly, of gutrot; and the one before him, the butcher, who had carved up his opposition and died of stab wounds; and the one before that, the filcher who minted coins for his own pocket and died in a dance with St Vitus in the very bedroom the honorary general, the state president, had recently left and where his wife now still slept.

Huh! he sneered. He was better than them all, a true father of his people – and he moved on to the vacant space where his own portrait would one day hang. For a long time, he stared at the blank wall until, heart jumping, his left side feeling strangely thick, he moaned and moistened his pouting lips. Lips that had become famous on poster and parade ground for their dour words of warning. Lips that were now blistered and cracked, caked and moist. Disgusted by the betrayal of his body, he limped into the high office where nightly he brooded about his republic and the evil of those who wished to overthrow him.

Why now? he appealed, drawing back the curtains on the dark tops of trees and the distant lights of the harbour. In between, invisible, inhabiting terrace and shack, men and women, his citizens, loved, hated, killed, gave birth, cleared their bowels in the hot, pre-dawn hours and knew nothing of his boils.

Never in seventy-three years of devout, unselfish service to God and state had his body given a day's trouble: not measles, mumps, pox, pimples, scarlet fever or flu had laid him down until the start of the heat, when he first heard of miracles in the sand veld and a prophecy of doom – nothing less than the end of the world – and remembered the vision of a fortune-teller. No, he vowed in the privacy of his high office, it would not happen, he would not allow it to happen, he would not be plagued by some soothsayer's fantasy. Then, overnight, as if cursed, his body erupted in red weals of agony.

Heat and diet, had diagnosed the state surgeon, prescribing water and fruit. To no avail.

It's the prophet, had predicted his wife, laying a round hand on his arm. They say he can walk through walls.

Which prophet? had responded the president. There are hundreds of prophets. For every imagined ill there is a prophet to stir up the people.

Enoch Mistas, had come the quiet reply.

Enoch Mistas.

Enoch Mistas!

He knew the name. He had heard it before.

I've heard he's foretold the day of judgement, his wife had added. The end – and she looked up at the ceiling where the fan-propeller slowly turned.

Another one, breathed the president now into the heat and stillness of the room. They all do that.

Day on day the city sweltered. In the streets the heat collected smelling of garbage and bad drains. Under the canopies of trees it festered, yellow, dripping. In the gardens of bankers and chairmen leaves wilted, hydrangeas, geraniums, violets faded from beauty. In houses, under roofs, even in high-ceilinged rooms, the heat grew thicker, suffocating, too stiff with salt and damp for the fans to stir even a hot movement of air. In the president the heat built up under tight centres of skin that screamed for release. Only his wife, large in floral print dresses, stayed cool.

Dream of dew, she advised him, and stop thinking of Enoch Mistas, he's giving you the boils.

But how could he stop thinking of Enoch Mistas? What was he doing right now: converting bandits, stirring up the poor to follow him into the promised land? And what had happened to the government agent, that nice young man with the blond moustache? He had stood here, in this room, eyes fixed on the walnut panelling behind the president's head, hands bunched at his sides, thumbs pointing down the seams of his trousers: a military stance. When he walked in, his smart black shoes had clicked together at attention on the Persian carpet and he had snapped a salute as sharp as the creases in his pants.

A good man, read the president in the dossier before him. Married. Two children. Courageous. Dedicated. Always does his duty. From a family of soldiers: father mentioned in dispatches during the Frontier Wars.

The president looked up at the eyes that gazed over his head. He pictured two girls in short dresses playing with flowers as this man and his wife picnicked on a blanket, beer and sandwiches in their basket.

Ja, Walker, he said, shaking the image from his mind. Don't play the hero. Just tell us what's going on out there. I have heard stories of perversions, sodomy, the sacrifice of virgins and the enslavement of women. These are people without morals who have lost the values of self-respect and no longer observe the rights of human dignity. It is our duty to stamp out such horrors. We rely on you to confirm our worst suspicions.

Yes, sir.

Another clap of heels.

May God bless you.

Thank you, sir.

Snap went the salute, about turn one two three, and out he went, cap under his left arm, right arm swinging shoulder height until the door closed leaving the honorary general, the state president, tapping a pencil on the vast plain of his desk.

What had become of the government agent?

The president sighed, scratched around the circles of torment on his backside, but found no relief. In the trees outside his window birds began their irritating chatter as they had done every morning of his boils, incessant, infuriating, ignoring inkwells, paperweights, doorstops, slippers that were hurled into the foliage to quieten them. Ignoring, largely, even a dawn squad with shotguns blasting blindly into the syringas.

Five dead sparrows hardly justifies such a hot pursuit, was his hysterical wife's only comment after the crack of rifle fire brought her screaming from her bed. At first I thought the servants were killing us. Really, little birds are God's children!

But they continued to twitter their morning devotions, supplemented by the sounds of the presidential house waking and changing guard. In the kitchen maids coaxed the embers into fires, set water on to boil, put food down for cats and pit bulls. The house began to steam. In her twin bed the first lady smiled, turned from her dreams of dew to the first faint light of a new day's heat and said: Don't forget the doctor is coming at eleven.

No, dear, he caught himself saying in his high office on the other side of the house. How could he forget? Wasn't he reminded by the slightest rasp of his silk dressing gown? Wasn't the mere formality of sitting down worse than the wildest excesses of his secret police? Didn't he have to sign orders of state standing up? Oh, the indignity, the gross indignity of a powerful man betrayed.

Into the corridor he shouted: Where are the morning papers? – and a servant, smiling stupidly, came running up the stairs with the news on a silver platter.

News that sat him down and stood him up just as quickly, that pounded his desk and clutched his heart as it skipped once, twice, leaving a useless left arm stuck with pins and needles. Not that he paid any attention, because there between the adverts for Mr Cohen, Gents Outfitter, Friars Balsam and the Union Castle Line was a notice from Our Military Correspondent that the army in helmets and fully armed had, when threatened by a rabble of vagrants brandishing sticks, fled panic-stricken, leaving food and equipment behind them – an event of unparalleled shame in the history of the force, indeed, in the history of the country. What next? And then he saw it, a dreaded reference to the prophet of the people, to the loathed Enoch Mistas.

Him! The epitome of evil, the stirrer of trouble, the unmentionable thorn in the flesh, the . . . the putrid Bible-puncher, the feculent king. Dammit, stamped the president back and forth: desk to window, window to desk. Hadn't he ordered that the man was not to be mentioned, he was banned, banished, he didn't exist? And now here was some treacherous editor defying all laws, reporting a humiliation, inciting the masses, even quoting the devil. For there, from the newspaper, Enoch Mistas spoke to him. Spoke straight to the president with all the impudence of the insurrectionists.

Remember, said Enoch Mistas, you are fighting God.

Aah, screamed the president, I will kill you – a scream that died in the waking ears of the first lady and took her gownless, nightdress billowing, out of the presidential chamber down the corridor of predecessors and into the high office where her husband, honorary general and president, massaging life into his tingling arm, puce at the impudence of editors and letter writers, was staring at the offending newspaper on his desk. And hot on her heels came Johan van Rooyen, the private secretary, head filled with presidential anguish, armpits flushed with carbolic perspiration, wrists flapping.

Do you see what this man writes? shouted the president at wife and secretary. This anarchist with a pen, this fool who thinks he knows more than I? He says I am weak, that because I have not backed up a small platoon – a bunch of runaways with no more courage than a muishond by the sounds of it – he says that I, me, the state president, am encouraging the people of the prophet in their defiance of the law. Have you read what he's said? Go on, read it, spluttered the president, thrusting at them the crumpled yellow press editorial.

They read:

If it is seen that a sufficiently strong body of vagrants and layabouts can flout the law with impunity, it will not be long before the example is followed in other parts of the country. If the government understood the native character a little better, it would know that a threat without power to carry it out is worse than useless. It is sheer folly to shake one's fist in a lawbreaker's face, unless one is prepared, in case of necessity, to deliver a blow. In the recent case the people of the prophet have already received the impression that the authorities are, if not afraid of them, at least unable to enforce the law; and naturally they have been greatly heartened thereby.

Such defiance is unheard of. I want him here, Johan. Within the hour I want him here. I will not stand for this, do you understand? This is treason, Johan. Treason.

Yes, Mr President, I will summon him, Mr President, replied quaking Johan van Rooyen, dashing out to put police into action, to arrange a squad from the Security Branch who, in twenty minutes, will shoulder into the newspaper office, overturning tables and typewriters, causing the cookery page sub-editor to faint, the cub reporter to choke on her tea, the social writer to remember a previous engagement and the book reviewer to crawl beneath his desk as they raise the fat editor from his chair and, scuffed shoes barely touching the ground, carry-march him to the kwela van waiting in the street.

And by the time they arrive at the house of colonnades the president will have been soothed by his gownless wife, taken back through the corridor of difficult deaths to his bath and given new dressings for those boils, red and inflamed, awaiting their eleven o'clock appointment with the state surgeon's knife. So when the fat editor, crumpled, breathing loudly through a forest of nose-hairs, bladder bursting with unrelieved morning brandies, is finally ushered into the high office he is faced with the healthy image of a president, smart in suit and starched shirt, stomach satisfied with eggs and toast, all rumours quashed that the man is ailing, stricken by weak heart and suppurating skin. Here is the parade-ground president, smirk-lipped, in charge. Also in full objurgation.

Thus: In my time, Mr Editor, I have tried to bring peace and prosperity to our land. – A scowl, a pout. – I am sure you will agree I have worked for the common good. In all fairness, before, I will admit, there were some, a few, who were poor, who did not have money for food or shelter or clothes, whose children died, who were consumed with cholera and typhoid, the wretched, living badly, dying miserable deaths. A great shame. There were others who were not free men, who were forced to work on farms, down mines, in factories, in the gardens and kitchens of the privileged for lowly wages. They were used, exploited, some were beaten when they had given every ounce of sweat. Others even died at the hands of their masters, and we never called those men to account for their sins. For that we are guilty and God will judge us. But he will also say that we have atoned, because those days are gone. And you know they have gone. You have even written that they belong to history. You have even reported that now all men are free to marry whomsoever they please, to go where they want, even to sleep in the top hotels if they can pay the price. Where is cholera and typhoid today, I ask you? Where is the honest man who does not go to bed on a full stomach? Come, Mr Editor, you know there is work for all, there is food in abundance, shelter, clothing. Let me tell you it is only the lazy, only the bone idle who have nothing to eat, who sleep beneath bags on the sides of rubbish dumps. Admit it, this is so.

But before the fat editor could speak, the president, raised finger, pouting lips, face suddenly livid, shouted: Why then do you write this drivel, Mr Editor? Look at this – he smacked the paper with his good hand – I will not be played with, Mr Editor. I do not wish to see such nonsense as bullets being turned to water by a raised hand and a prayer. What privilege do you think protects you when you print hearsay and rumours, and worse, far worse, blatant lies that incite ordinary people to rebellion? Other men have been jailed for less, Mr Editor. This is treason. Betrayal. Treachery. There are places, Mr Editor, countries not far from here where you would be locked up for that. Even sentenced to death. Who needs a trial when the evidence is here – he waved the newspaper – and everyone can see you are guilty, guilty of the worst crimes against the state, of sedition, of advocating revolution?

The president withdrew behind his desk, irritated by the rising heat and the smell of old alcohol on the fat editor's breath. What a poor specimen. Look at him standing there in his shabby suit, a face of blown veins, eyes downcast, hands trembling. Gutless, gutter pressman. What a spineless good-for-nothing.

Dammit, Mr Editor, I have had enough of you and your paper's insolence. You will get your house in order, or I will clean it up for you. I want no more of this scandal, do you hear, nor will I tolerate such flagrant disobedience from the likes of pensioner H. Gordon Turner writing that he will join a commando to oust Enoch Mistas and his rabble if I do not do my duty. In future you send such letters to me and I will remind Mr Turner of who pays his pension. Is that understood, Mr Editor?

The fat editor kept his eyes down, said nothing.

Is that understood, Mr Editor? screamed the president, stabbing at a button on his desk. Answer me, dammit.

But the fat editor had hardly time to clear his throat before Johan van Rooyen, rushing in, sweaty palmed, spun him out of the high office into the long arms of the waiting law.

Do you want him charged, sir? gasped the secretary.

No, no, Johan, waved the president, annoyed, dismissive, just get him out of here – and sat down on his good side, breathing heavily, overcome with heat. For a moment there was stillness. Stillness from pain, from the mortality of his heart, from the state of affairs. Somewhere a trumpet blew and guns saluted, distant sergeants shouted. The president put his head on the desk blotter and awaited the knock of the state surgeon.

He thought of horses, hooves clinking over stones, the weight of the rifle on his lap, dogs slipping through the spekboom following kudu blood. Behind him far hills at evening. He ached to be there. Until a figure, dark in a dark cloak, moved out of distant rocks on to the plain, casting a long shadow. Down-wind, the dogs paused, ears pricked, whimpering. Then the horse reared, whinnied, threw him and bolted. Across the valley floor all shadows thinned. It was Enoch Mistas. He knew it, could smell on the air woodsmoke and old sweat getting closer. The president stood up to face him, saw a man some fifty yards off, half turned away, looking out across the flats.

Why do you plague me? he shouted. Why do you boil my blood?

But the figure took no notice: didn't move, didn't turn, kept

looking across the scrub to where there was nothing but purple
thickening to black, lonely, a night on the veld. Or so it seemed.
And then the president could see them, too, rising out of a fold in
the ground as if they were the dead returned. A man on a horse,
two others carrying guns, an old woman, a young woman, lovely
and all suffering, a girl with sheep, a group of eight swinging
lanterns, and then the rest, tens, hundreds, with goats, donkeys,
wagons of fowls. Slowly they came towards the prophet, their
tiny lights growing sharper, the first murmur of hymns sinking
a new dread into the presidential heart:

We cannot sing the Lord's song

And from behind them, as distinct as voices over water, clearer
than a cathedral choir:

In a strange land.

Swelling, a balloon in his head, an echo in the valley of desolation
that once started never dies, bouncing back, now fainter, now
louder, booming in every crag, setting flight to starling and rock
pigeon, filling the sky with its frail message.

Brightly they passed before him: the crimson man on the
horse, the man with the necklace of teeth, the other pocked
and pitted, the smell of the old woman stronger than fecund
jails, the young woman, her skin as fine as dragonfly wings, the
sheep girl dribbling, and the rest: tailors, shopkeepers, their wives
and children, brigands, bandits, murderers, thieves and rustlers,
easy girls, Khoi Greek Jew Xhosa Zulu Griqua Portuguese, chiefs,
servants and slaves, each singing, each giving praise:

Having fought the good fight
By the name of the Lord.

Like a locust veld, when bushes move under the crawling mass,
so now the veld moved with humanity. Streams pouring out of all
points to join the people of the prophet. More and more, leaving
farmlands unploughed, big holes undug, laundry unwashed in

tubs, leaving stern husbands, proper wives, to heed the prophet's call of no taxes, promised lands and freedom. Of joy. An end to hard times, to the sting of words and the bite of sjamboks, to the crippling toll exacted by government men. Everyone was in revolt.

Running now across cracked river-beds, through cactus and thorn scrub, tripping over burnt-up meteorites, dead cows, the rocks of ages, dodging anthills and termite mounds, every time coming up against other people, laughing poking leering, calling Mr President, here, Mr President, coming at him with knives and hatchets. Murderer. Robber. Tyrant. Fiend.

Mr President!

Mr President, sir. The state surgeon is here.

And now how to choose the right reality? This confusion of mass movements, singing, chanting, praising the Lord is our Saviour, or the quiet heat of the high office where concerned faces bend over him with their breath of fried bacon, whispering: Mr President, sir, are you all right?

Ja, dammit, I must have blacked out. Here in the chair. Just now. Dammit. There were crowds, people everywhere out there in the sourveld. That's where they are isn't it, Johan? The prophet of the people? Hundreds of them. We must put a stop to it, do you hear? We cannot allow this. It is lawlessness. He is stirring up the masses. There will be trouble, I tell you. Deaths. Murders. Innocent lives lost. Even now it is quite out of hand. Impossible. Not so, Johan. Is that not so!

An exchange of glances between secretary and state surgeon that said: This is not just boils.

Yes, sir. Quite, sir. Impossibly out of hand.

We are being held to ransom.

May I take your pulse, Mr President, said the state surgeon, and – with a quick flick sticking thermometer into the presidential mouth – your temperature?

More glances, raised eyebrows, unspoken words about a leader fatigued, the chances of heart attack, the need to keep it secret for as long as possible because when he's dead who is there to take over?

A word, Mr Secretary, said the state surgeon heading for the door. And Mr President, you can undress, I need to look at those boils.

Outside in the corridor: What's this about crowds in the sourveld?

A small thing, doctor, nothing much. Nothing to get upset about. Nothing that can't be taken care of. Just a madman, really, who calls himself a prophet and, people say, has performed miracles. Whatever that means. But the president is obsessed with him. Talks of nothing else. He's even neglecting affairs of state. Cancelling banquets, threatens he won't take the salute. I mean, he sees everyone in the high office. He hasn't been out of here since you saw him last week.

He is not well, Mr Secretary. His heart is at risk. He must get away.

Replied Johan van Rooyen, shaking his head: There is no possibility of that. Not while Enoch Mistas is converting souls.

I shall talk to him – and the state surgeon returned to his patient lying stomach down in underpants and vest on the desk.

Ah, the boils: huge red filled-with-hot-pus hemispheres on rump and thigh, tucked in behind the knees waiting for the knife.

I shall have to lance them, Mr President, said the state surgeon, clicking his tongue, looking askance. This is quite extraordinary, he added, preparing knives and swabs, ointments and dressings, calling for boiling water. Quite extraordinary, I've never seen yellow mushrooms grow so quickly. It's as if all the water in your body is heating up. Hold still, sir.

In went the knife, peeling apart enraged flesh, releasing pressure, letting off steam, dammit, I will not tolerate this. There will be proper conduct. Enoch Mistas must be called to account.

Don't upset yourself, Mr President. Just another five to go.

Get Johan van Rooyen.

Here, sir, Mr President.

Aah. Dammit. Get Field Marshal Hedley Goodman, Johan. I want him now. This matter must be sorted out once and for all. Do you hear?

Yes, sir. Yes, sir. Right away, sir.

You must rest, Mr President. This is all getting out of hand.

Out of hand. Out of hand. Nothing is out of hand. I am in control. I have made a decision. Just finish your job, doctor, there is an affair of state to be attended to.

Thirty minutes later came Field Marshal Hedley Goodman in boned black boots, walking a little strangely but, being a good soldier, keeping his trials and tribulations behind a face of discipline.

You wished to see me, sir.

Ah, Goodman, said the president, lacing up a shoe, straightening his tie, pulling down starched cuffs to expose links of sapphire, quite recovered now from the ordeal with the knife, feeling better, in fact, than he had in weeks, because at last a decision had been taken and soon there would be action and a return to normality.

Sit down. Please.

The field marshal stiffly complied, sitting slightly to one side with a quick grimace, unmilitary, instantly hidden yet noted all the same by presidential eyes.

Piles, field marshal? – a wry grin.

Just so, Mr President.

It is the strain of life, Goodman. But we must not let these weak lapses of the body get us down. Must we.

Indeed not, sir.

Try parsley tea, field marshal. And dab the offending parts with a witchhazel infusion. I'm told these old remedies work wonders. Then, pacing from window to desk, desk to window: I'm sure you've heard of this man Mistas, some village lout who's proclaimed himself a priest.

Yes, indeed, Mr President. As a matter of fact I . . .

Good. Goodman, good. I like a man who has his finger on the pulse. Because then you'll also know he's small fry, hardly worth bothering about, but one can never be too careful where small things are concerned. Can one. Just to refresh your memory, the situation is this: he's gathering people, promising them the earth, and becoming a bit of a nuisance to the sheep farmers. It seems a local platoon tried to sort out the predicament and to their, indeed our, humiliation they were sent packing. And then the magistrates got in on the act and let these people go unpunished. Can you believe that? And worse, those law tinkers in their gowns and starched shirts conspired to keep this abasement from me. It's just a small matter, they squirmed, when finally word reached me. A small matter! A small matter, Goodman! Does it sound to you like a small matter when an army unit is put to shame by a scum of no-goods? Those damn interfering magistrates with their secrets and their cover-ups wanted to keep me – me, their president – in the dark. They wanted to pull the wool over my eyes, as if reality is not the stuff of my life. Just thinking about it now makes my blood boil. However, as disgraceful as it is, we have to live with this *fait accompli*. And then dammit, Goodman, I'm damned if those bench-warmers don't compound this major blunder by allowing the rag-tag mob unmolested passage out of the territory. Such decisions boggle the mind. Heaven knows what possessed them. But I suppose it is no good getting worked up about history. What's done is done. Except that unfortunately last year's secrets have a way of becoming this year's scandal and I wish to avoid that at all costs. Do you follow me? Good. Good. Well, as you may or may not be aware, this rabble have established themselves on some island in the great river in flagrant disregard of the statutes of our country. Obviously, we can't have that. And especially we can't have reports in the newspapers ridiculing government, nor old-age pensioners threatening to form commandos, as you probably read this morning. No! Perhaps it is best not to read the papers. Rumour-mongers, that's all they've become. However – thrusting the newspaper at the field marshal – sometimes they carry an idea or two. Read that. Go on.

Field Marshal Hedley Goodman read:

When dealing with natives and especially with religious fanatics like the people of the prophet, enough stress cannot be laid upon the value of moral effect. These people are looking for martyrdom. So why not save as many innocent lives as possible with as little bloodshed as possible? Half a dozen low-flying aeroplanes, using a few bombs or machine-guns, would clear up the trouble quickly, safely, and cheaply – besides creating a lasting impression on the rebel mind. An aerial strike would never be forgotten. Signed, Night Bomber.

Is it clear, field marshal?

Perfectly, sir.

Good. Good, Goodman. As soon as possible, you understand. I don't want this thing on the boil for too long.

Of course not, Mr President, saluted the field marshal, standing now at attention like the government agent long before him.

What had become of the government agent? But that was no more than a passing thought for a head of state, certainly not worth dwelling on, because it could conjure up a sad suburban house, a young wife in her kitchen, distressed, not sleeping at night, worrying about her disappeared man, and two little pink-frocked girls asking: When's Daddy coming home? None of which was high office concern in the grander scheme of things, yet he could not resist saying: We have an agent out there, field marshal, a good man. If he's still alive, bring him back.

End of interview, hands shaken in a powerful grip, eyes locked in the way of men and pacts, and the president escorted his servant, arm around his shoulder, across the Persian patterns to the mahogany door which he opened to usher this seasoned soldier into the corridor. Yet another handshake, and the parting words: God bless, field marshal. Then the heavy door closed leaving the two men to their destinies.

Press Clippings

STATE PRESIDENT WILL TAKE THE SALUTE AS
REGIMENT MARCHES THROUGH THE CITY

State President to Award Medals for Bravery

Parade honours those who gave their lives so that their fellow countrymen could live in safety.

by Our Military Correspondent

On Saturday, the honourable, the state president and his honourable lady wife will take the salute at the 71st anniversary parade of the Cape Royal Fusiliers as they have done every year since his inauguration 48 years ago. It will be a gala day for the city and all main boulevards and thoroughfares will be closed as the regiment, complete with the latest artillery, parades through the streets prior to the salute and presentation of medals.

National fervour

Once again the city is preparing for the event with excitement: flags and bunting in the nation's and the regiment's colours will adorn all buildings along the parade's route and from the Signal Hill a 21-gun salute will be fired to mark the start of the ceremonial occasion. Miniature national flags have been distributed among schools and hosts of schoolchildren will be on the streets to further enhance this impressive occasion.

THIS DAY AND AGE

Courageous tradition

Although the history of the regiment does not need to be reiterated it is as well to place on record oonce again that their military endeavours belong in the annals of the courageous tradition established by the defenders of Christian values on battlefields throughout the world. This must not be forgotten. Many are their valiant number who lie in unknown graves in foreign lands and their sacrifice must always be remembered because their names stand as an inspiration and a testimony to all that is dedicated and selfless within the human spirit. Also we should be reminded that even today the men of this regiment risk their lives to ensure that we sleep peacefully and that the values we hold dear are cherished. For although we are not at war, sometimes their presence is demanded in areas of unrest within the country if good government is to be allowed to exercise its democratic right.

Presentation of medals

At the end of the salute the state president will award medals and bars to those men who distinguished themselves when the moment to stand up for God and country came. On this year's honours list there are citations for extreme bravery beyond the call of duty, for bravery under heavy fire, for bravery under light fire, and for bravery as defined in the military schedule as Class I, II and III. Twenty medals for long service will be awarded. A special medal commemorating the efficient and humane manner in which the regiment has dealt with breaches of the country's sovereign rights and the maintenance of law and order will be presented to the acting commanding officer while Field Marshal Hedley Goodman is on manoeuvres. It is deeply to be regretted that the field marshal, who has been such a central figure in the regiment in the last three decades, will not be able to attend this parade, but unfortunately he and a number of divisions are participating in strategic exercises concerned with national security.

Additional festivities

Our editorial staff have been informed of a number of additional festivities that have been arranged to further enhance the spirit of goodwill and gratitude which prevails within the mother city towards her favourite sons, the soldiers of the Cape Royal Fusiliers. Tonight on the waterfront there will be a fireworks display to which all members of the public are cordially invited and our social editor reports that on Saturday evening a gala ball will be held to raise funds for those whose loved ones gave their lives in the call of duty.

On a lighter note we point out that the fair currently in residence at the Agricultural Showgrounds continues to draw large crowds and is an ideal outing for family members both young and old. Of particular interest are the cow with two heads, a circus of dwarfs, the Flying Family Pecorino, Maria the fuming fortune-teller in her caravan of ice, and a host of performing animals.

Congratulations

The editor and staff would like to take this opportunity to congratulate the Cape Royal Fusiliers on their impressive record in the defence of human decency and to record our loyalty to the president and the state.

REPORT OF THE COMMISSION OF INQUIRY INTO
FRAUDULENT ALLEGATIONS OF UNREST IN THE
INTERIOR PUBLISHED

Judge Finds Newspapers Acted Irresponsibly

THIS DAY AND AGE

'Beware that truth does not founder on the rocks of mendacity and deception,' warns Justice Erasmus de Blanc.

by Our Political Editor

The proceedings of a one-man presidential commission of inquiry conducted by Justice Erasmus François de Blanc, Judge of the Supreme Court, Appellate Division, into reports and allegations of a band of so-called vagrants causing disturbances in remote areas, have been published by the Government Printer, and find that there is no evidence of malcontents and that with the exception of a few isolated incidents involving farmers and labourers all reports and letters to the press of rapine and murder being conducted by disaffected marauders are quite without substance or foundation and were put about by people of malicious intent who conspired to criticise the good workings of government. Justice de Blanc's 18-page summation came after two days of deliberations during which time he heard testimony from a number of high-ranking officers in the Department of Police, the Bureau of State Security and the Department of Defence. Commenting on the newspaper reports which first fostered what have been proven to be false suspicions of trouble in the interior, the judge said he viewed with serious misgiving the irresponsibility of the press in not referring their information to the proper authorities for validation. If the due process of law and the sanctity of the state were to be preserved then it was the good citizens' moral duty not to disseminate hearsay and rumours, which, as in this case, were always devoid of truth. When truth was subject to the vagaries of individual inclinations then all that was inimical to stability, the dignity of human rights, and the rule of justice could 'founder upon the rocks of mendacity and deception', warned Justice de Blanc in his concluding remarks.

Commenting on the commission of inquiry's report, a spokesman for the office of the president praised the judge for his impartiality and noted that the integrity and independence of the judiciary was a cornerstone of the modern democratic state.

FIVE

The New Country

Imagine this: the sun shone brighter, the air was clearer, the ocean lay like a mill pond in and out of the harbour; people were friendlier, they smiled more often, they gave bigger coins to the legless beggar beside the flower-sellers. Or this: the yellow heat of summer was gone, the trees were russet, the days were drawing in, but there was goodwill to all men. It was a time of promise, of sweeping under the rug, of forgetting and forgiving, a time for shaking hands, for compromise and confessions, for wishful thinking, for illusion, magic, birth. And why? Because this was afterwards. The president was dead, long live the president. This was the time of hope, of cleansing, of purging, of witch-hunts, of catharsis. This was the new country. We must be open, we must be honest, we must admit mistakes and expose old lies, said the new president. Which was why Johan van Rooyen, against his better judgement, being still loyal to the old, unconvinced of the new but setting a brave face against this day and age, agreed to see the fat editor. And the fat editor, jubilant, put down the phone with a short, sharp burp.

Imagine this: he wanted information about the late, great and honoured president, the one who just a month ago had been wheeled on a gun-carriage down these very streets where the sun now shone brighter and the air was clearer. Imagine that, and he was going to get it. Such was the new dispensation that warts, let alone boils and all, were for public display. There was nothing to hide, nothing to be embarrassed about, nothing to be guilty of. That was how it was before, this was how it would be afterwards. Before was for nit-pickers, afterwards for pragmatists. Harping on old wrongs didn't repay foreign debt, create jobs, generate wealth, erect homes, educate, or feed the starving. Afterwards was for getting on with it, for pulling together, for nation building. Because afterwards life was easier. Afterwards repression was lifted, prisoners freed, demonstrations allowed. Afterwards was just wonderful.

So anything he wants to know, Mr van Rooyen, you tell him, advised the new president. But appeal to his good nature, his common sense, sketch in the delicacies of reconciliation.

But what if, asked Johan van Rooyen, dreading the thought, separating one afterwards from another, what if he asks about the . . . ah . . . ah . . . you know?

Indeed, what if, Mr van Rooyen? What if? Then you tell him nothing happened. It's just rumour, gossip, hearsay, if not downright lies to sabotage the peace initiatives. After all, there's been a commission of inquiry and they found nothing. But don't worry, he won't ask. Believe me, no one's in the least bit interested.

Except the historians and the moralists. But they need facts, not stories. They need graves, charred ruins, cartridge cases, eye witnesses, documentation. And there was none of that so it was easy to say nothing happened. It was easy to say: Prove it!

For everyone else, afterwards was just like before. There were births and deaths, marriages and love affairs. There was the seven-fifty train to be caught, the number sixty-eight bus on which to commute. Afterwards there was still inflation: the increasing price of meat; the outrageous price of vegetables. Property prices spiralled, the state demanded more tax, no one knew where it would end.

And imagine this: afterwards, there was still that other country. That other country of murder and rape and pangas and burnings. In this country, afterwards was as before: the sun was no brighter; the air was still thick with smoke.

On the hillsides the women lamented as they buried their sons: Greet those who have gone before you. And greet your brother who died this way, this time last year. Oh, our sons, our children, who are food for the guns.

And beside them stood their men, the warriors, calling on

the ancestors for justice, chanting: Death has no sting. Death is nothing. We will avenge.

Afterwards was the way it had always been: for the murder of my son, your son must die. You are a witch, you will be burnt. You are an informer, you will be stoned, hacked, knifed.

Afterwards there would be droughts. There would be floods. Typhoid, cholera, kwashiorkor, malaria, sleeping sickness, locusts, blight, tumours, pus would be in your days and in your nights. Ever afterwards.

Imagine this: afterwards was no different. Except. Except that afterwards held what happened like bones in a pit. All it took was a spade – or, as in this case, a letter – to realise we had been living afterwards.

Letters to the Editor

30 May

Dear Sir,

Why I am writing is because the other day I was told something that nobody has ever heard about. It is a great scandal. You would be horrified if you knew about it. It is an atrocity. You wouldn't think it possible in our time. But it's been done and I think it is a great crime. I will tell you about it if you are interested. My friends tell me you pay for this sort of thing. Because this is big news my price is four hundred green ones. That price is not negotiable. Please leave the money in Box 471, the Harbour Post Office before next Tuesday, then I will give you all the information.

5 June

Dear Mr Editor,

I can't understand why you won't trust me especially as I have such major news to tell you. My girlfriend says you're acting just like a suspicious journalist who never believes anything even when it's put on a plate before you. She says all you people ever want are facts, facts, facts or else you're not interested. Well, Mr Editor, I've got facts. I've got facts in black and white which will make your blood run cold. You see this story – that's your jargon for facts, isn't it? A story! Let me tell you this story is hot and when I say hot I mean dangerous. This story is playing with fire. You know what I mean. I mean death. There are people who will kill to keep this story quiet. But that doesn't scare me. I don't scare easy. I've been on the streets all my life so I know how to look after myself. Maybe you're scared, Mr Editor? Maybe when you hear about the real thing you also turn yellow? I don't blame you. If I hadn't been on the streets all this time I'd be afraid of what I know. I'd be afraid that someone would come and get me. Because that's what they do, you know. If you've got something they don't like they send in the special squad. How they find out about it beats me but they've got spies everywhere. Even your closest friend can turn out to be a spy these days. That's why I'm taking some precautions. As you will see I'm using a different post box this time. And don't think of hanging about waiting for someone to open the box because it doesn't work that way. I don't want you to know who I am. Because if they ever put the wires on your balls you'd squeal my name out first thing. At least that's what my girlfriend says and I don't see any reason not to go with that. Because you're taking such a long time, which is increasing the danger to me, I'm putting the price up to five hundred and fifty. This time you must leave the money at the Eastern Boulevard Post Office, Box 21. The deal's off if it's not there in one week's time. And don't ever expect to hear from me again.

16 June

I know I said I wouldn't deal with you again but my girlfriend and I have decided that because it's in the interest of our new democratic republic we're going to try one last time to convince you that we mean business. So, we're not going to ask you for money, we're just going to tell you this: my girlfriend used to work at the presidential palace. After the other president's death she found a message which will put your name into history if you write about it. But before you see it, she says you should talk to Maria the fortune-teller at the Agricultural Show. This is genuine.

The Tale of Woe

To believe a crank, sighed the fat editor, twisting a pencil in his ear, releasing a lump of wax. Such a weighty decision. Such an impossible position. He scratched deeply, viciously, at his crotch and rose to pace the room as all deliberating editors had done before him. Back and forth, forth and back, pausing only to break wind or to rub quickly at his pubic itch through the lining of his pocket, he shuffled, eyes fixed in concentration, bulging slightly like a frog's. Should he? Should he? He turned back to his desk and the letter. This was genuine. Should he? Should he? What was to be gained? What was to be lost? On the one hand it could be true. On the other hand he could never tell it. According to some all sins should be confessed. According to others muckrakers were scum. Trust us, said the rulers. They're lying, said the opposition. Who to believe? His story! Their story! The word of a crank? The word of Johan van Rooyen? Find out, barked the newshound within him, sniffing out a good story, uncowed by censorship laws, a state of emergency, press strictures, or the Act for the Prohibition of the Publication of Material Detrimental to the Security of the State. Dammit, this was afterwards. This was a new day and age. This was freedom of the press. This was the way journalism should be. Find out. Investigate injustice and state abuse of power. Right, he said out loud, slicking down his forelock, grabbing shorthand notebook and pencil, coat, keys and cigarettes. Right, right. I will. And he dashed out to the Agricultural Show.

Yet on the way he reconsidered: grew uneasy at the thought of fortune-tellers, squirmed at the choice of venue, blushed at his gullibility and almost, almost, turned off for a morning beer.

The Tale of Woe

But something kept him newshound-steadfast. Call it dedication, training, legwork, ego. It hardly matters. He was the voice of authenticity, he had a responsibility to the truth. This was what drove him on a fine winter's day to where the crowds streamed through the turnstiles clutching balloons, licking ice-creams, excited at a whiff of manure on the air and the bellow of a cow giving birth. Among them he wandered, preparing questions as he walked through the corrals of fierce bulls and bleating lambs, reflecting on the surprising turn of events as he passed down the halls of prize honey, jam, preserves, cakes, rusks, biscuits, paused to make a note at the racks of cured meat, salted fish, dried fruit, continued seriously into the stalls of quilts, bedspreads, mohair rugs, reed mats, cane furniture, tables carved in stinkwood with scenes of frontier life until, resolved to get to the bottom of things, he strode between the smiling farmers' wives, crocheting even while they waited for custom, and found himself in the fairground among dwarfs, the Flying Pecorinos, and shouts of: See the fat man. Lose your arm inside his flesh. Watch him eat a hundred pies and beer. Or cries of: Know your future! Let Maria foretell your fate. Here, where arms tugged for his favour, where dirty children picked bags and pockets, where mothers clutching babies plagued him for a coin, a banknote, a scrap of food – Oh please, kind Mister Gentleman, please, please . . . please – the newshound brushed aside all distractions, rolled determinedly towards Maria's caravan.

He knocked, got thrust aside – Witch, you lie, he'd never go with her, you devil, you ugly bitch of hell – as a woman came out sobbing.

Inside somebody laughed and called: Come in, mister, and hear the story of your life.

He did, stepped into a frozen world, ice underfoot, black frost along the couch. She sat among the skins of moles and rats, and was covered herself in fur and feathers, bones and teeth and beads. He took a cold breath, searched for eyes he could not find among the skins, noticed her fingernails – twisted, melted – like claws breaking through her mittens. She saw his glance and drew her fingers in.

Come, mister, sit down. I shall tell you what you want to know.

For what do these things matter now? They are history. For me it is all history. Even tomorrow is history. I can tell it and all that remains is for us to live out the telling. Say nothing, be still and you will hear a story.

With a sound of slopping water she moved beneath the paraphernalia of fate and fortune, settled among the frosted furs and held two blocks of ice at the holes that must have been her eyes. If she made a sound, it was a sigh, more imagined than real, more of relief than of sadness. Then she squeezed the ice until her fists steamed.

He was a man like other men, she began, neither good nor bad, neither weak nor strong. He was often wise and often foolish. He could love and he could hate. He could be hated and he could be loved. He was healthy yet pus boiled in his veins, he was both handsome and uglier than crows, he told lies when he told the truth and the truth when he told lies. He was a man like other men living through it. I did not know him well, and yet he sought me out. Not often. Once, and then before his death, again. But what help am I? I can warn, I can show the way of things, but that is all. There is no comfort to be taken there: what's said is done and we have to live with that. Come love, come joy, come murder, hurt or pain it makes no difference knowing it. You can't swap this for that, what's coming's coming, which I know as well as you. Once, years ago, he thought he could change the world. But he learnt otherwise. He learnt the best that can be done is to be ready for the worst. So he came to me again, to my coffin colder than the grave. Not long before he died, he sat where you sit now, such a troubled man, burned by his conscience, tortured because there was nothing else he could do. Maria, he said, and I can hear his voice even now, hoarse, like the last wind after a gale. I can hear him say: Maria, tell me I haven't sent a young man to his death.

What could I do? Lie? Pretend I didn't know? Or tell the truth? One thing I've never done, mister, is play with reality. You won't get pretty words from me, you'll get what happened, or what's going to happen. He knew that. He knew my trade is facts, events, not fantasy. That's why he came here. And why I wouldn't lie. For, mister, among all other deaths there is always one that wrings the conscience, one that demands justice for the rest. Don't ask me why. A life is worth neither more nor less than any other. All I can say is the world is like that; there is no telling what will trouble us. This one disturbed him. Tell me, he said, I haven't sent a young man to his death.

In those last words I saw it all. I saw the young man close the door of the president's office, I saw him march quickly down the corridor of great men's pictures, I saw him going down the stairs into the marble hall. Oh, he had glorious thoughts of serving president and country. He was a man on official business: he was to infiltrate the forces of evil and bring the redeemer to book.

And Maria described the government agent's last sad love-making in his wife's tears. How she felt him leaving, getting smaller and smaller, drawing away from her until she could no longer remember his caressing hands or recall his weight on her body. Could remember him only by the ache in her chest, the hurt of her heart. She told of his daughters saying goodbye as if this was any other morning of the week, when it wasn't, because there were sobs and tighter hugs and his raised hand at the end of the street was the last they ever saw of him. Because, when he should have come home, when dark was thickening among the houses and gardens and people went out to walk their dogs, when three women alone, mother and daughters, were curled up in one bed restlessly, he was in a train carriage of strangers playing cards, aces high, being dealt few good cards by a man named Bywooner Malan, calling weak hands as the night miles dashed through mountains on to the plains of scrub and stone. But what did he care for his dwindling coins? This was the first night between one life and another. The world was loose, a mad and dangerous place.

Ag, mister, this isn't your game. Give up, said Bywooner Malan.

But he wouldn't. He stubbornly persisted, put down his last money, watched the circle of faces, cracked, lined, cunning men used to the turn of cards and the unexpected favour, and bid against the odds.

At which Bywooner Malan shrugged, dealt him a five of hearts, two clubs, three spades, no ace, no king, no royal flush, no full house, only a black queen and a single diamond, as if to say see what I mean, life's not worth a gamble, nor worth a trick, hardly worth living. Give up, there are those handy at cards and those whose luck is elsewhere.

Just look at us, mister, he went on, sweeping his hand round the company of five – Smiley, John Smith, Boetman, Spooner, himself – a bunch of no-goods with not a prospect between us. Wives run off, if we ever had them. Children in so many places we can't remember. You tell me what sort of life that is for a man – nods, grunts, snorts from all. Not much! We've each one of us worked farms, dug, ploughed, sowed, shorn sheep from dark to dark for a mug of tea and crust without time to put seed in our own fields. We all had women die on us. All had to bury them beneath rocks because no farmer's going to let us lay them among his dead. There's nowhere for the likes of us, mister. We get good cards, but that's all. Life's down on us. But we're different types. It takes more than hard luck to stop our ways. What do you say, my mates? – at which they grunt and spit. So where we going now? I'll tell you, to search for diamonds, gonivas, brightstones, sparklers, fool's hope, kimberleys. Call them what you want, they're what give a poor man reason. They're hope, a chance, a better way of living. What'd you say! Join us. A man with no hand for cards must have a way with stones. With you we could find fortunes, make a tidy packet, clean up before the moneymen muscle in, if you get my meaning.

Which the government agent did, praising his lucky stars that he'd fallen among road men, rough men, plainsmen, who sooner or later must bump up against the prophet of the scrublands.

So where you going, mister? Maybe it's the same place as us?

Maybe, he replied.

They shook hands on it anyhow, returned his coins, pulled a bottle from an inside pocket, toasted their association, and fell back upon the jolting seats, open-mouthed, breathing loudly through black nose-hairs.

And for the first time the government agent thought of his wife and daughters: walked a familiar street, passed the houses of sleeping officials, bankers, draughtsmen and jewellers, turned in at the gate but could go no further. He stared at the shut door and curtained windows, knew that under a blue eiderdown in the back room lay three women who were his no longer. He heard the president say: You will never be honoured for this, but you will have done your duty. For that I salute you. I salute you. I salute you. And he turned from his house back to the train carriage with its square of light where he sat mirrored, sharp face, tight lips, deep eyes set close together, a man on secret government business travelling into the desert hours.

Until at a halt in the middle of nowhere which was no station at all, only a place of steam and water, the six got off in the greyness before dawn, stiff, unrested, cold to the marrow and, hefting their bags, turned from the spreading light and walked towards different things: for the five, diamonds; for the government agent, the start of a mission.

Out into the wastes they walked. Out into a land of red dune and black rock, of shale and stunted growth, of snakes, scorpions and horned lizards. A land given to the sun without shade and to the night with no comfort from the stars. A land of wind, a harsh wind carrying grit and twigs, whirling about the plains in search of the footprints of those who had been killed, who had been hunted here to death. For this is the heart of the country, desolate, bleak, and gathering on the sides of its hills and on the slate of its valleys are the people who once left footprints here. Among them the six walked, mostly in silence, chewing dried meat washed down with tea boiled from veld leaves. And the invisible people, in patience, waited for their revenge.

Which first came three days later when Boetman snatched his hand in horror from a high-tailed scorpion backing off, ready to strike again, not satisfied even with having done its worst – with having put a man a day's misery from death, a long day of crying for water, of ceaseless moans, of being uselessly attended by those who knew only that he could die and not how to treat him. While somewhere under a nearby rock his killer scuttled ready to strike again if need be, tormenting them with its life and a possible sudden unseen death should one for a moment sit down in the wrong place.

Find it, shouted Bywooner Malan, hurling aside rocks, poking in crevices. Kill it. It's not right he should die for an insect.

But right or wrong he died and was buried where he lay, under rocks through which could still be seen naked feet and Smiley's poor coat, the winding sheet, because coats and boots are the living's legacy, and the best gets handed on. So it was Smiley stepped out in a dead man's boots, doomed boots, that took him across mud mosaics, dinosaur rocks, calcium, lignite, asbestos, potassium deposits, quartz, uranium, but not alluvial ground, into dry gulches and beyond the red dunes to that inevitable place where, in the thin shade of a thorn bush, he would be bitten by a cobra before it was properly night and last twenty agonising minutes all rushing heart, collapsing lungs, blood, spit, dribble and froth, dead before the others, catching up from useless fossicking, even reached him.

There they stood, coarse men, black-pored, unshaven, Bywooner Malan, Spooner, John Smith, brooding on the same thought: that this was luck worse than droughts or locusts. That this was not a moment's misfortune, this was life under an evil star. They shivered and cursed hard fate. After all they'd been through, plagues and wars, jails and siege, it had never happened before. So why now?

So why now, mister, huh! Huh! Huh! They turned on the government agent hastening up at the sight of Smiley down.

He stopped. Bywooner Malan raised a fist; the others took out knives.

Get, they shouted. Get, you dog – and bent to pick up rocks.

Don't, ordered the government agent cold as evening wind, reaching inside his shirt. Just put them down.

They did, surprised by the gun he drew out, by the way he crouched, ready, fearless.

Back off. Go on, back, he told them, until they were beyond the corpse and he could see where the fangs had gone into Smiley's thumb.

It's fate, he shrugged. When the time comes, it comes.

They buried Smiley.

Spooner took the coat and boots, but he didn't wear them as Smiley had done, merely bundled them into his sack. Then they smothered the grave beneath stones and rocks being careful not to put their hands where scorpions or cobras could be. It was almost dark when they finished. Exhausted, they sat down to smoke. Only the government agent paced about, agitated, wanting to leave. The last light died quickly and they had no wood for a fire.

About them came to stand the shades of men, women, children: a patient host, neither angry nor forgiving, biding their time. In the scrub gathered quick men with bows and arrows dipped in root venom. On the plains milled zebra, eland, quagga, and from krantz to krantz passed springbok in their thousands, invisibly.

The four men saw nothing of this, although they shivered as the air turned cold.

The government agent cleared his throat. We should go, he said in a voice both hoarse and faint.

But no one moved because a lamp swung out of the darkness and a man approached, calling: I am a Christian. I am a follower of the only true God. He came up hesitantly, put the lamp down at the foot of Smiley's grave and greeted each man in turn, even bowing before the government agent. He wore a top hat and tails and a necklace of teeth.

Do you have food? asked Bywooner Malan.

No, replied the stranger. There is nothing left in these lands. They say that once you could shoot zebra, gnu, gemsbok, eland from your camp. They say that there was great abundance here, more than men have ever seen. But only old people remember such times. They say that all life has left here, that you will find only ghosts among the rocks. I have heard a story told that those who once lived here never die. That long after death their powers live on and no one dares call their names or speak of the time when they hunted peacefully here: a time before men came with spears, and other men came with guns to unleash death among them. And the death did not stop until they had all been killed. Even the children were not spared. It is said they were smashed against rocks until their heads exploded. All the bodies were left to be eaten, but no hyena, no vulture, jackal, crow would come near them. Nor worms either. Yet you do not find their bones here. Although so many were slaughtered you would not know it. This is the story of those who have become the spirit people. But I warn you, in the desert you shouldn't think of these things because the spirit people live in thoughts, they turn dreams into nightmares, in the dark they come to kill. Even those who do not know this story are driven mad. I have found men here who tried to kill themselves by beating their heads. I have found others who died from a poison only the spirit people know.

He paused to stare like the others at the lamp's tiny flame. Behind them, in the immense dark of the veld and the sky, nothing moved. For a moment they became statues, as old as the rocks.

Eventually, when the silence had turned into drumming hooves, padded feet drawing nearer, wings, a shriek of bats, he said: I have come to warn you. You are in great danger here. You must come with me.

And to the government agent he whispered: I am the redeemer's messenger, sent to fetch you.

All night they walked. All night. Across a valley and two river-beds, through a cluster of hills on to a plain that curved into the sky before them and slid down behind their heels like a black wheel where they stumbled, tired, aching, standing still even when they ran. In front went the stranger, now stopping to listen, now creeping, now striding out, or loping into a pace that had them spitting blood. Behind him the government agent matched step for step, until the desperate shouts of Bywooner Malan or John Smith or Spooner brought them up. Then they walked again, the prospectors coughing at the effort, crying out that they'd come far enough, that they couldn't go on. But the stranger never looked back, he forced them forward, only stopping at dawn beside a frozen puddle to rest. There they waited for the sun to melt the ice and give them water.

How much further? asked the government agent, feeling fatigue like lead harden in his legs.

The redeemer's messenger grinned, shrugged: Some time. Tomorrow. The next day. It is up to you. But such questions mean nothing. Ask rather if you are safe. He laughed. That is a good question, don't you think?

There is nothing out there, said the agent. Spirit people cannot harm a Christian.

The man laughed again.

The Tale of Woe

Later you will see, he said. When the sun is high you will see them.

After that no one spoke. The ice disappeared and they sucked up the brack water, being careful not to push their lips into the mud.

We must go, said the stranger, peering at each face, wondering if in those mouths lay gold-filled teeth, such highly prized necklace pieces. Those who lie down in the desert do not get up. Have you not seen people die as easily in the day as in the night?

He made them walk again but now the agent straggled. Sometimes even Bywooner Malan or Spooner lurched past him as he stood, head bowed, arms hanging forward, swaying slightly until the will came to plod on. The night's strength was gone; there was now just heat and thirst and distance.

See, the messenger shouted at him, when he, dazed, no longer agent or unsung hero or even husband father, caught up to where they waited at a heap of stones. See there – and he was spun from point to point. On all horizons floated mirages of buck and men like a ring drawing tighter. He saw them: animals clashing horns, wizened men fitting arrows to their bows. Everywhere they surged and shimmered, sometimes closer, sometimes further off, but always they danced wherever he looked. They promised water and food, encouraged him with smiles, but the redeemer's messenger held him back. Even when he struggled to break free, to run towards a lake or away from crowing women, the messenger held him in.

They'll kill you for sure, and my life's not worth losing you, he hissed between clenched teeth at the agent's vicious straining.

Only as the heat died did the figures slide back into the earth, and the agent stopped his protests. But now he would go no further.

We have won, he laughed, pointing at the empty horizons, running this way and that into the veld, punching and slashing the air. We have won, he howled, shooting at rocks, bones and the spectre-bushes leaning together like refugees.

You are blind, said the stranger, and he pointed at a group of three, watching, waiting: and there at a solitary hunter; and there at old men squatting in patience; and there coming out of the north others; and further back women and children hurrying forward.

No, no, shrieked the government agent, we are saved. We have won. Build a fire. We are saved.

And he and the others caught up in his madness gathered dry scrub and what wood could be found and fed the fire until the sparks leapt above their heads. Then, drawn to the fire, mesmerised by the flames, the government agent imagined his glorious arrival among the people of the prophet, bare-foot, in rags. An arrival of rejoicing, a clapping, swaying, praise the Lord welcome at a soul saved.

For even if only one comes among us renouncing the ways of evil the forces of righteousness will be strengthened a thousandfold and victory will be on the side of the just, prayed the redeemer, warming to the new recruit, offering him food at his table, a bed in his rooms. Lord have mercy on thy servants.

And he laid his hands with their red and weeping palms on his convert's head, saying: Accept this man, oh Lord, for he is one of us, hallelujah.

Hallelujah, echoed the people streaming out of the temple down to the great river to baptise him Simon, once, in the name of the Father, hallelujah, again, in the name of the Son, hallelujah, and finally, in the name of the Holy Ghost, hallelujah, until he rose dripping wet, gasping for air.

Now you are one of us, said the prophet, beaming.

So much one of them that after a few days of sitting on the prophet's right hand, suggesting this in the interests of unity, that on a point of legal rights, here a demand worth pressing, there a pitfall, one thing to be challenged and another ignored, this way to deal with government, there matters open for discussion, for talks, summits, possible negotiations, he had the secular ear. To what Simon said: So be it, announced the prophet, rising, dismissing priests, lieutenants, advisors, bidding Simon: Walk with me for there is no one I can talk to. These are all land people, know-nothings, used to seasons but not the affairs of men or God. I need a confidant, Simon, someone to take my mind off things. To organise, arrange, see to tabernacle administrations. What do you say to that?

Leave it to your servant, redeemer. I shall do my best, he answered in all humbleness.

And excelled in celestial matters also: devout with obedience in prayers, voice high at hymns, swooning with passion, talking in tongues, truly possessed of the spirit. A good man, one of them.

Who deserved a woman, for no man should have an empty bed. It was not right. It was not written. It is not the Lord's way and ours neither, declared the redeemer sitting back, closing his file, patting Simon on the knee. So let the fathers present their daughters.

Now? queried the priests, expecting morning prayers not beauty shows.

Yes now, snapped the redeemer. This is an important affair.

So be it. Chairs were arranged. In whispers men delegated, hurried off, smiling, delighted, leaving the cabal to wait while anxious fathers eager to find favour fetched daughters from the fields, from the laundry pool, the chicken runs, and mothers, wielding brushes and powder, in the one to twenty queue of beauties ordinaries and dowdies outside the tabernacle door, hardly dared hope let it be mine, when the redeemer, eyes partly closed, hands composed over the good book, commanded: Will the first present. And a father and his daughter entered to a rising hum of approval. A bow, a curtsey, a swish of skirts, front view, back view.

That's worth a second glance, said the redeemer. But let's see them all first.

Next.

Next.

Come closer, Simon. What's nice from afar is often far from nice. Now we want to see unsplit hair, white teeth, the shape of hands, translucent skin, and smell only a milky warmth upon their breath. Otherwise reject it, Simon. There's no point in a bitch gone in the teeth, all you'll get are nights of foul clouds. Nor much sense to one with knotty fingers and pus scars. Believe me what's outside is inside too.

So we'll see more of her and her and her, but the rest aren't worth raising blood. Believe me, Simon, mine is the eye of experience.

But now compare these three – standing on chairs in a circle of men, skirts dropped, blouses off – compare ankles, calves, thighs. Note the tone of muscles, any bruises? varicose veins? Move up to the spread of bums, the overhang not loose but firm. Ah, good. Very good. So far a difficult choice. And on this side value the width of thighs. Oh, here is too little flesh and too sharp bones. Step down, sister, you will not do. But look at these – guiding Simon's hand over pebble smoothness, the slight swell of stomach, the deep navel – and, ah, notice waiting breasts, blue nipples. But check first for strain in the muscles, the stretch runnels of breasts too quickly formed. Nothing. Well, that makes things harder. But so much the better, it's worth taking time. Let's step back, distance, too, is needed. Observe now the line of that throat rising from rounded shoulders. Come down to ensure no sudden infelicities, no showing ribs. These are things to look for, Simon. And, finally, the most important: that veil of worth. Ensure a virgin thicket, a maidenhead intact: as it is in her but not in this one. Out, whore! I won't have one who has already spilt her blood.

And then the image in the flames became that of the president and the government agent shrugged helplessly: What could I do, Mr President, but for duty and country play along, take the girl to my bed, love her, or at least pretend to, live out my husband's role, thinking every time of my own wife, asking forgiveness of all those who are deceived, even this trusting, willing woman, for otherwise how was I to do my job?

At which the president gravely nodded, eyes closed, the pain of man's ways and his boils weighing deeply: Go on, my boy, go on. It's worse than even I imagined.

So he was told what he wanted to hear of life among the redeemer's people: of thieves with amputated hands, adulterous women stoned to death, blasphemers with their tongues put out, whippings, pulled nails, drawn teeth and other tortures, solitary confinement, mock trials, dawn executions and, even worse, perversions, sodomy, orgies in the tabernacle, horned priests, the sacrifice of virgins, devil worship with children and goats, the blood of babies, until he cries: Stop. I've heard enough. What's happened to our people!

The Tale of Woe

And in the flames the government agent also saw the houses of tired wives and men without work, children in the dog-turd streets playing with fire, and the old brought out to do their dying on the stoep. Here his wife in overall and slippers took in laundry – two and six for five shirts, five bob for a full tub – spent all day scrubbing in the concrete yard, her hands in the zinc tub cleaning other men's shirts, their wives' dresses, underwear, socks, blown handkerchiefs, her head bent to it, hands wrinkled, the hard days passing in sheets of washing.

But I'm a hero, he muttered at the fire. I have sacrificed for president and country.

Words she doesn't hear in the slop of scum and water, not even feeling his presence, grown so hard in the years of absence she cannot even remember his face.

And our daughters?

Oh, your daughters leave from here each morning for the clothing factory. Both unmarried and not likely to, hurry up this street of corrugated houses towards the mountain, take the number sixty-nine down Main Road past furniture and radio stores and second-hand vendors into the industrial sector, and their sewing machines one behind the other in the line doing sleeves today, legs yesterday, jackets tomorrow, working from siren to siren.

But I'm the government agent. A hero.

And in the flames the agent saw a night of arrows, his glory gone, his great deception over. Instead, men blamed him for deaths, for riding out on horseback to gun them down. And women, their breasts cut off, their stomachs sliced open, carrying children – smashed boy-heads, crushed girl-heads – passed mutely before him from darkness into darkness, stopping once in the flames to cast an angry, accusing look.

It wasn't me, he screamed. It wasn't me – and ran into the night, followed by a flight of arrows, and among them, one, a branch from a tambuti tree, smoothed, weighted with iron, fashioned on a peaceful day, washed in the poison of forgotten roots, flew swifter, surer than the rest, cutting first the fibre of his coat, then splitting the skin, piercing through and through to nestle in the warmth of kidneys and intestines, liver and gall, spreading a dull yellow into the bloodstream. Out there in the immensity of karoo night the hunted one stumbled among rocks and small bushes, coughing, retching, confused by bright lights and odd shapes: the whirl of stars, clash of triangles, dots, the jagged zip of heartbeat. Stopped. Fell. Lay on a sandy patch where yesterday a beetle had walked leaving its particular trail and the day before a lizard had run out after flies. Breathed his last, moving a few grains of sand with the rush and suck of his air until even they were still.

Here the redeemer's messenger found him in the morning, bent down to look quickly through his inauspicious teeth, and left him with the short tambuti arrow sticking in his back. Around the dying ashes he left, too, Spooner and John Smith, dead to the world, with the life drained from their cut throats.

Just he and Bywooner Malan set out for the island in the great river, but they walked differently from the day before. In front went the prospector, his arms pulled sharply back and tied. Behind him followed the redeemer's messenger, deaf to all protestations of innocence, all pleas for mercy, all tears of frustration, all whimpers of: Believe me, please believe me, I'm only a diamond digger.

Maybe, said the messenger, but now I'm giving you a chance to be someone else, someone important, a government agent, no less.

All I've Got to Say

That was all I could tell him, mister, Maria said at last, shifting beneath the frozen skins, reaching a charcoal hand into a bucket for more ice. That was all he wanted to know. As I said, he sat where you sit now with his Homburg on his knee, and when I'd finished he said: Maria, if you're the Maria I once visited, in these things you were right. But I chose to put my trust in others. I used the logic of professors, advisors, generals and men of wit who all, without exception, lied or blundered, couldn't tell rumour from reality, couldn't forecast even with the best computers tomorrow's weather let alone the country's mood. I should have heeded your warning. I should have searched out this evil when it still suckled on a woman's breast. But I forgot. I thought there were more important affairs. I turned to good government, to law and order, to development, fiscal growth and the collection of taxes, when all along a demon fed off my flesh, sucked at the very life I created. I have had my revenge now. I have cleared our nation of this cancer, but at what cost, that such an innocent man should die so lonely, so unmourned, unburied in the wastes, his bones scattered? I have had my revenge but nothing is put right.

That was what he said, sitting where you sit now, such an old man, only days from death. I could see it all, the ocean liners in the harbour, the city in a festive mood, hung with flags and bunting. Bands in the street leading platoons and cannons to his last salute. I could see him pinning medals when the moment came . . . but what could I tell him? I have seldom had words of comfort. What good is it to know that what happens happens and can happen no other way. It's no good at all, is it, mister?

So don't ask me any more. That's what I know, that's the last I saw of him. Standing, as you're standing now, clutching his hat, saying: I'm sorry, Maria, I should have listened to you. He did, though, because listening is all you can do to the likes of me. Then he went, but this time it was no good trying to warn him about his heart.

So, mister, that's all I've got to say. Just leave your money and go.

A Further Letter

28 June
So now you must believe us, Mr Big-Shot Editor. Now you know we mean business like we said. We don't mess with people, Mr Editor, not when we're talking about atrocities like this. This is history, this is the stuff we're going to tell our children in the years to come so that they won't forget how we struggled against the oppressor. In our new democratic country everybody is going to know about this. About the hurt of our history. We're talking about pain, Mr Editor, the pain of people who have no rights, no voice, nothing. But now the oppressor will start to hear our voice. You must help us to give the struggle its voice. In our new democratic country people will praise you as a hero. Viva the struggle! Viva! I have talked to my comrades and they say you must give us seven hundred for the information. This price they say is not negotiable. Pay in two days at Eastern Boulevard Post Office, Box 21.

Hot Air

The fat editor, letting slip a wind, thought he was on to a good story. On this fine, sun brighter, air clearer winter day he could see headlines revealing plots and conspiracies, boxes detailing the tyranny of a president, sub-heads exposing deceit, cross-heads screaming misfeasance, highlighted quotes of malevolence, column centimetres laying bare crimes against humanity. As he rolled along the pavements he dreamt of awards and international citations, fame and the adoration of cub reporters, especially the young thing on courts. Oh ho ho how he'd like to get his hands around those tits and squeeze. Oh ho ho what head she'd give. Oh ho ho and he clawed deeply, viciously, at his groin before disappearing into the curry gloom of the Maharaj Restaurant where Johan van Rooyen, pensive, worried, picked without relish at a roti.

Jo-han, sang the fat editor waddling up, putting out a clammy hand which the roti eater took briefly, limply, all too aware of how that hand scratched, wiped, fiddled, constantly, in dark and fetid places. How good to see you. Right. Right. Well, ah, how very good to see you, my friend, right, right, he said, sitting down with what could have been either burp or fart.

Smiled the one. Grimaced the other.

Then: Well. Right. Right. And what will you have, huh? You know, what's it to be? asked the jovial journalist, skimming a menu, remembering a day when this very same man spun him out of the high office like a top. How times changed. Who would ever have thought then that there would be this now? Right. Right. What do you think? What's it to be, huh? Fish

224

biryani? They do a very good, you know, biryani. Chicken tandoori? Right. Not bad, not bad. Or if you're vegetarian, I mean, you know, there's chickpea dhal? Mushroom pilau? No! Right. Right. Then how about, you know, spicy shrimps? Or crispy sheep's brain? Huh! What a choice. You know. A fine establishment. What a pleasure. And ah . . . ah . . . it's on me, of course. On the paper. That kind of thing. No argument, it was my invitation. I mean. My pleasure, you know. Right! Right, right.

What they ordered was: a bottle of Riesling, neck of lamb soup for the fat editor, chicken soup for the former presidential secretary, mince tarkhari garnished with coriander leaves for the windy one, mutton masala chops served with dhunia chutney for the once and faithful aide, followed by Bengali sweetmeats for the former, Kashmiri milk dessert for the latter, and coffee, thick, caramel-flavoured coffee.

What they talked about, after the wine had been poured but before the soup arrived, was:

Well, cheers, your health.

To the president.

Ah. Right. Right. Yes. The president. Right. He's a good man.

He *was* more than a good man. He *was* a patriot.

Right. Oh yes, yes, of course, that one. You knew him sort of so well.

For forty-eight years.

Forty-eight years, hey. Right. Right. A long time. Right. Right. Er, listen, Johan, you know the way things are these days, no sort of secrets, open administration, right to know, all these things, you know it's not like it was. I mean, we can say things now, things that wouldn't have been allowed before, critical things you might say, but truthful, you know, facts.

No. Actually, I don't know. What do you mean?

I mean. Well. I've been told, by respectable sources, you understand, what I'd call honourable men with no axe to grind, I've been told, certain things.

Certain things?

Yes things . . . About the former president. Things.

What sort of things, exactly?

But the editor was gone between the tables, fighting the wind within him, the demanding itch in his crotch, until in the privacy of the men's cloakroom he farted, burped, scratched and emerged much relieved. By then soup had been served.

Bon appétit.

They drank four spoonfuls in silence, until:

Er, listen Johan. Ah, right, these things, you know what I mean, these certain things, ah, how shall I say, these allegations, yes, you follow me, these allegations, well maybe I can help put the record straight. Give the other side of the story, so to speak. You know, objective reporting, that kind of thing.

Johan van Rooyen finished his soup, wiped the corners of his mouth with a napkin. He felt tired, suddenly very tired, and cheated. Why should he be left to eat curry with disgusting journalists in back-street joints? Why should he have to face the stupidity of newspapermen? For heaven's sake, enough was enough. He took a sip at the wine.

I think you should realise that I am here only because of the new dispensation. Only because the president, the new president, especially suggested, suggested, you understand, that I see you as a small example of the new approach, as a gesture of goodwill towards the press. If he had not expressly wanted it, I would have turned you down. As you know, I do not have much time for the press. Nor do I want to listen to slander about the former president, and certainly I do not want to end up sounding as if I am defending his good name. He needs no defence. He has nothing to answer for. He was head of a wise and just government. He had his way of dealing with matters which is not the way of our new president but these are merely differences in style, not content. So do not expect me to justify past decisions. I won't. However, if you want impressions of the man, of his deep concern for the nation, of his love, of his tolerance, I would be more than willing to help you.

Yes, yes, that's it. That's it exactly. Your impressions, you know, how he responded to the demands of high office. That sort of thing. That's what I'm after. A profile. A portrait of a head of state. I mean, you know, the things that make a man . . . ah, a statesman.

When the mince tarkhari garnished with coriander leaves and the mutton masala chops served with dhunia chutney were half devoured, Johan van Rooyen made these observations.

I think you must understand that the president was a most serious man. In outlook and disposition. He took his office extremely seriously, he was concerned to ensure that he had all the information before he made a decision. He consulted all the relevant people. He would go to great pains to know all points of view. And for this he paid a price. His health suffered. In the last months he was in great pain. Great pain. I would find him almost weeping with pain at his desk early in the morning. He would still be in his dressing gown, papers everywhere, the pain etched into his forehead. Such was his attention to duty. Such was the seriousness with which he took his position. The presidency is a privilege, Johan, he used to say, it is conferred by the people, it is the highest honour they can give, so it must not be treated lightly. Those were his words and I'll never forget them. Nor will I forget how he bore that pain. You wouldn't have known he was suffering, you wouldn't have known that his body was shot with fire every time he sat down, every time he took a step, every time he lay down to sleep. Often he couldn't sleep because the pain was too great, and that's when he'd get up and work. Other men would have taken pain-killers, morphine, anything to relieve the agony. But not the president. No. He wanted a clear head. He felt it was his duty to be able to deal with an emergency should one ever occur. Luckily that never happened. But he was prepared for it. Prepared for it through sheer grit and courage. This is my cross, Johan, he used to say. And I must bear it alone. In fact I am breaking a confidence now, because he made me promise never to tell anyone about his suffering. The only other people who knew were his wife and his doctor. Otherwise it was a closely guarded secret. Not even his children knew the state of his health. But now, let me tell you this, and you will see what sort of man he was. There were times, quite a number of times, when he saw high-level delegations, not only delegations from within the country, but heads of state from abroad, shortly after he had been treated by the state surgeon. Nor were these treatments mere consultations as you and I know them. It was usually surgery. Minor, admittedly, but surgery nonetheless. It meant scalpels and lancing and swabs and stitches. All without anaesthetic, mind you. If he was going to deal with affairs of state afterwards he would not have an anaesthetic. In fact, so far as I know he never had an anaesthetic. And where do you think this surgery took place? Not in some private clinic, not in some lavish theatre with nurses dancing in attendance. Oh no. It happened on his desk. On the very desk where he ratified treaties and death penalties, where he signed laws into the statute. On the very desk where he sat across from foreign dignitaries negotiating for oil or weapons or low-interest loans. That's where the doctor treated him because he didn't have time to spend a few hours, let alone a day, in hospital. He was that sort of man, sir, dedicated to serving his people no matter what the sacrifice. But it cost him dearly. It cost him his life. It was that dedication that killed him, I'm convinced of it. That extraordinary sense of duty which is so unfashionable nowadays but which he upheld to the end. Johan, he used to say to me, I must set an example. I cannot expect people to work hard if I don't show them leadership, true leadership that is prepared to roll up its sleeves and set to. Not this sham leadership they all talk about, this hot air that sounds off and gets nothing done. Let me tell you, my boy – he used to call me 'my boy' in private, such was the intimacy of our relationship – let me tell you, my boy, there is only one way to run the world and that's to work. You can quote that, that is what he said, and you can quote that I think that's why his heart was overtaxed. If he had been less concerned with the state of affairs, more interested in trivial pleasures like playing golf or bird-watching, he would be with us today. He would still be our leader in these troubled times. I tell you, he died for us all, he died in the knowledge that he had served his nation, that he had left it a better place. His conscience was clear because he died knowing that his country was at peace. Let me tell you something . . . I know there are lots of people, some of them his former colleagues, oh yes, you don't have to look surprised, I know these things, who speak badly about him these days. They say he was autocratic, that his marriage had collapsed, that he acted irrationally without listening to what people advised, that he ran down the economy, that he has catapulted us into mayhem. I know people say these things. But I also know they are wrong. Perhaps our currency isn't worth as much as it used to be on the world markets, but that is not because we are less productive, it is because of hypocrisy abroad; perhaps the price of cigarettes and whisky has gone up, but these are luxuries which can be done without, certainly the staples, bread, milk, maize, meat, are not dearer than they were ten years ago, not in real terms. Perhaps there are some voices raised in anger, but there have always been malcontents and there will always be the disenchanted no matter what you do. Perhaps there is killing in some out of the way places, but this is hardly new, it is part of the human condition. It occurs wherever there are men in the world. So to judge the president by these measures is wrong. They do not show the worth of the man, all they show is the poverty of mankind's imagination, our inability to follow inspired men. Believe me, nobody, perhaps not even his wife, knew him as well as I did. I'll tell you something in confidence, off the record. I loved that man. I loved that man in the highest meaning of the word, I loved him the way I have never loved anyone else in my life. If it had been necessary I would have died for him. If during a cavalcade an assassin had lunged at him with a knife I would have stepped in to take the blows. He was a good man. A man you could follow unquestioningly. He was proud, he was humble, he could be strong, he could be tender. I remember there were many times when he would smile at me and say: I think it's time you went home, my boy, you're looking tired, and there would be such concern in his voice and in his face. At other times, when we were alone in the high office at the end of the day or working late into the night, he would break the silence and, laying his hand on my arm, he would say: Johan, I don't know what I would have done without you, my boy. You have been more than a loyal colleague and friend to me, he used to say, you have been . . . But he never finished that sentence. His eyes would cloud, he would look away and squeeze my arm. Those were precious moments. Emotional moments when you felt how the responsibility of high office weighed on him, when you felt the loneliness of great men and their love.

Johan van Rooyen sipped quickly at his wine, bowed his head, marshalled the remains of his lunch with a piece of roti and clumsy fingers, but couldn't bring himself to eat any more.

Yes, yes. Right, fascinating, stuttered the fat editor. Do go on. Don't let me put you off. Lovely treats these, aren't they? And from the three thick syrupy goolab jamuns before him, he lifted one and slid it into his mouth, leaving a sprinkle of desiccated coconut on his chin. Johan van Rooyen bent to his chilled milk pudding.

While the fat editor chewed on the jamuns, the former presidential aide said: I think, sir, there are certain, how shall I put it, certain misconceptions I need to clear up. Misconceptions about the president's state of mind, the supposedly ruinous state of his marriage. Perhaps these were even among the . . . ah, certain things . . . you referred to earlier?

The fat editor nodded, wiped coconut from his chin, messed syrup on his tie: Right. Right. I'm sure. I'm sure. Rumours. Stories being put about. Things like that. You know how it is. You know, ha ha. That type of thing.

Categorically, you understand, quite categorically I can state that although the president was under exceptional pressure – who wouldn't have been in his situation? – his thinking was as clear as yours and mine. Of that I have no doubt. He knew exactly what he was doing. He made his decisions in the last months as calmly as he had ever done. I am not saying that he didn't agonise over them. He did. Some of them were not easy. They cost him sleep, they cost him his health. But he always had the strength of character to make the right decision. You understand what I'm saying, don't you? I'm saying that right up to the end he was in control, he was always man enough for the job. It is true that he became more, how should I put it, self-reliant, more unorthodox towards the end. Some have gone so far as to accuse him of isolationism, but that makes it sound as if he wasn't in touch with what was going on. And of course he was. He had his feet on the ground. He knew exactly where the problems were and he focused his energy on solving them. So although he ran the state of affairs from his high office in the latter years, that is not to say he had become autocratic, or, as some will, a dictator. He still sought opinions, he still explored every avenue before he took a final decision. Nowadays you have to. These days even one human death from the most innocent of decisions is inexcusable.

Johan van Rooyen scooped up two spoonfuls of the chilled milk pudding in quick succession. The fat editor, released from his source's unwavering gaze, clawed at his crotch through the thin lining of his pocket and asked: Er. Right. Right. I hear you. Extraordinary. Extraordinary. Right. Right. Er, listen, I heard, you know, you know the way these things happen, I heard that . . . well . . . that he wasn't even going hunting any more. I mean, you know . . . people said, you know, people said he was beyond it. You know, beyond . . . beyond coping?

Johan van Rooyen, the chilled Kashmiri pudding finished, dabbed at the corners of his mouth with the napkin, responded: I think I've shown you at some length how competent the president was in the later months. If these people, your confidants, are implying that because he declined hunting invitations he was incapable of running the country, then those assumptions are false. It is true that the president had been a great hunter. At one stage it was a sport which gave him much pleasure and enjoyment. He enjoyed being out on the veld. He enjoyed the open air. He valued hunting because this is a country which has a strong hunting tradition. But, and I must emphasise this happened some years ago, he came to find gratuitous killing unacceptable. If a man had to hunt to feed his family that was one thing, but to kill for the mere thrill of killing, to kill merely to satisfy a bloodlust, that the president found morally indefensible. You see, he believed that all animals, all men too for that matter, had a right to live and a right to live the way they wished to live. By hunting he was violating those rights, and his conscience, his humanity could no longer countenance that.

Right. Right. Amazing.

The fat editor shifted on his chair and eased out a fart that stayed trapped beneath the tablecloth.

Coffee, thick, caramel-flavoured coffee, was served. Johan van Rooyen, unaware of the rotten air circulating about his knees, looked at the viscous fluid without enthusiasm. And while he wished for a bitter espresso, the fat editor knocked his back with two lipsmacking swallows. Johan van Rooyen sighed and decided to offer one last insight.

Let me tell you something. Let me tell you of one of the last cherished memories I have of the president. It says many things, not the least of which is to vindicate what I have told you. As I recall this incident, not so much an incident as one of those moments when you feel just for a second that the world is at peace, that there is no killing, no unhappiness, that goodness has given us a brief respite, this moment, this particular moment I'm referring to, occurred some months ago during the hot spell. You remember how choking the days were, how listless they made us all feel? They were difficult days for the president. He was riddled with pain, he had a serious state of affairs to attend to, and he needed to make a decision. If I remember rightly you even incurred his wrath at the time. Do you remember? You published some letters or an article which almost jeopardised his negotiation process. But I suppose you weren't to know that and fortunately nothing untoward came of your, ah . . . indiscretion.

Johan van Rooyen drew at his coffee and suffered its sweetness. He swallowed quickly to suppress thoughts of nausea and wiped his lips.

As I was saying, that hot weather was a burden to us all. It raised tempers, it raised problems where no problems should have been. It added yet another difficulty at a time when we needed cool heads. I must admit that those of us serving the president floundered in that heat. Only he seemed able to rise above it. He was always immaculate, always white, always perfect. Despite the delicacy of the issues he faced daily, not once did he jeopardise the nation's history with a rash decision. Not once, sir. I can assure you, not once. And those were testing times, as you well remember. I have told you already that the president was not a man for self-indulgence. He would rather sacrifice his own time, his own family life, than neglect the affairs of state. The only relaxation he allowed himself was every twilight before dinner, when the sprinklers had dampened the air and brought some life back into the garden, he and his wife would walk across the lawns, between the beds of rhododendrons, fuchsias, roses, wild herbs, and sit on the bench beneath the linden tree. He valued that time. He valued that time to such a degree that he would let nothing interfere with it. It was the only time in the day that was his, and quite rightly he guarded it jealously. My cherished memory is of standing in the long window of the downstairs reception room as the twilight deepened. I suspect there was some matter I had to discuss with the president, but what it was escapes me now. Nor is it important. What is important is this image I have of them – and remember, they could not see me, for the room was dark, so they were behaving quite naturally. They were walking across the lawn arm in arm, so at peace with themselves and the world that you could feel it. I thought then how striking they looked. Halfway across the lawn the president bent down, picked up a peacock feather – the presidential residence has always had peacocks in the grounds – he picked up this beautiful feather and gave it to his wife. Briefly they smiled at one another, kissed, and continued serenely across the grass. It was a wonderful moment. It was a human moment, a moment of caring and concern, a moment to inspire us. So now you see why . . .

But the fat editor, unable to contain himself any longer, interjected: Yes. Yes. Revealing. Can I quote you? As it were, directly. Portrait of a president, that kind of thing? You know.

Johan van Rooyen nodded.

Excellent, excellent. Then, leaning across the table, the fat editor added: One thing though my sources say, you know, that the president saw a sort of fortune-teller, that type of thing, now and then?

Categorically, replied Johan van Rooyen rising, I can deny that.

Ah. Well. Right. But. But Johan ah, you know, my information is sort of how shall I put it, irrefutable. You know, accurate. Confirmed, that type of thing.

I tell you it is lies.

Right. Right. I hear you. I hear what you're saying. You know, I mean, well maybe, you know, you didn't sort of know about this.

Impossible. If it were true I would have known about it.

Right. Right. I have the woman's name. She's told me about it, you know, that sort of thing.

I'm sure she has. But people will say anything for money. And now I must go. Thank you for lunch.

Right. Right. A pleasure. You know, grateful. Sorry to raise these sort of unpleasant things – and even though still seated, he extended his hand.

But Johan van Rooyen had gone without a backward glance through a door that opened on a bright world of noise and traffic. In the gloom of the Maharaj the fat editor scratched at his crotch, burped, strained to blow out a stubborn fart and called for a waiter.

Closing Correspondence

1 July

What are you playing at, Mr Editor? You know we're genuine. But are you genuine? The comrades say the security men have got to you. They say you've been told to drop all this, or else. They say that when it comes to the crunch you liberals always chicken out. They say it's not worth bothering with you any more. That you don't really care and that this crime against humanity, that's what they call it, a crime against humanity, will be paid for with blood after the revolution. But I'll give you one last chance because I don't think you're like that. Maybe you have been intimidated. But I've read what you've written and I know you are a man of principles. Look, I'll tell you one thing: this is about the former president. It's about a crime against humanity. It's true, I swear. I've got evidence. This is urgent so I'm delivering the letter by hand. If the price is too high we can negotiate. Pay us whatever you think. Use the Harbour box number.

4 July

Dear Mr Editor,

Help us, Mr Editor, please. We are waiting across the road. You must help us, please. We are just poor people. My girlfriend has been without work since the new president moved into the big house. He had all the staff fired. Just like that, he told them they must all go. He said he wasn't going to have anyone

235

working for him who worked for the other president. My girlfriend hasn't had a job for two months and yesterday my boss told me to go. He told me I was lazy and drank. But I swear I never drink on the job. He was a good boss but he wouldn't look me in the eye when he told me to take my wages and go. When I asked him why he had made up these lies about me he got angry. He said I must get out, that he didn't want political troublemakers in his factory, he said I was a communist, a terrorist who was just out to destroy everything good that had been built up over the years. It is not true, Mr Editor. I have never caused political trouble. When the comrades came to me I listened, but I never did everything they wanted. I told them Mr Barney was a good man, that he always paid fair and listened when you had troubles and needed a loan. Only he wouldn't listen to me when he told me to go. He wouldn't let me talk to him. He pushed me out of the office. Nobody pushes me, Mr Editor. I see red when people push me. So I pulled a knife and stuck him in the arm. But that's all, I swear, just once in the arm. He asked for it. He shouldn't have done that to me. He shouldn't have pushed me. He only did that to me because I'm the oppressed. He can do anything to the oppressed because the law is on his side. Last night the police came to where we stay. But we were expecting them so they never caught us. But now we can't go back there ever again. All we've got is the clothes we put on while the police were banging at the door. Won't you give us some money, Mr Editor, for the fact we've been telling you about? I swear to you without a lie, and so does my girlfriend, that this fact is genuine. She found it in the president's office when she was dusting. It was hidden under the pad on his desk. I promise you we're not lying. Didn't we tell you the truth about the fortune-teller? Just give us some money and we'll never bother you again. We just need money to take a train to another town. In another town we can start again. Please, Mr Editor, my girlfriend is crying. She says the police will kill us. We have nowhere to hide. I know you are in the office, Mr Editor, because the man at the door told us. He said if we wrote out a note he would take it to you personally.

Closing Correspondence

Please come down to us as soon as you have read this. We do not want people to think we are vagrants or they will call the police. We beg you, Mr Editor, come to our help. We are not comrades. We are just poor people.

SIX

Another Story

This is another story: one not to be found in regimental records, history books, a traveller's diary, letters home, memoirs or biographies – one to be heard only at a mother's knee or on a night of beer when old men's tongues loosen, and at funerals where the young go badly to their graves. Because this is a story of shame, a grim chapter in the lives of prophets and presidents, indeed, in the lives of us. Because often history records only what it wants to, never mentions the cries of peacocks or the resonance of dragonfly wings. Never sits down at the fire on a night of stars to hear the stories people tell their children. A story of once upon a time on an island in the great river . . .

. . . Enoch Mistas is at prayers in the tabernacle as he is every morning, while in the rooms behind, uncomplaining, forever virginal, Tasmaine washes the helpless Ma-Fatsoen and hears Jabulani Mximba unlock the grille doors of the cellar beneath her feet. Oh that she, like others, could hear only celestial voices, for in her ears ring the cries of the living. Beyond, in the fields, Simple Martha lies cocooned in silence with sheep and dragonflies, oblivious of the hymns of hoeing women or the drilling feet on the settlement square where Dead Das and Allermann parade seventy-two knobkerries, spears, Mausers and Enfields into discipline and attrition, into army. Truly a glorious morning, with P.T. George lost in his past, a morning clean and fresh before the end of the world, all sinners repentant, rejoicing in the glory of God and the coming of His kingdom, when out of the bushes on the southern bank four horsemen in khaki ride down to the sluggish water's edge. There they stand, tight-reining the horses from drinking, two, through telescopes, scanning the paradoxical scene.

A sign of war, declares the field marshal eventually, half standing in his stirrups to ease the anal knot. What do you say, Trotter?

Undoubtedly, sir, replies Captain Trotter, collapsing his telescope, wiping sweat and dust from his stinging eyes.

Sergeant-major, commands Field Marshal Hedley Goodman, announce our presence.

Which is done by point three-oh-three shots at the heavens, sending peacocks from their bluegum roosts in full cry, fowls to the henhouse, pigs off, sheep fleeing, leaving only the dragonflies perfectly still, quick-winged above the dew. And it brings P.T. George back to the here and now with a what the hell! – and, turning from his peaceful past on the promontory to the sight of distant horsemen, a further: Oh Christ, I knew it would come to this as he sets off, run-lumbering, heart pounding in his fat, to stop Dead Das and Allermann doing anything rash like unloading a dozen bullets at the delegation as they are preparing to do. Through potato and onion patches, over pineapples, vines and bolting sheep he goes, soft flesh screaming, eyes streaming: You bloody fools – racing in his head when the men go down on one knee, rifles pointed at four mounted targets too far off, thank God, to be even slightly alarmed.

Stop. Stop, he shouts, coming up gasping for breath. Let's (pant) hear them out (wheeze) first.

Please to stand aside, Mister P.T. George, motions Allermann. This is no time for negotiation. Turning to his soldiers: All men are to prepare to fire. Take aim. Looking back at the rasping man: This is the time for war, ja. This is the time to fight.

No, heaves P.T. George, spitting blood from torn lungs, knocking Mausers from shaking hands, Enfields from quivering shoulders. It is not what the prophet wants.

The prophet says there will be blood, screams Dead Das, red-faced, snake-mad at such defiance before his force. He says that is what the Lord wants. He wants the blood of all evil men.

No, pants the anxious emissary bent double for breath: No, first we must talk.

Blixem, howls Allermann, what is there now to talk about.

Another Story

We have been hounded from the land. We have been chased out like plague-rats. Those men do not come to talk, they come to fight. But like cowards they will not fire the first shot.

Enough, enough, says P.T. George, his breath back, hand raised in authority, setting off with a summoning wave to Dead Das and Allermann. We will meet them.

On the island's bank they wait, Dead Das with pistol drawn, Allermann with a ready Mauser, P.T. George hands clasped behind his back, face set for tough talks, watching four horsemen under a white flag ford the morning river, splash clear, and field marshal captain sergeant-major corporal dismount in the mud.

The field marshal winces, pulls at his pants, wants to know of P.T. George: Are you Enoch Mistas?

No, he is told. Who wants him?

A sniff, a purse of the lips, reins thrown to the corporal, then: Field Marshal Hedley Goodman, officer commanding Cape Royal Fusiliers. And who the hell are you?

A pause, a weighing up: P.T. George, advisor to the prophet.

Don't make me laugh, sir. Mistas is no more a prophet than I'm the Virgin Mary.

A half-turn from P.T. George about to walk off: If you cannot keep a civil tongue, field marshal, we have nothing to talk about.

Listen, you fat runt, hisses Field Marshal Hedley Goodman stepping close up with bacon breath, grabbing lapels: Where's the government agent?

Let go, whispers P.T. George, tight-lipped, if you enjoy sunsets.

Impasse. How to handle this one? wonders Captain Trotter, fed up to the back teeth with short-tempered haemorrhoids and religious nuts, about to step forward and separate the eyeing dogs when his top brass retreats all smiles and changed tactics, with: This is no way to discuss matters, Mr George. Let's talk like gentlemen. And offers a sweaty hand. Which is briefly, limply, taken.

Now to business. Put simply it was a warning: disperse.

Why?

Because here are harboured vagrants, bandits, deserters, murderers, traitors and other undesirable elements considered a threat to the well-being of citizens and a danger to the state. Not to mention the avoidance of tax, incitement to civil disobedience or grand blasphemy.

And to resist?

Is to face the consequences.

Which are?

The total clearance of this place in terms of the Slums Act, the relocation of people according to the Orderly Settlement of Peoples Act, the repayment of back tax plus penalties following the laws of internal revenue, and an admission-of-guilt fine for constituting an illegal gathering. Also, and in addition, says the field marshal unfolding a paper from his tunic pocket with a crisp flick of the wrist, an order for the arrest of Enoch Mistas upon the execution of which all the aforementioned would be waived. Especially if, you understand, my good sir, a man we believe to be here, no more than believe mind you and of course we could be wrong, by name of Jimmy Walker, could be returned, no matter how battered and bent, to his wife and two daughters, surely a compassionate gesture of the highest order, wouldn't you agree, Mr Advisor?

Umm. And how long do we have to consider these demands?

Until four o'clock, replies Field Marshal Hedley Goodman. And consider them well because the consequences will be on your heads, says he, swinging with a grimace of pain into the saddle, snapping a salute and leading captain sergeant-major corporal with white flag back across the river and into the bush.

Huh! say Dead Das and Allermann turning for the settlement with P.T. George, thoughtful, sorrowful, following a dozen paces behind along the sand path that leads through sheep, at-ease platoons, anxious women, milling children into the quiet dimness of the tabernacle where Enoch Mistas is still on his knees. What to do now?

This is absolutely no deal, announces Dead Das, chewing tobacco, spitting on the dung floor. The prophet is not an object for bartering. There is only one thing to do, which is to fight.

Ja, grins Allermann.

Oh if it were this easy, thinks P.T. George looking up at the tabernacle thatch where mice crawl and starlings quarrel. They will decimate us, he responds.

The Lord, He is with us, declares Allermann. We cannot be wanting for more.

No, ponders P.T. George to himself, we cannot be wanting for more unless it is guns and bullets. And what of the women and children? he asks. Should they not be allowed to leave?

Weakness that you can say that, Mr George. It is the duty of all believers to fight for the Lord our God who has taken us out of the land of oppressors and promises us His kingdom. That is what he demands. You will see, when the prophet speaks no one will go.

With all his followers called to the temple of the redeemer, thus spake the prophet: Oh true believers, oh people of the prophet, in our struggle for the kingdom we have been hounded into the wilderness, but the Lord is blessed, the Lord is good – He has given us an island of plenty, He has shown us the way into the promised land. But now, I tell you, the forces of Satan, the armies of the enemy, are gathering even now beyond our walls. Already they have sent spies and tempters into our midst but we have found them out as our Christ Jesus knew of betrayers among his disciples. Of all this I have dreamed and in my dream Jehovah appeared. Fear not, He said, for my time has arrived when there will be bloodshed on earth. But whosoever dies in my name will enter the kingdom of heaven and sit upon my right hand. So fear not, brothers and sisters, rejoice, rejoice, for our King whose works are great and marvellous is at hand. And soon you shall see His sign that the end of the world has come, and you will give hosannahs to the highest. Let us now give thanks unto the Lord who has told us to break our fast and taught us to sing:

> I hear a sweet voice calling
> Oh listen to the sound
> It is the voice of an angel
> That God through His promise has sent down . . .

There you are. Do you hear what we told you? leers Dead Das from the prophet's left side at P.T. George on the right.

These are his people. Who would now think of forsaking such a man?

No one. Because no one really believes that just behind the dunes and bushes there are regiments of death with machine-guns and rifles and cannons and tacit understandings of loyalty to the state and what must be done in the name of law and order, or peace, or freedom from tyranny. So no one goes, instead they prepare an end to the fast, gather brushwood, chop logs, light fires, sing as they pick oranges and grapes, draw wine from the caskets and bring a slaughtered lamb for feast or sacrifice to the roasting coals.

Where is fear now? Where the imminence of massacre, the last hours of heartbeat? Where the intimations of mortality?

Certainly not to be found in the eyes of Simple Martha gazing in rapt wonder at such happy times: children there and here between mothers and fathers carrying bread, butter, jam, eggs, goat's cheese, peanuts, biltong, laying out a long table under the bluegums for an evening of giving thanks. Nor in those sad pools, the haunted eyes of Tasmaine at a window behind the tabernacle, can be seen the pain of tomorrow, instead, mirrored there, are smiling women, lovers, proud men secure in the knowledge of deliverance, of redemption, of going about the business of the Lord. As is Enoch Mistas, shepherd among his flock, curing warts with a blessed finger, laying on hands to stop fevers, colds and gout, offering his chained Bible to be kissed, praying with the aged, playing with the little boys and girls. And with him go Dead Das and Allermann, smiling, benign, meeker than mild, dishing out comforting pats, encouraging words, dates and prunes. Only P.T. George stands aside, worried, sucking his lower lip, unable to think of anything else except something awful's going to happen here. Why such innocence? he ponders. How come such absolute belief, such fundamental faith in God's good office? Why oh why? Especially when in him beats the expedient heart, reasons the logical brain that tells him all is not well. But how to tell others that? How to advise the prophet basking in such glory and adoration? How even to approach him, until, fortuitous circumstance, the prophet beckons him over and they walk alone across two fields and an onion patch.

So, the servants of Satan are massing, he begins. It is as well.

246

Another Story

They are in force this time, redeemer, replies P.T. George, trying to warn but wary of his prophet's sudden temper.

No matter, says Enoch Mistas, dismissive, unconcerned. I have dreamt, I have dreamt of all this and the end. I have dreamt there is to be bloodshed: horrible deaths and bad dying.

So easily said. So quickly accepted, thinks P.T. George. And out loud, hoping against hope, suggests: There are ways to avoid it.

No, sighs the prophet of the people. No. It is God's will.

And the two men walk on, mud clinging to their boots and bottoms of their trousers, deep in thoughts as different as: All my life of danger and adventure to end it here in a miserable massacre; and: This is not the end, the Lord will provide, thinks Enoch Mistas looking up at an afternoon blue that is everywhere and endless unspoilt by high cloud or summer thunderheads. Indeed a glorious future awaits. Walk on the overweight man panting for breath from the age in his bones and sluggish blood, walk on the tall man, the young man, eyes alight with the zeal of mission and coming glory.

Perhaps, hesitates P.T. George, perhaps we should leave . . . or . . . or at least let whoever wants to go, go . . . or the women and children could be taken elsewhere?

Jehovah will not have us run, declares Enoch Mistas, quietly, confidently. Show faith, P.T. George, show faith. We have run far enough, we have been downtrodden and scorned, we have been forced from our land, we have been taxed when we had nothing to give. All that we have borne with patience and fortitude, and now Yahweh will lead us to victory. Show faith, P.T. George.

I have faith, redeemer. But you know there will be bloodshed, you know there will be death. Must everyone here – a great sweep of the arm taking in distant smoke and laughter, running children, calling mothers – must everyone here die?

It will not be death, P.T. George. It will be a new life. This is not the end, this is the beginning.

What now? How to talk sense into such a fundamental head when it needs to be shaken, clipped across the ear, made to see that these are lives being so lightly squandered, that this is it, the number's up? Of course there is no way round it, P.T. George is stymied, he hasn't got a chance. Yet still he persists.

Perhaps, he begins, perhaps we could release to them the spy, the government agent? I think then we might have room to talk.

This strikes home. This brings up blood to that young head. This makes the prophet see red.

No, he screams, stopping, rounding on his breathless advisor. I will not be spied on. I will not be treated like some common gangster. I will not. I will not. That man will be tried. Tonight. He will be tried, he will be sentenced. He has sinned against God. He and the president must take the consequences.

Then, quietening down, regaining his composure: This afternoon you will tell them, P.T. George, that there will be no barter. We will not give in to devilmen and dictators. In the eyes of the Lord we have done no wrong and we acknowledge no other law. Now, please return, I wish to pray alone.

That's it. Off across the field goes a dejected P.T. George thinking: Maybe I should get out tonight, leave them all to this mess, take off for southern savannahs and a quiet end to my days. What's it to me whether they live or die? I've no prospects here any more.

While behind him, a tall man, and thin, shrugs into his coat although it is far from cold, scratches at the reddening itch in his palms, clutches at the Bible dangling from his wrist and walks off towards the northern shore, as inscrutable as ever, his face still as young as a child's with not so much as a maniac's narrowing about the eyes. And there he sits all through the afternoon discussion, all through the fading light until Dead Das, ever respectful, approaches beggar-like whimpering: Redeemer, holy prophet, the trial is about to begin.

But first, what transpired before? What happened at the four o'clock river meeting?

This.

There, standing at the designated spot, were P.T. George, Allermann, Dead Das and, slightly back, Jabulani Mximba, grinning, when out of the dune grass on the other side of the river came the horsemen. Once more from the waters waded the glistening beasts, wide-nostrilled, silver-flanked, prancing sideways to the command of army spurs which had no intention of dismounting because: We are not here to be messed with, misters. We came for Enoch Mistas and the government agent. Without them the consequences for you, for you all, are dire.

So resounded the words of the field marshal in P.T. George's ears, and he, tired of it, soul-weary, but the redeemer's man to the very end, said: Field marshal, threats won't get you anywhere.

Which left Hedley Goodman, officer commanding, appalled at such insolence, bluster-faced with indignation, hardly listening to the further words of provocation: By Jehovah, we will not allow you to arrest the prophet. We will not allow you to scatter the people from this island. We will not allow you to burn our huts or the temple of the redeemer.

God Almighty I've never heard such nonsense, he stormed. Arrest them, sergeant-major. Arrest them all now.

But before Sergeant-Major Bloodstock could move, Allermann swung rifle to shoulder and Dead Das drew a pistol.

Does this mean you intend to fight? queried Captain Trotter, ever diplomatic, his handkerchief raised.

That, answered Dead Das shifting targets, is your business, not ours.

Oh good lord, man, burst out the field marshal, bum-sore and irritated, can't you give a straight answer?

It would be better if you could, Captain Trotter encouraged the sullen faces grouped around. You quite understand, don't you, sirs, that if you lay down your arms and allow us to enter the village and carry out our instructions there will be no harm done to you. You have our word on that.

Huh! said Dead Das. Your word! Your word is worth less than a sparrow fart in the doldrums. Don't give us that.

The horses shifted, shivered their skins, dropped dung during that tight conference of conditions which got nowhere and left P.T. George downcast, smoothing the sand with his boot, sick at heart at the way of things.

Sir, implored Captain Trotter turning to P.T. George, we must ask you again, are you going to fight?

And he said: You have heard them, captain. It is God's will.

Come, commanded Field Marshal Hedley Goodman, words are wasted here. But you, misters – pointing one by one at Dead Das, Allermann, Jabulani Mximba, P.T. George – must know what you have done. You must know that camped not five miles away are the armies of the state come to put things right. And it is you, each one of you, who has ordered them to do so. You stand no chance. I ask you for the last time, surrender.

Never, shouted Dead Das/Allermann firing pistol-rifle-shot into the air behind the wheeling horses. And added: If it is to be a fight, we warn you that Jehovah will fight with us and for us. You confront the armies of the Lord.

In mid-river Field Marshal Hedley Goodman, his face grimacing for pain of piles, disgust hardening his heart, looked back at the four men, the fat one already turned and walking away, the others waving fists and weapons at their retreating backs, and vowed: I'll wipe those grins from your stupid faces, but just remember you asked for it. Whatever happens is your responsibility. You've only got yourselves to blame.

Not that P.T. George was grinning, far from it: a moroser mood he'd never been in. All about him people sang and laughed as if this wasn't their last day on earth, their final sunset. But he could feel the vibrations of lead in the air and a new smell of soldiers' sweat just noticeable under the roasting lamb but to his nostrils as acrid as poison.

Having It Out

Oh to have done with it. To pack up, walk off, get out, cross the sea, leave them to field marshal, president, the terrors of state.

But he couldn't.

For in P.T. George too much had already died. In the cemetery of his past lay the graves of this one: a gentleman traveller who had set out from a grey manor on a day with grey snow underfoot and a sharpness in the air that caught his breath. A young man inspired by travels and camp life in the southern continent, eager to cross the equator, to stare on bluer seas and lands that offered no pity, were indifferent to blood, tears or the screams of the dying, an optimistic man finding himself by new stars, who died of mosquito bite – unmourned. And here, alongside his headstone, stands a neglected cross inscribed: scientist, in honour of a man intrigued by rhinoceros and elephant, keen on Le Vaillant's barbet, Griffith's vulture, Mungos mungo, Kobus leche, Lipus capensis, Manis temminckii and Otocyon megalotis, or the head of the king protea and the riverine cycad. A Darwin admirer, a Newton man from an age of steam and engines who died young in a chaotic country of sangomas, witchdoctors, bone-throwers, tokoloshe; where the past interfered with the future and the present was nowhere, where what was real at midday proved a mirage in the afternoon, where in the lives of men moved animal spirits and the shades of ancestors with no need of logic – also unmourned. And in this corner of the cemetery marked only by a white stone is the grave of the hunter, untended, disgraced, who, stirred blood-mad at the sight of so much life and the death he could bring, shot all day at trek springbok, aiming again and again into the moving hordes, firing with eyes closed yet still striking flank, belly, shoulder, head, what did it matter when there was so much? A plain of antelope pouring through the valley for three days and nights until, when it was over, when the last hooves churned the final dust, there was only his carnage to record that here had been a spectacle. Spare no sympathy. He, too, is unmourned. As will be this one, the corpse of the adventurer, now entering the gate in a cheap box carried by gravediggers. Yet he deserves a thought, a moment's silence. He is newly dead, still warm, but then no body can wait about in a hot land, unhymned, without priest or laity to say a few words, that this was a curious man, an unconventional man, who did many things out of no deep conviction except that they were there to do and always proved enticing, but who died disillusioned, believing at the last that it was all a cheap trick, poor entertainment devised by poor minds. Mourn him. Grieve for this man who in his ending showed compassion for the helpless, who argued for another way. Pause here and consider his humanity. Only one plot, already dug, remains to be filled soon by an artist with a small talent and a bad eye for colour, but one who gained pleasure from sketching among foraging giraffe or seeing in his brushstrokes the colour perceived or the rise of mountains he believed he saw, who finally withdrew into these softer worlds when about him men killed and his words had failed.

It is this last P.T. George who stands now on a grassy promontory at the further end of the island delicately painting the sunset colours of the river as it curves away. There is not a ripple of wind on the surface. He remembers the same promontory with hippopotamus in the river, women coming down to collect water, and a younger man who stood here painting the scene, and shakes his head. Too many dreams, he thinks, too many bloody dreams.

But at least I had dreams, says the younger man glancing up. Look at you, what have you got now? Not a dream, not a belief, not a hippopotamus, not a country of adventure left before you. So don't accuse me of having too many dreams. Accuse yourself of destroying them.

Having It Out

There was no other way to live then, says P.T. George eventually. No other country but a land of macchia and stones, marabous and cobras. They were dry dreams, dreams of deserts. You will find out.

Bah! spits the younger man. You told the pastor you wanted to see it wild. You rode into the veld on a horse. You had faith then.

I have faith now.

This is not faith, bursts out the younger man, gesturing at the distant tabernacle. This is the madness of charlatans and mercenaries. I am talking about the faith of tomorrow.

It is the plan of God, sighs P.T. George, too tired to think, too fatigued for anything but the easy answer.

Was it the plan of God that made you join the redeemer? chides the younger man. Was it? Or was it weakness, that when all about you people spoke in tongues, you gave in to their babbling too?

The younger P.T. George gets no reply from the person he can now only dimly see. Yet, firm-fleshed, his cheeks not blown in veins, hands steady, he accuses again: If we had met in the backlands I would not have known you. If someone had pointed you out, if someone had said, see that lard of flesh, that is the man you will become, I would have laughed at him. You are a failure, old man, you have only a failed world to paint.

And you, snaps P.T. George, suddenly angry, for a moment high-tempered, do not have to kill springbok, do not have to forsake cause and effect for this chaos. But you will. You will know the suffering of others; you will make small gestures against despair.

To which the young man has no answer, can only fade as those vanquished must fade into the night. Must disappear as the river has disappeared and the country gone dark around him, blacked out, silent: no frogs, no distant jackal howl, no quick shriek of a bat, no movement in the reeds. Only curving over him a night thick with stars and old light: the passing of life a million years ago. So the hump of the man becomes a rock, losing the day's heat, picking up a fine dew on its moss.

The Man They Want

Beyond his wits and now almost beyond his time, the government agent – a lonely, frightened man twisting the hairs of his beard, casting from side to side like a chained marmoset at the laughter and happiness about him – stands on trial outside the tabernacle.

All afternoon, fists clenched to the cellar grille, he has watched roasting lambs move through their slow revolutions and people prepare to feast.

He has shouted: I am innocent. I am Bywooner Malan, diamond prospector, farm help, a nobody, briefly a soldier but wanted for desertion, for failure to report, for absconding on duty, a hounded man working the edges of towns, sleeping rough, not bothering anybody, an outcast, a vagabond, a jailbird, but guilty only of poaching sheep, stealing fruit and a barrel of wine, not a deceiver, not a spy, not a government agent. I am innocent. Believe me. Innocent. Innocent. Innocent.

And he would sink down, cower away from the children come to stare. But only until his sobbing stopped, until he had fear enough again to beg for mercy in the name of the Lord, to plead: Ask this man – pointing at Jabulani Mximba – where he found me. He knows the truth. I'm not the president's man. Do you hear? I spit on the president. I spit on his wife. Oh, please, believe me.

No one will, says Jabulani Mximba moving off, fingering the necklace of teeth he'd once cut from the mouths of his victims. You've got to be the man they want.

But I am not the government agent, comes a last protest, the final words of the condemned man also become like stone, transfixed, staring at the indifference of cooking food, oranges, pineapples, bunches of grapes.

You should believe you are, whispers Tasmaine, in long black dress and bare feet, standing at the corner of his cell offering a little wine and dates to the shaking man. It will be easier that way.

But I am not.

Nor am I the woman you see. I am elsewhere with children and a farm man, soil in his squint lines and under his nails, I see us standing among shrivelled crops in another drought, we pray but there is no rain, only at night we still have tears to wipe from one another's faces. At least there I can love, draw water from deep wells and not feel the blisters. Come, take this.

I am the wrong man.

I go to the fields because there is too much work even for a man. Since the horse has died he has to pull while I plough. You must know what it is like to break soil for the first time, the weakness of flesh against that crust, the tiredness beyond mind, then at last the triumph of one furrow. A triumph without words, with just one glance that we did it and must do it again. I am that woman, government agent, despite everything, I am that woman.

And pushing the wine and dates through the grille she searches in Bywooner Malan's eyes for a glimpse of resignation then quickly leaves, striding across the clearing scattering children before her like chickens.

Oh yes, laughs Jabulani Mximba, it will be better that way. For you at least. You may as well die someone, someone who's got people worked up enough to judge him. Think about it. That's more than can be said for ordinary men. For men like Bywooner Malan. No one's going to listen to them. No one will even hear them. Who wants to? They don't matter. So play the game, it's going to happen anyhow.

The redeemer says bring out the spy, commands Dead Das.

Shackled and bound in the lantern light, arraigned before the feasters, mocked by dog barks, cat hiss and the screams of roosting peacocks, he is still Bywooner Malan, son of a goldminer, son of a waitress, who played in the winter dust of Chinese Camp. He cannot raise his head even to look quickly at a good meal – the pile of sheep bones, chicken bones, orange peel, bread crumbs – or above that at the faces, not really serious, too content for grave business, who see him now suddenly for the first time and point, whisper, joke. Or search through them for the one bowed head that may consider his suffering.

Instead he stands condemned and to all about him is without question the government agent, this deceiver who has come among us to spy, to report our lives, what we do, what we say, what we eat, who our children are, to release figures to the government, to lie about us, to slander us so that other men will not raise a finger in our defence, will merely say they had it coming, and this is that man, that informer, hoping we would take him in so that he could take us in, hoping we would love him, cherish him, invite him to become one of us, trust him, have faith in him, take him at face value and say, here, eat, drink, worship with us who are scorned, hounded, threatened with death, vilified throughout the country for wanting to praise the Lord in peace, for wanting justice, tax reform, to be counted man for man, woman for woman, for wanting dignity and a decent future where we are not refugees, where we are citizens of our own country, but, my people, that is not what the president wants, he sends his spies among us, he tells them to go out and find this riffraff, live among them, become one of them, and report to me everything because they could throw us into disruption, spoil our lives, destroy our law and order, so we must destroy them first, wipe them out, forget them, pretend that they had never been, that there never was a band of people who rose up, a mere handful who challenged the mighty for a minute, an hour, a week it doesn't matter, but for him it must never be recorded that there was a voice against his, a voice saying there is another way, a better way, because he knows such voices will be heard again and again and again long after his is dead, it will be heard until the powers of suppression are ended and there is light on earth which this man, this stooge, this government lackey, this presidential puppet who enjoys the good life, who has everything he wants, who has been promised the world if he will betray us, which he wants to do, oh yes, he wants our obedience to the president, he wants our death, he is here to say we are not free, that we cannot be free, that wherever we go there will be one among us who is not what he seems, who reports, who lies, deceives, makes sure that when the time is right we will disappear, vanish, and it will be as if we had never lived. Look at this man and judge.

Crucify him, shout the people of the prophet, coming up to spit food and gob in the downturned face. Crucify him.

And from the carpenter's shed they bring spades, ropes, nails, hammer, the cross to erect it right then and there before his horrified eyes and their laughter, relief, thanksgiving that the days of bread and water are over.

Dig, they command. Dig three foot here, because you wouldn't want to fall flat on your face.

But who can dig his own death, break the first crust of earth that is diamonds not gravel, take out one foot, two feet, three feet of soil that has grown grass and flowers and now a cross, that has waited for this moment, as it has waited for the rain of tears, sweat, blood of a man dying? Others have, but not Bywooner Malan. There is no strength to hold the spade, let alone dig, there is only one thought, one plea in his eyes: I am innocent. Please believe me. Innocent.

You are worthless, hisses Jabulani Mximba pushing through, taking the spade. You can't live, you can't die. How could you expect anything else but this?

This: a cross, black and tall against the bonfire, sturdy as a tree, facing west.

Tomorrow, announces the prophet, quietening his people, pronouncing sentence: Tomorrow, at sunset, let the Lord's will be done.

Come, says Jabulani Mximba leading off the captive, you've got a chance to change your mind.

Later there are overturned benches, broken bottles, leftovers. The lanterns are out, the dogs have buried bones, the fire has become ash, only a porcupine sifts debris. In the huts and shacks and tents sleep the people of the prophet: here a man talks in his dreams, there a woman groans as she turns over, children cry out from nightmares stalked by monsters, even a dog yelps at its own fears. In the cellar beneath the tabernacle the government agent

257

alias Bywooner Malan tosses closer to his death in a blackness filled with terror. On the promontory at the end of the island P.T. George, his head lolling forward, dozes off. And about him come to stand Simple Martha's sheep, baleful, their eyes unblinking.

God's Plan

Because Simple Martha slept with the sheep she was always the first awake, the first to gaze up into the heavens each morning, waiting for the angels her brother said were soon to come. They would come, he said, at daybreak, drifting down.

Once he had drawn pictures for her in the sand that showed the sky torn by lightning and out of the gap – a white gap she often saw when there were storms – came the angels like a host of dragonflies, multi-coloured, some riding on the backs of others.

Dragonflies, he had told her, slowly mouthing the words, are the angels of the Lord made visible. They will be there on the morning of Judgement Day.

On the morning of the massacre Simple Martha is the first to see the aeroplanes skim over the palm trees and soar upwards in an enormous loop. Wing to wing they climb, getting smaller and smaller until in the clear summer air they disappear with a flash of silver. Once again, above her, the sky stretches endless and blue.

And then from nowhere they pass over her once more and are gone in that quick high spark.

At the noise sheep flee in terror but Simple Martha, wrapped in her silence, creeps out from under the hedge to get a better view. Sucking on the hem of her dress she squints into the harsh light that covers the sky at sunrise, the effort puckering her face, her fists bunched in the folds of material that hang about her waist. Above the village the aeroplanes have left white trails in the sky like sloughed snakeskins, twisting, dropping back towards the ground.

Simple Martha closes her eyes. Surely this is the sign her brother has been waiting for. In the perfect darkness she holds her breath, lives blissfully in the black silence, happy that this time it is the plan of God. Only when her heart begins racing against her chest and the darkness in her is shot with stars does she, gasping for breath, open her eyes. Even then she doesn't expect to see the aeroplanes again, but they come out of the sudden brightness straight towards her.

They fly low across the fields, rocking slightly, until as they reach the hedge where she stands they bank and go out over the river. Simple Martha croaks with joy and lifts her skirt as she spreads her arms like wings.

And then the aeroplanes thunder over the island and bank for their third approach.

The shriek of engines coming down and the tap of a Bible against her shoulder brings Tasmaine up from her dreams into the face of Enoch Mistas, low over her, smelling of communion, lips pulled back in half sneer, half grin. His eyes hold her face like mirrors, blank, reflecting, loveless, until Tasmaine shuts out the hurt, turns quickly inside to her farmer, the man he should have been, standing where her dreams had ended in a ploughed field on a day with rain. But even there the aeroplanes reach her: the pitch, the shrill whine closer, closer, closer until she can dream no longer, until she is back in the small room with its bed and her only chair at the window and the roar becomes the fear in her, becomes a hard scream echoing the full throttle swoop and pull out.

No, yells Enoch Mistas, lashing her with hand and Bible: No. It is the plan of God. It is the day of judgement, the time of their blood.

But Tasmaine cannot hear him, she is singing softly to herself, neither lost in dreams nor aware of the anguish and terror beyond her window, or the white pleading face of Bywooner Malan. Instead she goes about her ordinary morning: empties the pot, folds back the kaross, rubs her teeth with yellow root, washes

from the jug, singing all the time under the long stare of Enoch
Mistas, the redeemer, the prophet of the people who once led her
by the hand into the sea that ticked in her ears with the language
of crabs.

Go, woman, he shouts, again breaking memories, again casting
aside soft times. Go to the fields. Prepare to meet your Master.
And he goes out into the excitement of Dead Das, Allermann,
Jabulani Mximba and his army of the Lord awaiting his word,
his order to kill, to fight in the name of the Almighty, herald the
everlasting kingdom, as the aeroplanes come in once more.

P.T. George still hunched against the cold looks up to see three
biplanes, bright, silver machines with blue and red insignia like
targets on their fuselages, tearing down the sky. He sighs, folding
in to the pain that tightens across his chest, that squashes his
heart and lungs. He hears ribs crack and feels the side of his
face loosen and drop away from the skull. P.T. George falls
backwards gasping for air as the cage of his chest collapses. With
his one good eye he looks up into the early-morning heavens and
sees that the swallows have become crows and marabous. Already,
he winces. It's hardly begun and they're here already. It takes P.T.
George a whole massacre to die, but he hears it all, and finally the
singing.

As the aeroplanes circle, Simple Martha claps her hands, dancing
with delight. This is the sign the prophet has been waiting for:
hadn't he broken the fast the night before, hadn't they feasted,
drunk wine, worshipped the Lord? Now there would be sacrifices,
perhaps he would even want some of her lambs, the fat ones she'd
fed on river grass. And after the feasts of thanksgiving, would the
priests lead a procession round the altar, anointing everyone with
the blood of the lambs? Perhaps the tiny flames she'd once seen
flickering over her brother's head would return. So much was
possible if this was the sign.

High above her the aeroplanes come together again and fall
towards the horizon in a silver arc. Just as quickly as they had
appeared, so they are gone.

Simple Martha looks towards the village. People are running

into the fields, there are cattle among the vines, goats in the wheat, the peacocks beat past her so closely she can feel the wind from their heavy wings. Then, just as abruptly, the people running towards her turn and run back into the village. Many fall. She can see children being trampled by the cattle, old people thrust aside, mothers dropping babies, men so crazed with fear they knock over carts as they flee to the shelter of the houses. Only in the square, among the panic of cats, hens, chickens, dogs, stands Enoch Mistas, the chained Bible flapping like a useless limb, cursing the armies of Satan who dare to invade his province. Know this, sodomites and unbelievers: the wrath of the Lord will be on your heads and flies will feed from your carrion. Heed you Ezekiel who foresaw the appearance of wheels and wings in fire, who foretold the creatures of four heads who heard trumpets and saw the desolation of cities. Heed this you armies and take fright.

But the armies cannot hear him and his words are nothing in the noise of engines.

Again the aeroplanes come, this time from behind her, flying so slowly and low that their sudden size and shadow sends Simple Martha skidding into the hedge. She looks up at cockpit heads smiling, grinning, laughing down at her before they pull up and up into the blue.

A tearing sounds down the sky but Ma-Fatsoen with ears only for the voices of her lost daughters could be as deaf as Simple Martha for all the notice she takes of three plummeting aeroplanes. She sits up in bed, her head cocked, her lips trembling in expectation.

What's that, Sissy? she is saying, as Tasmaine enters the room. There are dragonflies on the dam. But there are always dragonflies on the dam in the good years. Look, look at their lovely wings.

Come, Ma, coaxes Tasmaine, breathing through her mouth to avoid the old woman's stink. We must sing. We must go into the fields.

Obediently Ma-Fatsoen puts her arms into the coat, then, hitching it all above her puckered thighs, crouches over the bucket and lets loose a spray of urine. Tasmaine turns from the sight, languid after the days of fasting. She remembers watermelons.

How when the rains stopped the first shoots would push through the sand and swell, drinking from a deep red stream until they were the size of babies. She remembers the crush of pink flesh in her mouth and the sweetness that burst through her nose. There are no watermelons on the island. Although she had planted seeds they never grew.

Outside the aeroplanes scream down their fall, wings vibrating like those of dragonflies.

Once more the aeroplanes swoop on the village and arch up into the sky, climbing until they are little silver dots, then spin madly back down towards the huts and shelters. Again and again they soar and dive, always getting closer and closer to the tabernacle, the temple of the redeemer, always pulling up.

Dead Das, Allermann and the seventy-two army of knobkerries, spears, Mausers and Enfields threaten, hurl, shoot at the hated wings of Lucifer, the devil's advocates, who only mock them, even coming so low they can hear their laughter.

Now we will see, yells Allermann, red with rage, hurling down Mauser and pistol, running into the store: Now we will see how they laugh at the Lady Schwarzlose – and he emerges with the machine-gun cradled in his arms like a bride.

Hidden in her hedge, Simple Martha can see children crying, women curled up under carts, their skirts over their heads, while Dead Das and the priests shoot at the aeroplanes. And in the centre Enoch Mistas, her brother, at the foot of the big cross where the government agent was to die, waves his arms at the heavens, the Bible flying about his hand like a bat. Then Allermann starts firing with the machine-gun and she can see the little flickers of flame at the barrel blasting remorselessly away until all the bullets are spent. And the planes become crazier and crazier, roll across the sky, chase people down the fields, knocking them over with a brush of wings.

Run, Simple Martha, run, shout people uselessly, pulling her, tearing her out of the bush. It's the forces of evil.

Come, Simple Martha, come, pants Nick the Herd, pausing to catch her hand, until she breaks free when the aeroplanes send him howling down to the river, crazed with terror and fright.

Sing, Simple Martha, sing, says Tasmaine leading Ma-Fatsoen, Mrs Naald, Mr Zimri, women, children, old men, a small band, a sad procession led by her skirts along the sands: Sing because there is nothing else we can do:

> By the rivers of Babylon
> There we sat down yet we wept
> When we remembered Zion
> We hung our harps upon the willows
> In the midst thereof
> Great and marvellous art Thy works
> Lord God of Israel the Everlasting King

But Simple Martha knows there is something else to be done: she must follow the sign, wait for the end of the world as the prophet had predicted. So she pulls free to the safety of the hedge to watch the whistling, glinting, spinning rain that falls on the temple of the redeemer and among the houses.

All about her people stream towards the river: mothers with babies strapped to their backs leading young children and grandmothers, fathers carrying bundles and spades, old men with hens under their arms, old women leading goats. No one is running any more; no one sees Simple Martha, no one sees anything but the colour of flames and burning, fire and smoke. Behind them houses crumple, flames leap in the tabernacle, hands at the cellar grille and a pleading face begs mercy, protests innocence, screams when the floor gives in. And the long whine of more bombs falling and the explosion of metal, earth, fire, feathers, flesh. Bodies in flame, running towards the river, arms thrown wide, hearing the crackle of their skin and hair, breathing the smell of their own burning. Then among them again the small band singing, calling: Join us, sisters, come with us, brothers, see the plan of God unfolding, worship the morning of justice, the coming of a world without end. By the waters of Babylon, there we sat down. Between them Simple Martha dances from one to the other, smiling in their faces, pointing at the sky, touching the blood of their wounds, the raw stumps of wasted limbs. Until she hears the thunder, until she hears the only sound since her father's endless words: the voice of destruction, the tearing, the howls of terror and pain. Impossible noise, pitched and clangorous, that not hands, not cloth, not mud, nor her own screams, louder than all else breaking through her years of silence, can stop.

Now she runs, beating her head, trying to keep out this hell she's never heard, over stones and thorns, sobbing, stumbling, running away from hymns, howls, the panic of hearing, until in a field she falls among her sheep, clasps the old ewe about the neck, cries louder than bombs and bullets. In the wool there is some silence, only a muffled noise that fades as she calms, as she looks up to see her brother, the redeemer, letting free his coat-tails, come striding towards her. Beside her he kneels down, strokes her hair, cups her ears in his thin hands, croons a song Ma-Fatsoen used to sing in the mission years, until Simple Martha is deaf again. Together they sit in silence and noise, back to back, dreaming of pools, bells, tents of cloth, the syrup of figs, dried meat, porridge, living elsewhere in their lives before a boy became a prophet, before there were signs and voices and the plan of God. A last moment that ends in a last quick smile when he stands up, hesitates at the sight of soldiers, then turns towards the village, the flames, and is gone.

Simple Martha lies down among the cropping sheep, content. In the sky she sees the aeroplanes come together the way dragonflies do, and disappear.

Even at the last Simple Martha didn't hear the singing, became completely her silence, uncomforted, dying with her slaughtered sheep while the voices came to all the others as they did to P.T. George, quietly, under the rush of blood, easing in between the pain of being alive and almost dead. It was no song they knew, just voices chanting, reciting, lilting, stronger than cries and explosions yet little more than a sadness upon the breeze. It sang across the fields, through the settlement flames and smoke, along the river sands as bunched together behind Tasmaine and Ma-Fatsoen, bare-foot, in rags, bloody, shuffled the small band, singing.

THIS DAY AND AGE

The soldiers come out of the small dunes along the river's bank where they have waited all night, lying on the sand in the desert cold, unable to smoke or talk, stiff with frost and boredom. In the early light, they too watch the aeroplanes, see the chaos, grin, squint down their point three-oh-three sights and wait until the people of the prophet flee into the river. Then, as ordered, they fire: shoot people in the shallows, kill children mothers fathers, fix bayonets and wade in among the bodies that rock on the currents, float gently away.

And there, on an island in the great river that runs through the driest part of the country, the soldiers massacre all the people of the prophet.

A Parting Shot

Just beyond the heat of the blazing village Field Marshal Hedley Goodman swung gratefully out of his saddle. Dapper soldier, veteran campaigner, follower of orders without question, all the same glad to hear finally the occasional shots as his men killed those curled up under bushes, scrabbling into aardvark holes, playing dead without anticipating a bayonet-all-corpses command, because he could at last get off his seat of great discomfort.

Surveying fields, craters and smouldering ruins, he thinks: Bastards, what a mopping up this is going to take.

Because there are bodies everywhere. Only three hundred and five people this morning, but now bodies all over the place, and a good many of them his own troops.

The dead always number more than the living, he grumbles, waving off a dragonfly and, turning to his aide, says: Pour me a bath in the shade of my horse.

Orders are shouted all the way back to base camp, wagons trundle up, the tin tub is brought out, a fire stoked, water warmed, while Field Marshal Hedley Goodman, focusing his binoculars on chaos and mayhem, fires and slaughter, asks: Any trace of Mistas yet, Captain Trotter?

None, says Captain Trotter unhappily, fidgeting with his lanyard, eyes cast down at this singular defeat in a morning of triumph.

We must have him, Captain Trotter, says Field Marshal Hedley Goodman listening to that most welcome sound of water being poured into his bath tub, anticipating the pleasure of sitting submerged without pain. We must have him dead or alive, you hear? He fixes the captain with grey eyes: a steely glance that has nailed many subordinates before.

Yes, sir, salutes Captain Trotter, springing to attention, eager to be off and kicking incompetent arses.

Oh, and captain, calls out the field marshal after him, lowering now bare-bummed into that soothing water, sighing with relief: Oooh aah that's more like it, as the water eases aching piles, then, looking up at the anxious captain, adds: Send a message that our mission is accomplished; and get the men to start digging a hole. I want no signs of carnage, I want just burnt-out ruins. I want historians to say the tabernacle caught fire and the people of the prophet went out into the desert where they died. I want them to record such things in passing.

Yes, sir, field marshal, sir.

Soon the heliograph flashes its codes of triumph, and the soldiers set to with a will. But what it takes is an afternoon to dig a large hole and a day to bury the dead. Because it's not an easy task. Fires have to be extinguished, ashes poked through, riders must go downriver to retrieve bodies. All severed heads, limbs, torsos are gathered up, collapsed walls dug through, whatever valuables collected, all crosses, crucifixes, religious paraphernalia packed for transport, captured weapons of assault – rifles, machine-guns, pistols, knives – listed in the state inventory, no trinkets taken, an absolute assurance made that never in the future, never at all, will some ploughing farmer, caught by a glimpse of white in his field, climb off his tractor to find teeth, a splinter of femur, praying hands, broken bones. Let him wonder about a cartridge case, even a shard of metal, let him wonder at the ruins when he returns from planting pineapples, or the pea-cocks and the dragonflies that never leave the island, but let him never hold in his rough hands the small rifle-smashed skull of a child.

Never.

So all afternoon Field Marshal Hedley Goodman, naked from the waist down, wearing cap and tunic, sits in the tub bothered only by dragonflies to make sure that never really is never ever. As the sun falls westwards, his aide moves the horse round to rearrange the shadow, keeps the water tepid, tries to chase the dragonflies away with the sweep of a palm frond. But it's useless, they always come back again riding three decks high.

Damn this goddamned campaign, curses the field marshal. I told them it would be playing with fire. Thirty-eight men dead for a god-struck madman. Damn everything. Fetch Captain Trotter. Bring me Enoch Mistas. All this bloodshed is on his head. Where is Enoch Mistas?

Just how to explain that one to an inflamed field marshal, Captain Trotter doesn't know. Although he has searched everywhere: in the fields, upriver, downriver, turned over every corpse, scoured the now burnt-out ruins, even found in the cellar beneath the tabernacle the suffocated body of a probable prisoner . . . although he has put a reward of two shillings on the elusive prophet's head, all has been in vain. He has learnt nothing more except that Enoch Mistas is gone.

Gone! What do you mean gone? he had yelled at the dying woman. There is nowhere for him to go.

He is gone, was all the woman would say, and laughed or cried: The Lord cometh, hosannah in the highest.

Captain Trotter looked at her, a handsome young woman despite the splattering of blood and the poor clothes, with breasts like doves and thighs as smooth as sausages. Should he, he wondered, then caught the grin on a soldier's face and turned away.

He is gone with the Lord, the woman cried out again. The Lord came down and took him away.

And that, after a fashion, is what he told Field Marshal Hedley Goodman, who was still sitting in his tub to ease the pain of his piles.

He is not here, he is not anywhere on the island, Captain Trotter reports. He seems to have disappeared. According to the woman he escaped.

Soldiers stop swatting at dragonflies, others rest on their spades or pause in the dragging of corpses towards the open mouth of the pit. The sun slides out of the sky but the heat stays.

Seems to have disappeared! Field Marshal Hedley Goodman flushes as red as a bubble of haemorrhoids. People don't just disappear, captain. They don't just go up in a puff of smoke, they don't just vanish into thin air. Nor do they escape from an island in the middle of the day with soldiers crawling all over the place.

Overcome, furious, forgetting the sharp centre of pain between his buttocks, the field marshal almost stands up to command: Bring the woman.

So they bring her, arms draped over two soldiers, feet dragging, her breasts – the doves – blood-splattered, clothes in shreds, those sausage thighs dripping semen, seemingly dead to the world. Field Marshal Hedley Goodman looks at her and forgets the pain that focuses his every breath. She is beautiful. She is lovely. She is the most astonishing woman he has ever seen. Even through the grime of devastation she has no equal. He stands up, sheer good manners force him to his feet, force him to grimace with hot pain, but to stand rigidly to attention while an aide wraps his loins in a towel.

You haven't . . .? he says, raising an eyebrow at Captain Trotter, leaving the question hanging between the dragonflies.

No, of course not, field marshal. No, no, she's asleep, tired out after the interrogation, that's all, isn't she – blustering, blushing, seeking support – isn't she, sergeant-major?

Yes, sir, captain, sir. Asleep, sir.

And who is she? demands the field marshal.

His wife, sir. At least, what passed for a wife in the prophet's eyes, sir.

Prophet, captain? Not prophet. Surely you mean renegade, bandit, outlaw, anarchist, saboteur, blasphemer, homosexual, devil-worshipper, the scourge of the nation, captain. Nothing less than the scourge of the nation.

Red-faced, stretch-necked, Field Marshal Hedley Goodman, drawn to the limits of his tolerance by the ache of his piles and a prophet of doom, bellows: Just find him, Trotter. Just find him or you'll be a captain for life.

Yes, sir. Yes, sir, salutes the trembling Trotter.

And get that woman cleaned up. I want to talk to her.

But before Field Marshal Hedley Goodman can lean back in the relief of water-soothed haemorrhoids, a peacock cries in the bluegums and a soldier, his brown hair turned suddenly white,

A Parting Shot

fires a volley at the form of Enoch Mistas. And Enoch Mistas, dressed in black frock-coat, his Bible, as ever, chained to his wrist, glowers at the soldier, steps between the trees and is gone. On the far end of the island a peacock cries and Enoch Mistas bends down to close the eyes of the uncollected dead. There, in the half-light, he is seen by a cook come to draw water from the river.

He's a holy man, are the gibbering cook's later words. A holier man even than the highest archbishop. No one's going to kill him.

That night he is there and here and here there simultaneously: fired on by Sergeant-Major Bloodstock in the fields; and at the same time shot at among the ruins of the village by Captain Trotter, who sees him walking with his Bible clutched to his chest among the smouldering embers.

Halt, Mistas, challenges the captain, drawing his pistol: Halt or I fire.

But the praying prophet walks on and Captain Trotter fires three times at nothing.

Such a commotion: shots, shouts, commands, countermands from all over the island with peacocks crying the cries of the dead, horses rearing in terror at the sudden appearance of ghost or man – who knew? – but he is everywhere. Out go cooking fires, lanterns and lights. Men with their pants down over steaming latrines fall back among the faeces; others wake in the grip of cold or hot fingers, stare into the eyes of Enoch Mistas, deep, fundamental, black. And the field marshal's tent collapses about his tub when guy-ropes fray in an instant, unravelling just like that. Which once again brings the veteran campaigner to his feet with a scream of frustration, anger, piles of pain: For Chrissakes, Trotter, what the fuck's going on?

What's going on is gross regimental pandemonium. Never in the field of battle, never in the most abject rout with an enemy blazing dumdums into their fleeing flesh have they behaved like this, soldier, non-com, officer alike: undisciplined, firing wildly whenever a peacock cries, bayoneting carcass and corpse, crazed, hysterical, as Enoch Mistas appears and disappears all over the place.

Get my breeches, roars Field Marshal Hedley Goodman into

the mêlée, spinning the chamber of his pistol, thumb testing the edge of his sword, apologising to the now washed and dressed in army khaki but even so dazzling beauty of a woman who waits, head lolling forward, tired of it all, slipping in and out of this world and the next, for his pleasure. My pardon, madam – ah, woman – your husband and I have unfinished business. With that he is gone into the chaos.

Perhaps the woman smiles, perhaps it is nothing more than the grimace of pain which twists her mouth, for she knows Field Marshal Hedley Goodman has no more chance of killing Enoch Mistas that night than does anyone else in the Cape Royal Fusiliers. Yet forgetting the haemorrhoids that chafe between his buttocks, brandishing sword and pistol, he chases the prophet, or is lured by him, through pastures, potato fields, the stand of bluegums, into the ruins of the tabernacle where no one else would go.

And there, standing at what had once been the holy end and is now again, the prophet of the people, the backlands bandit, the redeemer, the scourge of the nation, Enoch Mistas, miracle-worker and saviour, waits arms outstretched, Bible dangling, blood oozing from hands and stomach. Field Marshal Hedley Goodman, triumphant at his wounded quarry, pistol pointing, steps into the gloom and hears behind him a door that had once been, and is now again, close heavily.

Silence.

Then: Welcome, field marshal.

Enoch Mistas raises his head and opens his eyes. He searches the half-light until he sees, partly hidden behind a pillar, the figure of the commanding officer. Once more he closes his eyes and seems to pray. Field Marshal Hedley Goodman, seizing the opportunity, scuttles forward like a rat one two three pillars. He stops, heart pounding, thoughts wondering: Should I shoot from here?

Weapons are useless in the House of the Lord, preaches Enoch Mistas. In the House of the Lord swords are melted and bullets turn to water. Put down your futile tools, officer.

For a moment, a strange uncharacteristic moment without will or way, the field marshal almost obeys the command. Had he not clenched his teeth, which clenched every muscle in his body right down to that tight little ring of eina anus, he might have surrendered his arms to the dung floor. But with rectum pain reality returns. He stands his ground.

You are an impostor and a murderer, Mistas, challenges the military man, slipping forward pew by pew. You are no more prophet than I, but at least my God is the God of mercy. He pauses, noting the stains of blood on the wooden boards at Mistas's feet, feeling confident, adding: It is time you atoned for your sins and the bloodshed of innocent people.

Enoch Mistas lowers his arms. Field Marshal Hedley Goodman stops, crouches, straightens the line of sight down the barrel of his revolver. Should he shoot? But again he hesitates.

Of course there must be bloodshed, roars the prophet, stepping towards him, pointing at the spread of blood that glistens in the fabric of his coat. Is it not written that men shall be drunk with blood?

His quarry, the very scourge of the nation, is no more than twenty feet away. Hedley Goodman, dedicated soldier and decorated officer, prepares to launch himself across the final gap, to drive his sword straight into the belly of the beast. He deserves to die slowly, reasons the officer commanding, with ants creeping into the spilled yards of his innards.

Enoch Mistas roars again: There must be bloodshed. The whole world is going to sink in blood.

He glares into the gloom at his opponent.

But I am not the cause of it. God is going to cause it. The time of Jehovah has now arrived. He laughs. But what do you know, soldier? You take your orders from men, from a bald man infested with boils, with a bad heart and a limp side. You send him gifts of massacres and you think you have triumphed. But let me tell you, when people rally round the word of God, people must die. So it is written and so will it be.

Deliberately, slowly, Enoch Mistas turns his back, walks to the altar.

They will hang you, Mistas, shouts the field marshal. There is no judge who will not wear the black hood when he sees you.

But that veteran of fights, battles and wars, that man of conviction wavers, hesitates, loses the moment and so much else.

Again Enoch Mistas raises his hands as if crucified, blood still seeping from the wounds: I won't die, infantryman. I shall never die. Already I am told to children.

And then it seems to Field Marshal Hedley Goodman, who believes in God and the Holy Ghost, who understands the workings of the steam engine and the theory of flight, who is seen every Sunday in the regimental chapel, who acknowledges the miracles, especially the resurrection and the appearance of Christ to his disciples, who accepts without question the principles of gravity and the mechanical universe, who has no time for mystical rope tricks on the promenade, hot-coal walking or daggers through bloodless cheeks, that the prophet self-proclaimed, the hero of stories, begins to shimmer and lift lighter than air, floating above him, hovering, raining blood on to his khaki uniform. What can a man trained in the science of killing do but raise his pistol, squeeze the trigger, fire a parting shot before he loses his mind as his enemy disappears through the roof that before had been and now is no longer? Loses his mind utterly, completely, and is found by Captain Trotter the next morning trying to wash out blood-spots that no water will clean from his uniform. There on the banks of the great river, Captain Trotter, Sergeant-Major Bloodstock and the regiment's two champion wrestlers try to pin down Field Marshal Hedley Goodman, if only literally, because there is no hope of their ever getting to hear what happened in the tabernacle that night. And pinning him down is no easy task. Puny field marshal before, now he lashes out with tight fists, butting like a goat, blackening eyes, loosening teeth. Such strength in a madman. But in the end they succeed in lashing his arms to his sides and push pull him back to his re-erected tent.

Enough, says Captain Trotter waving off dragonflies as the sun rises on scenes of carnage and an old man's will: Bury the passed on. We're not spending another night here.

Weary footsloggers who have killed all morning, dug a pit all afternoon, chased a ghost all night begin to drag and shovel on empty stomachs even before orders are shouted. There is no point in denying the dead any longer.

That's it, soldiers, encourages Captain Trotter, going among the men with the flick of his swagger-stick and a kindly word. For a Christian burial, history will always turn a blind eye.

A Parting Shot

And what about the woman? asks Sergeant-Major Bloodstock, second in command, keeping pace.

She comes with us, replies the captain. Make sure she stays alive.

But how to keep alive a dying beauty? May as well try to save a sunset or stop a river because this one is going, like colour from cloud, like passing water, drifting off. All the same, the regimental doctor who should have been attending to gutshot soldiers, gangrene wounds, amputations, keeps her in this world with morphine, brandy, hot tea, even face slaps for much longer than decency allows. There she sits all through the burials, nodding in her camp chair beside the twitching Field Marshal Hedley Goodman, reliving the life she had to lead, until in the middle of the afternoon the exhausted column is told: Forward march.

By then the scene is this: one large pit on the fringe of a burnt-out village filled in with bodies, topped with soil and the company minister's prayer for the fallen. Fording the river are the last of the Cape Royal Fusiliers with rifles above their heads; and leading the column Captain Trotter on horseback, Field Marshal Hedley Goodman in a cart and Tasmaine getting weaker by every jolt of the first-aid wagon.

Out into the karoo, out among black rocks and macchia, rising crows and the shades of the vanquished, out into the waterless wastes march the Cape Royal Fusiliers, ghost-stricken, unreal, lost. Men never again to know the arms of lovers or the happiness of children, men condemned never to make it across a hundred miles of locusts and dustdevils to the train that could have taken them back to barracks. Men who must now march for ever over this rough territory. Because this is afterwards, this is the new country. And afterwards there are no rousing cheers, nor even messages of a job well done from a president who had once lived in a house of shaded rooms. Instead, afterwards, there are versions of events: the word of a drunken editor in an hotel bar, the talk of a cleaning woman, a vigil of prayers for what happened or what may have happened or what people heard happened. Afterwards there are the facts according to one, the truth according to another: secrets uncovered, confidential files exposed, a message revealed. Afterwards there is outrage, duplicity, denial and exaggeration.

There is the condemnation of the guilty and the veneration of the just. For the one the unchanged landscape of flat-topped hills and ironstone, the howl of wind among scrub and the march that is endless. For the other statues and street names: the place of martyrs and heroes. Afterwards, for the one as for the other, there is the future. There is history. Afterwards is where the story begins.

THE END

Printed in the United States
by Baker & Taylor Publisher Services